PRAISE FOR "MALIGNANT ASSUMPTIONS"

(LIZA LARKIN BOOK 2)

"an exciting and … satisfying read"

— KIRKUS REVIEWS

"the suspense kept me on the edge of my seat … fantastic novel"

— READERS' FAVORITE

"a fun mystery novel that will keep audiences guessing until the end"

— FOREWORD CLARION REVIEWS

PRAISE FOR "FATAL ROUNDS"
(LIZA LARKIN BOOK 1)

"Rubin makes the most out of an uber-creepy premise in this superior medical thriller"

— *PUBLISHERS WEEKLY* (STARRED REVIEW)

"A knockout that's just what the doctor ordered for thriller enthusiasts."

— *KIRKUS REVIEWS*

"A brisk, page-turning read."

— RACHEL HOWZELL HALL, *NEW YORK TIMES* BESTSELLING AUTHOR

PRAISE FOR "BROKEN HOPE"

"Rubin's revenge thriller is fast-paced and full of plenty of unexpected twists and turns … a true page-turner"

— KIRKUS REVIEWS

"This brilliantly clever, thought-provoking plot will keep the reader engaged from start to finish."

— READERS' FAVORITE

"clever cat-and-mouse games … highly recommended"

— D. DONOVAN, SENIOR REVIEWER,
MIDWEST BOOK REVIEW

PRAISE FOR THE BENJAMIN ORIS SERIES

THE BONE CURSE: "A strong medical thriller—inclusive, skillfully written, and inviting."

— FOREWORD REVIEWS

THE BONE HUNGER: "The reveal is a real shocker, and Rubin's winning lead is well-suited to sustain a series. This is just the ticket for Robin Cook fans."

— PUBLISHERS WEEKLY

THE BONE ELIXIR: "The author's pithy writing keeps the story popping all the way to the rousing final act. A chilling supernatural tale with indelible characters."

— KIRKUS REVIEWS

MALIGNANT ASSUMPTIONS

MALIGNANT ASSUMPTIONS

CARRIE RUBIN

INDIGO DOT PRESS

Indigo Dot Press
indigodotpress@gmail.com

First edition, 2024

Library of Congress Control Number: 2024914816

FIC031080 FICTION / Thrillers / Psychological
FIC030000 FICTION / Thrillers / Suspense
FIC031040 FICTION / Thrillers / Medical

ISBN 978-1-958160-10-7 (hardcover)
ISBN 978-1-958160-11-4 (trade paperback)
ISBN 978-1-958160-12-1 (ebook)
ISBN 978-1-958160-13-8 (audiobook)

Cover design by Lance Buckley Design

PROLOGUE

LIZA LARKIN, AGE 15

My knuckles split open, but I keep punching. I should have worn gloves or taped up my hands or something, but I didn't take the time. My fury needed someplace to go.

The heavy bag barely withstands my pummeling. It's not the best. My dad bought it from a big-box store. It doesn't even hang from our basement's ceiling, but its sand-filled base keeps it upright, and today it's serving its purpose.

I kick hard with my foot and yelp. Then again.

"Hey, hey," a voice calls out to me. It might as well be a thousand miles away.

"Liza!"

This time my father's shout reaches me, and my bleeding hands and bruised shins finally fall still. Sweat drips down my face, and my sweater reeks of wet wool. I haven't even changed out of my school clothes yet.

"Liza, honey, what are you doing?" My dad reaches for my hands and examines my wounded knuckles.

My chest heaves from exertion. Every cell of my body is on fire. "This is what you bought it for, right?"

My father stares at me with that crease in his brow, a crease that says, *We definitely have more work to do with this one.* "Well, yes, I bought it so you'd have an outlet for your…emotions. But I didn't mean for you to pound the stuffing out of it until your hands break."

"Better than breaking someone's arm, isn't it?" I'm referring to last year, when I broke a girl's arm with a bat because she was a psychopathic bully. The consequences for me weren't pretty.

My dad envelops me in a hug. "Oh, sweetheart, it'll be okay."

I don't like hugs, but my father—and my mother when her schizophrenia allows for them—gets a pass.

Dad leads me to a worn sofa against the concrete wall of our brownstone's unfinished basement. "Sit. I'll be right back." A minute later, he returns with a glass of water. "Drink this."

I do, and with each swallow my frustration eases, and my body heat cools.

When I finish, he takes the glass from my hands and angles his body toward me. "Now. What's going on?"

"It's…my…" I want to tell him, but my anger rises again, and the words stick in my throat.

"Remember what Dr. Lightfoot taught you. Inhale deeply through your nose and exhale through your mouth. Five seconds in, eight seconds out."

Together, my father and I breathe in and out, and finally, after a dozen rounds of this, my words form a sentence. "It's Mrs. Dixon."

"What about Mrs. Dixon? Is she leaving the school?"

I shake my head. I wish that were all it was. Although losing my favorite teacher, the only teacher who makes me feel like I'm not a walking mutation, an emotionless freak who needs to "come out of her shell," would make me want to kick my boxing bag into Mars, it would still be better than what happened.

"Then what is it?" my father asks.

"She…her house burned down."

"That's awful. Is she okay?"

I shake my head.

"Did she…die?"

"No. She's in the hospital in the ICU, but her husband and son did. Smoke inhalation."

My dad's posture sags, and he leans back on the old couch. "Oh, Jesus."

"Principal Fisher told us at the beginning of fifth period. Let us all out early."

"How is her daughter?"

"She was staying at a friend's house last night."

"Oh, tiger," my dad says. "I'm so sorry. I know how much you connect with Mrs. Dixon, and I also know how rare that is for you." He tucks a strand of hair behind my ear. "You guys are two science-minded peas in a pod."

"She once told me she was on the autism spectrum, and—"

"You're not autistic, Liza. Dr. Lightfoot has told you that many times."

"Whatever. But Mrs. Dixon...I don't know...she..."

"Got you?"

I nod. I don't remember ever crying before, although I'm sure I did as a little kid, but I fear I could now.

"It's okay to be sad," my dad says. "It's okay to cry. Accidental home fires happen, but it doesn't make it any less tragic. It—"

"No." I shake my head forcefully. "They think it might be arson. They're still investigating, but that's the rumor." My body grows rigid, and my split knuckles strain into fists. "If I find out who did it, I'll—"

"Rumors mean nothing." My dad's tone is sharp. "Don't talk like that, you hear me?" When I don't respond, he grips my chin and repeats, "Do you hear me?"

"Yes." I thump my head against the wall behind the sofa. "But I feel useless. What can I do? How can I take away her pain? That's what you and Dr. Lightfoot are always trying to teach me, right? To feel other people's pain? Well, now I am, and I don't like it." A teardrop finally falls. Others follow.

My father folds me in his arms and rocks me like he did when I was a child, whenever my anger threatened to overwhelm me.

"Oh, tiger," he says. "You can't take away anyone's pain. Having empathy for them doesn't mean you can fix their hurt."

"Then what's the point of it?" I rub my wet face into his shirt collar. He smells of Axe bodywash and the sweat of a day in his law office. "Why would anyone want to feel this way if they can't do anything about it?"

He pulls me away from him and stares into my eyes. "But you *can* do something about it."

I blink. "I can?"

"Yes. You can help them. In whatever way they need. You can visit Mrs. Dixon in the hospital. You can organize a fundraiser to get her the money she'll need to make a new home. When she's out of the hospital, you can take her a big plate of my barbecue ribs. You can babysit her daughter."

This last one makes us both laugh. He knows as well as I do that I'd be the worst babysitter in the world. Last year I forgot to feed my brother's fish when he was away at music camp. The year before too.

"You might not know how to relate to people," my father says. "You might not even care about most of them. But you can always help them, Liza."

He squeezes my hand.

"You can always be a helper."

1

PRESENT DAY

With gloved hands, I pluck the dead man's heart from the gaping Y incision. At the same time, Waseem Ahmad, my fellow second-year pathology resident, enters the autopsy suite. I'm surprised to see him. He's rotating through lab medicine this month, which means no postmortem duties. I plop the slippery organ with its severed arteries onto the scale to weigh it.

Across the stainless-steel table, dressed in the same protective yellow gown and face shield as me, stands another one of my colleagues, Megan Carlson. She greets Waseem. "Get bored analyzing your flow cytometry? Looking for a piece of the corpse action?"

"Hardly." Waseem's tone is devoid of its usual pep and charm. "Liza has a visitor."

I do a double take at my coworker. *A visitor? Me?* That's like a woman telling Ted Bundy she's happy to see him. It just doesn't happen. "Who is it?" I ask.

Waseem scratches his dark stubble. "I don't know. Some guy. Looks kind of tough, like he eats bricks and craps machetes. Pretty sure he's not the CEO of Titus McCall Medical Center."

Here my stocky colleague smiles a little. I'm relieved to see it.

When you're as poor of a people reader as I am, you need others to be who you know them as.

Megan's eyebrows lift behind her plastic shield. No doubt she's full of curiosity, but I can offer her nothing. I have no idea who the brick-eating machete crapper is. The only thing I know is that it can't be anything good.

Waseem's phone trills. He checks the screen and, with a quick wave, shuffles out of the room and disappears into the morgue hallway.

I study the partially autopsied body between Megan and me, the cadaver's chest now minus a heart.

"Go ahead." Megan's voice carries the nasal remnants of a cold she's been fighting all week. "I can finish on my own. You were nice enough to help at all. I appreciate that."

I shrug. "It caught my interest. He might be another fentanyl overdose, the third one in a week."

Megan lightly touches the deceased man's shoulder. "He was only twenty years old. It's so sad."

Hearing Megan's compassion makes me check myself. *This is a person,* my father would say. *Not just a case of clinical interest.*

It's not that I don't care or feel bad for the young man's family. I do. It's just that the mind of a person with schizoid personality disorder doesn't dwell on feelings, at least mine doesn't. Instead, it flies straight to the puzzle.

"My aunt Fiona works at an addiction center," Megan says.

I start removing my protective clothing.

"Well, she actually works in HR for a company in Boston, but she volunteers at the center. A teenager there died a few weeks ago from a fentanyl OD. It hit her really hard."

I make to leave, but Megan isn't finished yet. Her gloved hands knead each other over the corpse. "I'm worried about my aunt."

"Why?"

"She hasn't been returning my calls or texts. That's not like her."

"No?"

I'm itching to go see who my visitor is, but Dr. Lightfoot has trained me well enough to know that bolting when Megan is visibly upset would be insensitive.

"No, not at all. My aunt can be challenging, but I'm the only one she has. She calls me every Thursday but didn't last night. Today I've been texting and phoning, but she's not responding. Called her office, but her voicemail message says she's out for the week. I'm kind of scared. Maybe I should drive to Boston and check on her. I just…"

She stares at me over the lifeless body on the autopsy table. I sense she needs something, but I have no idea what it is. "Maybe she went away for Labor Day weekend," I try.

"She'd still respond to my texts."

"Maybe she's camping and doesn't have reception."

"Aunt Fiona is *not* a camper." Megan pauses. "I know you're going to laugh at me, but I have a bit of a sixth sense, and it's telling me something is wrong."

I don't laugh. I have no idea about a sixth sense, but I do know that Megan picks up on more unspoken cues in one day than I could in a year.

When she says nothing else, my late father's words resurface. *You can always help them, Liza. You can always be a helper.*

"Can I do something to help?" I ask.

When Megan's hands unclench and her shoulders relax, it's clear I've said the right thing.

"That's so nice of you, thank you. Maybe you could drive to Boston with me tonight? I'd just like to check on her. Make sure she's okay."

"I can't."

"Oh." Megan lowers her head.

"I have a late meeting with Dr. Silverstein. We're discussing my grant proposal for our research project." To avoid disappointing Megan, I blurt out, "But I can go with you tomorrow morning."

As soon as the words leave my mouth, I regret them. Weekends are my time to decompress. Peaceful hours where I don't have to play the social game. Tomorrow was meant for a solid workout at Brian's Gym and then a day devoted to my grant.

Now I'll have to struggle to make conversation. But…be a helper, right?

"You would?" Megan says. "That'd be great. Really. A huge relief. I just have a bad feeling."

"I'll even drive," I add, because apparently I don't know when to quit. "As long as you don't drag me to Nordstrom."

This makes her laugh, and, like Waseem's smile, I'm happy to see it. Balance is once again restored with the people in my life.

"I promise I won't make you go shopping," she says. "But I'm definitely going to buy you lunch."

Yay me.

I toss my personal protective equipment into the bin. Just as I'm disinfecting my hands and about to leave the autopsy suite to hunt down my visitor—I'm convinced the man has asked for the wrong Liza—Megan calls my name. I turn in the doorframe, hoping my impatience doesn't show.

"I know this is ironic," she says, "considering I just asked you for help, but don't feel like…"

"Don't feel like what?"

"Don't feel like you have to help people to get them to like you. There. I said it." Megan removes the cadaver's heart from the scale. "You can tell us no sometimes. Waseem, John, Jen, me—we'll all still like you. Whether or not you're fixing our tech problems, or helping us with tissue dissection, or driving to Boston with me to check on my aunt, we'll all still like you."

I scratch the back of my pixie cut, unsure what to say.

"And," Megan continues, peering into the severed aorta protruding from the muscular heart, "it's okay for *you* to ask for help for a change. It doesn't have to be one-sided."

"Um, thanks, but I'm good."

"Well, just remember that. You never know when you might need a hand other than your own."

With that, I escape Megan's sermon and head to the second-floor path department.

Time to meet my unwanted visitor.

2

———————

F ew things rattle me. I'm normally pretty calm, but as I trot up a flight of stairs to the pathology department to confront my unknown guest, my fight-or-flight mode kicks in. As my shrink would tell you, that's not my best mode. I'm rarely a flight person. It's always a fight. And I have a lifetime of poor choices to prove it.

Probably it will be nothing, just some stranger looking for the wrong person. If something was wrong with my mother, Dr. Dhar or one of the center's nurses would call me. Besides, her schizophrenia has been less chaotic of late. She enjoyed a stable summer and even took some day trips with me. My brother is doing well too. His indie band has seen recent success. They're currently on tour through New England, and Ned's uncharacteristically good spirits make him almost unrecognizable.

So, no, I doubt this visitor has anything to do with me.

I open the door to the path department to find out.

And immediately tense at what I see.

Near the end of the carpeted hallway, leaning against the wall across from my program director's office, stands a tattooed man sporting a crew cut and a black metal T-shirt. His face, a grim rictus of viciousness, makes Waseem's brick-and-machete description spot on. Although Dr. Thomas's secretary, Mrs. Dejean, isn't visible from inside the two-room office suite, I imagine the man's presence spooks her. The fact it's on my account makes me want to buy her some expensive chocolates and do her paperwork for a week.

As I approach the stranger, his gaze bores into me. His squarish mug and deep-set eyes spark no recognition in my brain, but my pulse ratchets up nonetheless.

When I pass the office suite's door, Mrs. Dejean rises from her desk chair. "Oh, good, you're here. Mr. uh…" She stares at the man and fidgets with her broach. "I'm sorry, what was your name again?"

"Trevor Jones."

I roll the name through my mind. It means nothing to me.

"But Liza here might know me as *Chopper.*"

Chopper.

Shit.

Chopper hasn't entered my thoughts in over a year, and never once have I met him.

I skip the polite greeting. "Let's go outside. Mrs. Dejean doesn't need us invading her space."

Chopper pushes away from the wall. "Fine by me. Wouldn't want me airing your dirty secrets in public now, would you?"

Questions pellet my brain:

When did he get out of prison?

Why is he here?

How did he get the nickname Chopper?

That last one is particularly troubling.

I lead Trevor "Chopper" Jones down the stairs, through the hospital's eight-story atrium, and outside toward the fragrant gardens. They're pretty and serve as a nice retreat for overworked employees or patients' family members, but they're often deserted.

As we weave our way past evergreen walls and into a shrubbery maze, I'm acutely aware that retreating into hidden gardens with a recent inmate, especially one who has six inches on my five-eight frame, not to mention pounds of muscle, is exactly the kind of poor choice that made my late father pinch the bridge of his nose and shake his head. But I can't afford to be seen with Chopper. It doesn't matter that I've never officially met him. He smells like bad news.

With that thought, an idea occurs to me. I point him in the direction we're headed but slow my pace and fall behind. I open the voice-recorder app on my phone without him noticing and press *Record*. Who knows what he's about to say? Or do.

At last we descend the concrete stairwell into a tranquil sitting area with a jade fountain and four wrought-iron benches, all of them empty. The steps trigger an unpleasant memory for me, but I push it away, unable to go there right now.

I sit on the nearest bench and get right to the point. "What do you want?"

"What, no foreplay? Nice nose, by the way. You get that from one of your dead guys in the morgue?"

Chopper is referring to the boxer's nose I earned last year after a brutal fight, another memory I'd prefer to forget.

"Does April know you're out?" I ask. I can't stand the idea of my neighbor or her daughter having to deal with this loser again. "She hasn't said anything to me, and that seems like something she'd mention."

"Maybe she's too busy baking. At least the moron is good at something. Well, that and…"

He makes a lewd expression, and I cut in before he finishes the sentence. "It's tough to find your footing after serving two years in prison for your boyfriend's drug crime. Do you even care that your kid went to foster care?"

"April doesn't know I'm out yet." Chopper scratches a pink scar beneath his jawline. "But depending on how this conversation goes, I might have to pay her and Jasmine a visit."

Fire burns in my belly. "You stay away from both of them. I mean it."

Chopper laughs, exposing two silver fillings in his molars. "Ooh, I'm so scared. I might just—"

"What do you want?"

He edges closer to me on the bench, his thigh inches from my own. I'm eager to move away, but I refuse to let him think he's rattled me.

"Hmm, what do I want." His words are a statement rather than a question as he stares up at the sky. "What do I want. Such a philosophical concept."

I stand. "I don't have time for this."

He yanks me back down. My flame shoots higher, but a mental calculation tells me a physical battle with him wouldn't be in my favor. Not by a long shot.

"You're going to listen to what I have to say. Got that?" Chopper sniffs, covers one nostril, and leans over to blow snot onto a nearby rosebush.

"Classy," I say, wanting to smash his face down into the disgusting blob.

"The way I see it, you owe me."

I snort. "I owe you? How's that?"

"Hey, tough girl, how about we don't dance around? I helped you out last summer. Completed a task on a certain someone, a task that…let's just say wouldn't do your doctor career any good if it came out. In fact, I bet it would end you. Dump you in a nice little prison cell like the one I just left."

"You're full of shit." My normally robotic voice—at least according to my brother—develops a tremble of anxiety. "I never asked for that."

"You didn't, huh?" His own snort follows but thankfully no more snot balls. "Whether you asked for it specifically or just put the little birdie in April's ear, I came through for you. The guy is gone." Chopper scans me up and down. "April seems to think you're pretty special. Wanted to help you out, I guess. Looking at you, I don't get why."

I should have seen this coming. Not sure why I didn't. Probably because it's been over a year since my awful experience with Dr. Sam Donovan, and I wanted nothing more than to push the whole thing from my mind. So I did. Buried it good and deep, just like the surgeon himself got buried good and deep. I should have known his sick soul would claw its way out one day, and here it is, in the ugly form of Trevor "Chopper" Jones.

"What do you want?" I ask for the third and hopefully final time.

"It's not easy starting fresh after prison," Chopper says. "Takes resources, resources most of us don't have."

"You mean money."

He snaps his fingers, and his lips curl into a smile. "Whad'ya know? The girl with the butch haircut and Gap wardrobe is smarter than she looks."

"I'm not giving you money. If that's why you came here, you're wasting your time. I'm not about to finance your drugstore."

"Nope. Those days are behind me. I'm making a fresh start."

"Yeah. Right. April didn't waste much breath talking about you, but the little she did share was that you were more rotten than the banana peels in her trash. Her words, not mine."

He ignores me. "So here's what I'm thinking. I'm gonna start a business, one right here in Morganville. Rich asshole tourists love coming our way. Leaf-peeping time, ski season, summer festivals, it doesn't matter. They flock to us like maggots."

"Wow, use that in your marketing material. They'll line up in droves."

"I got real good at woodwork inside. Made all sorts of things: benches, birdhouses, garden tables. You name it, I made it." Chopper's face softens in the sunlight, lessening his scary countenance by about five degrees. "The prison has a deal with some local churches. Inmates make the goods. The Jesus lovers auction them off for charity."

"So, what, you're going to sell birdhouses?"

"Damn right." Chopper's hardness is back. "People will buy my stuff. They're always looking for high-quality shit to take back with them."

"But why here in Morganville? Why not Boston?"

"Are you deaf? I already told you—people love it here." He kicks a pebble toward the fountain. "Plus, this is my home. My mom's here. I'm her only kid, and she needs me. I can't leave her again."

Well, well. Chopper has a soft spot.

"Besides," he growls, "who wants to buy handcrafted souvenirs in Boston? People want that stuff from quaint little shops in quaint little New England towns like quaint little Morganville."

I can't argue with him there, but I don't know what he expects me, a pathology resident making $66,000 a year, to do for him.

As if reading my mind, he says, "That's where you come in. You're gonna give me fifty grand to get my business up and running."

I bark a hearty laugh, which for me is rarer than a chimp piloting an aircraft. Chopper is a fool if he thinks I'm forking over fifty grand. That would wipe out the remaining inheritance from my dad, and the only time I dip into that fund is when my mom needs treatment her insurance won't cover.

"You think helping me is funny?" he asks.

"No, I think you blackmailing me is funny. You're delusional if you think I'm going to give you a dime."

"And you're delusional if you think I won't start singing about what happened."

I study him, trying to discern if he's bluffing. "If you sing, you implicate yourself, not just me or April."

Chopper shrugs. "Not if I pass it off as a rumor. You know, I heard from a guy who heard from a guy. My name doesn't have to come up."

"Unlikely."

"Even if it does, what've I got to lose? My life is already messed up. But you? A doctor? You've got plenty to lose."

I press my fingertips against my temples. This can't be happening. I don't care about much, but I do care about my reputation and the only career I've ever wanted. My goal is to become a neuropathologist and study the brain inside and out, microscopically and macroscopically, chemically and hormonally. Only then might I figure out how the same organ in the same family can make a mother a delusional schizophrenic, a brother a depressed void, a late father a steady-state carer, and a daughter a deranged and schizoid misfit.

But as much as I want to remain on the pathology wagon train, I can't give this ex-convict money. There is no guarantee it would be a one-time thing. It never is with blackmailers. (Unless *I'm* the black-mailer. I always keep my word.)

"I'm not giving you anything," I tell Chopper. "I can't risk you coming back for more."

"You think you can risk *not* giving me any?"

I sit silent for another spell, mindful I need to get back inside the hospital for my meeting with Dr. Silverstein but too thrown off balance to do so.

This could ruin me. Not only me—April, too, if what Chopper is saying is true. And what about Jasmine? April would rather die than lose Jasmine again. I picture the two of them in their apartment across from mine, April getting the baking pans from the kitchen cabinets and Jasmine dumping the flour into a giant mixing bowl. April rolling the dough into balls and Jasmine putting a chocolate kiss on top. April handing me a plateful of warm cookies and Jasmine giggling while I snarf them down.

No, I can't bring April into this. How brainless was I to think this wouldn't come back to haunt us? I didn't ask any questions at the time. Just lied to myself and considered it serendipity that my nemesis had ceased to exist—literally.

From six feet under in a cemetery in Boston, my dad closes his bony orbits at my stupidity. A few miles over, my shrink heaves a heavy sigh in his home office. I don't blame either of them.

Sometime during my stupor, Chopper has stood up and is now running his tattooed hand over a hedge near the bench. "I can see you're deep in thought, Doc, so I'll let you chew on things a bit. Enjoy the long weekend." He winks. "See you soon."

With that, he lobs another nasty nose blow onto the rosebush and strolls out of the hospital gardens, back into his blackmailing, woodworking world.

3

———————

On Saturday morning, I exit my apartment complex in southeast Morganville and steer my Civic to our historic town center to pick up Megan. My desire to drive to Boston to check on her aunt hovers around minus ten on the desirability scale, but my word is my word, so off I go. If traffic is light, the drive will take forty minutes. If it's heavy, I'm looking at eighty. At least I got a good sweat in at Brian's Gym. My hour of circuit work and heavy-bag boxing pumped out enough endorphins to get me through what lies ahead. Hopefully.

No doubt Megan's aunt will wonder why her niece and an odd excuse for a human being are showing up on her doorstep, but that's on Megan to explain. If proving the woman is okay helps assuage Megan's worry, then it's the least I can do. Besides, Dr. Lightfoot's cancellation of last night's session saved me from making the drive to Boston twice in as many days.

On a tree-lined street still boasting the greens of summer, I pull into one of Massachusetts's millions of doughnut shops. Okay, maybe not millions, but there seems to be one on every New England corner, so you do the math.

Once armed with six pastries and two sleeved cups of hot drinks

—coffee for Megan, Earl Grey tea for me—I navigate the labyrinth of downtown streets toward Megan's loft. She moved here from Boston a few months ago, where she'd previously been living with her sister. With its cobblestone roads and colonial holdovers, Morganville's downtown area is scenic. This weekend it's congested with Labor Day tourists. They dart between parked cars and jaywalk, and twice I have to brake to avoid hitting them.

I visualize Chopper inside one of the gift shops, sculpting his wooden birdhouses, smirking because he thinks he's found a bank account in me. Well, he hasn't. Not only do I have the recording from our conversation yesterday, but I also made another copy should I need it. With a few edits.

But I can't think about Trevor "Chopper" Jones right now, so down deeper, deeper into my cerebral cortex he goes.

In the parking lot behind Megan's building, which is a renovated brick structure from a century and a half back with rent too pricey for me, I text her that I've arrived. While I wait, I dig into a vanilla-cream doughnut.

No sooner have I licked my fingers clean than she swoops into my car with her signature floral scent and her skillfully applied makeup. Her hair's golden highlights carry the shine of a recent touch-up. "A partial foil," she told me last week. Whatever that is.

"Thank you again for driving me." Megan buckles her seat belt and settles her giant tote bag on her lap. "It means a lot."

"It's okay. I've got nothing better to do."

"That's a lie, and you know it."

It is, I think but don't say.

"I'm keeping you from working on your grant, and I know you've already been slowed down by Dr. Silverstein's personal issues."

I nod but remain silent.

"I promise we'll just check on my aunt, have a quick lunch, and then get you back by this afternoon." Megan spots the coffee cup in the beverage holder between us. "For me?"

"Yes. Doughnuts in the back seat too."

Her eyes light up, and she reaches around for one. "Just what the doctor didn't order. My nose is still stuffed up, but at least I can taste again." After chewing a bite of a chocolate glazed, she says, "I almost drove to Boston last night. I also thought about calling the police for a welfare check but realized that might be an overreaction. Aunt Fiona would be horrified if a cop showed up. Just wish I could shake this feeling."

"What's your aunt's address?"

Megan tells me, and I tap it into my phone's GPS. I check the estimated time of arrival and say, "In fifty-two minutes you'll feel better."

"I hope you're right."

As we drive away, Megan begins telling me about her aunt. I play the role of the mute chauffeur, which is just how I like it.

"Maybe I already told you, but my aunt doesn't really have anyone. Never been married. No kids. She's forty-six, so children aren't likely in her future, not that she seems to want any. Her only sibling, my father, lives in Florida, and they don't get along. Same goes for my sister, Ellen, who avoids Aunt Fiona completely, even though they both live in Boston."

Before I have to ask why, Megan continues. "Ellen is a defense attorney for a prestigious law firm. Aunt Fiona, social-justice crusader that she is, doesn't understand why my sister defends rich white-collar criminals. Guys who bend the system for their own gains. The two of them argue all the time, so Ellen no longer visits her. Wouldn't even check on her yesterday. Says my aunt is flighty and flaky and lives in a fairy-tale world."

Megan eats more of her doughnut. Her bites are like rabbit nibbles compared to my hound dog chomps.

After a sip of coffee, she says, "My aunt isn't flighty or flaky, at least not in my opinion, but she is a bit…New Agey. She's into some different things. Crystals, energy healing, that kind of stuff. My sister, on the other hand, is more…well, she's more like you."

I doubt that. No one is like me.

As Megan resumes her one-sided conversation, I pass a slow-moving Saturn, its rear-passenger window replaced by a sheet of cardboard.

"Aunt Fiona is a total professional, though. Been working in HR for a party-supply manufacturer for years, and like I told you before, she volunteers at an addiction center. She likes to give back to the universe."

While Megan talks, my mind wanders to the grant proposal I'm not preparing. My research involves the electrophysiological properties of white matter interstitial neurons and whether they contribute to the development of schizophrenia. As lead author, it'll cement my first footprint into the academic world of neuropathology, but I have to snag the NIH grant first. In order to do that, I need to draft a killer proposal. I'm supposed to present my outline to my program director, Dr. Thomas, on Tuesday.

Unfortunately, my research advisor didn't show up for our meeting last night, which I'd been happy to schedule since my psychiatry appointment had been canceled. As Megan mentioned, Dr. Silverstein is struggling with personal issues, namely her husband's spiraling dementia. As a result, we're falling behind on the grant. My goal for this weekend was to evaluate the existing research to help draft a solid introduction and guide our methodology and objectives sections. I'm nowhere near finishing, and my stomach twists at the thought of missing the grant's deadline.

"…not sure if she has any work friends," Megan is saying.

I tune back in, mindful of the increased holiday traffic. I merge onto I-93 and head south toward Boston.

"Or even a boyfriend. Aunt Fiona is kind of tight-lipped about those things. So, to make a long story short…"

Short?

"…my sister Ellen and I have different viewpoints on family. I'm in the camp that says family is family, and unless they're abusive, you stick by them. Ellen, on the other hand, says there's no reason to keep people in your life whose company you don't enjoy, blood relative or not."

I think about which team I'd be on if I were the type to join teams. No doubt the first one. I don't particularly enjoy my brother's company. Don't even see him that much. But if you go after him, you go after me. Same for my mom or anyone else in my limited circle. Then again, if they were toxic and sucked the life out of me with neediness and selfishness, I'd probably bolt.

To my surprise, Megan pulls knitting needles and a ball of yarn out of her designer tote. Maybe it's a purse, I don't know. I just know it's big, and she apparently has everything but her microscope in it.

"Since when do you knit?" I ask, the first words I've spoken since we left her place.

"Since I started feeling like I'm close to a breakdown."

Uh-oh.

"Feels like my head is exploding."

Ask her what's wrong, my father says in my brain.

"Why is your head exploding?" I ask.

Megan's hands start working the knitting needles. Her project appears to be a scarf. "I don't know. Ever since Amy died, I can't quiet my mind."

Amy was Megan's best friend from med school at Johns Hopkins. Despite doing residencies in different hospitals, they kept in touch.

"Here today, gone tomorrow. One distracted driver—or drunk, or whatever—is all it takes." Megan drops one of her aluminum needles and snaps her fingers.

"They still don't know who hit her?"

"Nope." Megan returns to her knitting, the needles working so furiously the yarn might catch fire. "That's what makes it even worse. Some vile coward got away with murder. It's so unfair."

I squeeze the steering wheel more tightly, my own anger rising at the thought.

"I think that's why the morgue is getting to me lately—there are just so many deaths." She scoffs. "Doesn't bode well for a future forensic pathologist, huh?"

Once again, I'm clueless as to how to respond. Help in the form of action I can give—like driving Megan to Boston to check on her aunt. Help in the form of reassuring words, not so much.

"And there's so much inhumanity and ugliness in the world,"

Megan continues. "Online, on the street, in the news. Sometimes I just want to crawl into a hole and hide."

I merge into the middle lane and take three big swallows of tea. Megan is the social one, the upbeat one, the glass-half-full one. After fourteen months of working together, I've finally learned how to navigate her. But this newer, sadder version of Megan Carlson unsettles me.

We drive the rest of the way in silence. Thirty-five minutes later, I squeeze my blue Civic into a parking spot on a narrow street off Boylston near Fenway Park.

From the passenger seat, Megan points to an eight-story building with bay windows and ecru siding. "My grandpa bought a unit here in the nineties. Rented it out for extra income. He left it to Fiona after he and my grandma passed. Fiona could sell it for a lot more now, but whenever someone suggests that, she says 'over my dead body.' It's just a small studio, but she loves the location."

I glance around in both directions. Given all the restaurants, parks, and university offerings in the area, I'm going with Fiona on this one.

We exit my Civic and spill into the September sunshine. After dodging a few passing cars, we cross the street and head to the condo building's entrance. Megan presses the call button for Fiona's unit. When there's no answer, she shakes her head.

"Something's not right." Her hand cups her abdomen. "I feel it."

I shrug, which, according to Dr. Lightfoot, is not a helpful response, but while I don't know what to say, I do know that Megan is weirdly intuitive, and it would be unfair to dismiss her anxiety.

She punches a four-digit passcode into the keypad: 2175. "Every unit has their own code to enter the building. Aunt Fiona uses the same four digits for everything." The door buzzes, and Megan holds it open for me. "It's the year Aunt Fiona would time travel to if she could."

I stare at Megan, confused. Then I realize she means the code— the year 2175. I'll admit, it's the first thing that's piqued my curiosity all morning. "Why that year?" I ask.

"Who knows?" Megan leads us to the elevator and smooths her linen pants. "Aunt Fiona said she just had a feeling that would be her best time."

Ooookay. Maybe Auntie is a bit flighty after all.

The elevator smells of almonds, and its handrails suggest we'll be catapulted into space if we don't hold on. I examine my Nike T-shirt and jean shorts in the smoky mirrors and hope they'll pass Flaky Fiona's muster.

We get out on the fourth floor. As we approach unit 405, which is halfway down the corridor, the almond scent disappears and something less pleasant takes its place. It's faint, but it's there.

Megan says nothing about the odor, simply knocks on her aunt's door. Maybe her nose is too congested from her lingering cold to notice it.

"Aunt Fiona?" she calls out, knocking louder.

The growing concern on Megan's face is obvious, probably because it mirrors the feeling in my gut. The rotting, almost sweet scent of decay—albeit subtle—hovers near the apartment door.

Should I say something? Am I overreacting?

Megan digs inside her enormous bag, pulls out a key, and inserts it into the lock. "Aunt Fiona gave me this in case she ever locks herself out. I hate to invade her privacy, but…"

She looks at me, and I nod. We need to get in there.

After she opens the door, we step inside the apartment, its air warm and stagnant. About the size of my own studio, it's smartly decorated with antique furniture and accents. I get little time to examine them, because the deeper we cross into the unit, the stronger the smell.

"Don't you smell that?" I finally say. "It smells like…decay."

Megan snaps her head toward me. "Smell what?" She inhales deeply through her nose. "I don't smell anything." She scans the room and makes a complete turn, her wedge sandals bunching up the tasseled edge of an area rug. She darts to the back of the unit to a door on the left. "Fiona?"

It's the bathroom, but there's no Aunt Fiona inside. Megan whips open the only other door, just opposite the bathroom. Inside is a deep but narrow closet stuffed with clothes and household objects. A window lies at the end. Megan opens it and sticks her head out. I stand behind her and see it leads to a fire escape. Together we scan the metal staircase and the narrow alley below. No Fiona.

But that smell. Where is it coming from?

When we return to the studio's main living space, it dawns on me that the unit has no bed. Where does Fiona sleep? The couch?

"Oh good, she's not here," Megan says with obvious relief. "Whatever you're smelling must be a dead mouse or something." She opens the kitchenette's blond-wood cabinets and searches each one. "Nothing here. Maybe it's coming from the bathroom."

I shake my head. An unusually tall upright piano stands next to me. It appears to be an antique, with distressed wood carved into elaborate curves and patterns. I sniff it. The scent is definitely stronger here.

"It's coming from the piano," I say. When I touch the massive instrument, I realize there are no ivory keys.

Megan laughs. "That's not a piano."

"What is it then?"

"It's Aunt Fiona's bed. An antique Murphy bed."

I study it, acknowledging that a piano/bed combination makes sense. A bed would take up valuable space in a studio apartment, leaving little room between it and the plump sofa Fiona has pushed against the wall.

"She bought it at an auction." Megan runs her fingers along the wood. "Fits a double mattress."

I lean in closer to the faux piano and sniff again. My muscles tense. *Oh yeah.* The smell is coming from there.

Two rounded handles project from the wood about a foot above where the keyboard would be. I wrap my hands around them.

"Do you think a mouse got in there?" Megan asks. "Maybe I do smell something now."

I open the antique Murphy bed and let it fall flat.

Aunt Fiona lies inside.

4

———————

I blink at the woman I assume to be Fiona Carlson. It takes me a second to register what I'm seeing: trim body in pink pajamas pressed into the mattress, legs slightly splayed, one arm crossed over her chest, the other against her side. Her blond head grazes the piano's upright back, and her bare feet sink at odd angles into the mattress at the foot of the bed. Although her eyes are closed, they appear sunken in her ashen-blue face, and her nose is smashed where the opposing wood closed in on her. A patch of urine stains her pajama bottoms, its ammonia residue mixing with the scent of death.

Megan utters a strangled cry. "Oh my God, oh my God!" She rushes to her aunt's side and shakes her shoulder. Then she presses a finger to the woman's carotid artery.

The pulse check is pointless—I think we both know that. Fiona's coloring, not to mention the early scent of decomposition, confirms it, but I understand the reflex.

"Oh my God," Megan wails again. "I can't believe this. I just can't believe this. Call 911!"

My phone is already in my hands, the numbers punched in. No social training is required to know this is the next move.

While I speak to the 911 operator, Megan rocks back and forth near the open bed, her hands cupping her nose and mouth, her gaze never leaving her aunt. "I should have come last night," she repeats several times, her voice muffled behind her hands.

When I end the call, I say, "It wouldn't have made any difference. The rigor mortis is gone. She's likely been dead for over thirty-six hours, and with the pressure of her body against the mattress, the livor mortis—"

"I don't need a fucking pathology lesson," Megan shouts.

I've never heard her swear before, but I realize too late I deserve it. I shouldn't have veered into the clinical. I've learned better than that. Someone finding their loved one dead deserves empathy and compassion, not a misfit blowhard pontificating on the stages of death.

Even though comforting words don't come easily to me, my chest pinches for Megan all the same. I, too, am disturbed at finding a dead body, but any consoling I give her will feel forced.

Do it anyway, my late father says in my head.

So I do. I put an arm around Megan while we wait for the ambulance. She stiffens at first, as if she, too, is thrown by my unexpected touch, but then she leans her trembling body into me and starts to cry. Not howling or sobbing, just a few quiet tears and a soft, "I don't think I can go through this again." I assume she's referring to her friend's death last spring.

She wipes her eyes with the back of her hand. "I should have come Thursday night when I didn't get her call."

"One missed call doesn't mean a person has…" I fear I'll say the wrong thing again, so I let my voice trail off.

"I know, but my aunt always touched base with me. I should have known something was wrong."

"You can't blame yourself. Seriously. This is not your fault."

She nods and pulls away from me. When she reaches for her aunt's hand, I'm about to tell her she probably shouldn't touch anything else, but another forensics lesson from me is not what she needs.

"Oh, Auntie." She strokes Fiona's forearm and looks over at me.

"I warned her about getting this bed, but once she saw it, she had to have it. She said it was the antique find of the century." Megan gives a sad little laugh and then releases her aunt's hand and stands back from the faux piano bed. "Shouldn't touch anything else, I guess." Her words echo my earlier thoughts. "Then again, it's clearly an accident, so I suppose what's the harm?"

Is it? I wonder.

"People have died in Murphy beds, you know." She reaches into her pocket for a tissue and blows her nose. "That's why I warned her against it, especially an old one like this. They can snap shut on you. It's rare, but... And look here." Megan points to the backboard. "There's hardly any room between the mattress and the wood. You can see how she got, she got…"

Megan shakes her head as if unable to speak the word, but I imagine she was going to say *crushed*.

"The medical examiner can sort it out. For now, you just take care of you." It's a stupid platitude, I know, but it's all I've got.

Megan retreats to the sofa and grabs her aunt's purse off the velvety cushion. After digging around inside the bag, she pulls out Fiona's cell phone. Other than the case's bold purple color, the only thing I register is that Fiona's mobile is still in her purse. Wouldn't she keep it near her at night?

"I'm going to need her phone to notify people." Megan enters a passcode onto the screen. "Two one seven five. Figures." She rummages around in the purse again.

"I better go down to let the police in," I say. "I told the 911 operator they could just buzz the unit, but in case it doesn't work or something."

"Okay."

Megan now retrieves a black object from Fiona's purse. Rising from the couch, she slips it into her own tote bag, near the murderous piano bed. She dropped the bag after seeing her aunt's dead body. Her ball of yarn and half-knitted scarf spilled out and remain strewn on the area rug.

"What's that?" I ask, regarding the dark object.

"Fiona's stun gun."

"Um. Okay. Why are you taking it?"

"They're legal now in Massachusetts, but you need a firearms permit, and my aunt hasn't gotten one yet. She bought it at a trade fair in Ohio and carries it for protection when she's out doing her social crusading. She keeps putting off registering it, though, so I don't want her to get in trouble."

This seems a moot point now that Fiona is dead, but I refrain from voicing it. My father would revel in my restraint.

I open the door and head down to usher in the police.

5

———————

The next couple of hours go by in a blur. Uniformed police officers snap pictures, ask questions, and make phone calls to various death services. Curious neighbors hover in the hallway, hoping for a peek at the drama whenever the door is opened. Having not known Fiona Carlson, I'm a useless appendage at this point, but if my presence helps calm Megan, I don't mind being here.

After the coroner finishes up and two body-removal technicians transfer the body down to a transport vehicle, Megan and I follow them out.

A small crowd of spectators has gathered outside the building. Some appear to be passersby. Others are tenants who trailed behind us for a show. With hushed murmurs all around, we watch as the removal techs wheel the mortuary cot holding Fiona's covered body down the accessibility ramp.

Being crushed by a Murphy bed seems unambiguous enough, and the cops didn't find anything suspicious, but Fiona's death raises red flags in my mind. Although the coroner, a tall man with slouched shoulders, declined to make any definitive statement, he did confirm that deaths of this manner have occurred in the past.

"It's an antique bed with an old spring system," he said. "One of the locking legs looks faulty. It's possible the bed simply closed while she was sleeping. We'll know more after the autopsy."

We stand with him now on the sidewalk. He tells Megan once again he's sorry for her loss. "How tragic to lose your aunt in such a senseless way."

Megan thanks him, and together we—and the bystanders, doubled in size now—watch him duck his body into his Prius and drive away. The transport van carrying Fiona Carlson pulls out shortly after.

An elderly woman who followed us out of the building takes Megan's hand. "I'm so sorry, dear. Your aunt was a lovely woman. Brought me amethyst crystals to help with my anxiety after my husband passed."

Another woman gives Megan a hug. "I'm sorry too, sweetie. Your aunt helped me as well, but with Reiki instead of crystals. She told me she used it on some of the people at the addiction clinic."

Crystals? Reiki? I'm beginning to understand why Megan's sister accused Fiona of being a flake. But who am I to judge? If these things help people get through life, then good on them. I vent my own crap by beating up a bag full of sand in the gym. How's that any different?

Megan introduces me to an egg-shaped man with wire-rimmed glasses that glint in the sunlight. "Liza, this is Chuck, my aunt's neighbor down the hall. He brings"—Megan's voice hitches —"*brought* my aunt dinners. She didn't have much time to cook, so she really appreciated the wonderful meals."

Chuck brushes off Megan's praise, but a blush springs to his cheeks. "Too much food for a single guy. I was happy to share."

I study him. Despite the postmortem state of Fiona's body, it's clear she was an attractive and fit woman of forty-six. This man seems her physical opposite. I wonder if his food offerings carried with them the hope of a relationship. If so, I imagine it was an unrequited desire.

Dr. Lightfoot says I'm too suspicious of people. I suppose this is what he means.

A few more tenants gather around Megan to offer their condolences. How many of them actually know her or are just getting in on the action, I'm not sure. I'm also not skilled enough to detect if their sympathetic words stem from true sincerity or from the weird thrill people seem to get from tragedy—tragedy that happens to someone else, that is.

A woman with lined lips and a tight sweater approaches. She tells Megan her aunt will be missed. I swear she says it with a slight smile. Maybe, like Megan's sister, she didn't find Fiona so likable.

Abruptly, a beefy guy who looks to be in his forties darts out of the building and barrels through the crowd. Is his brusqueness out of ignorance of what just happened? Or is it because he doesn't care that a woman in his building died? Either way, we make eye contact as he passes.

Another man, this one with wavy blond hair and a physical build more in Fiona's league than Chuck's portly corpus, tries to dodge the crowd of onlookers on the sidewalk. I'm not sure whether he lives in the building or is just passing by, but I pull Megan to the side so he can get through.

"Oh, sorry," she says to him. "Thanks, Liza."

I need none of my shrink's emotion flash cards to deduce that Megan is growing overwhelmed by all these people. She chews her lower lip, blinks rapidly, and clutches her designer tote bag against her side so tightly the tendons in her forearm pop out. I don't blame her. I'm not enjoying this macabre social hour either.

"Do you want to go?" I ask her. "You already locked Fiona's unit, right?"

She nods. "Yes, let's get out of here."

I part the crowd with a no-nonsense exit, creating a path behind me for Megan. When we cross the street to my car, I glance up at the U-shaped building and frown. A skinny guy in a hoodie is climbing down the fire escape on Fiona's side of the complex. He's passing a seventh-floor window, but whether he came from there, the eighth floor, or the roof, I don't know. I only know it seems odd someone would exit the building that way.

Is he avoiding the crowd at the entryway? There must be a rear entrance. Couldn't he have gone out the back instead of shinnying down narrow stairs into an alley full of dumpsters?

Megan is already in the car, but I keep watching the man. He trots down the remaining steps and spills into the alleyway. Then he saunters off toward the sidewalk on the other side of the building, hood up, hands stuffed in his pockets, his back to me.

Something is off with him. I sense it. I might not understand typical human behavior well, but I know a thing or two about *a*typical.

"Liza?" Megan calls from inside my Civic. "You coming?"

I tear my gaze away from the departing man. He's not where my focus should be right now. It should be on getting Megan home. It should be on my grant proposal. It should be on Chopper, my blackmailer.

I climb into the driver's seat, willing my brain to comply.

6

The drive home from Boston seems to take forever. Megan's frenetic knitting (as if twisting the needles fast enough will turn back time to when Fiona was still breathing) leaves me searching for something comforting to say. My well of learned responses has run dry.

With each new wrap of yarn, Megan mumbles about the fleetingness of life. "Everything we have can end just like that. Everything." When I nod and take the exit for Morganville, she adds, "There's so much ugly out there. I'm not sure I can take it anymore."

By the time I drop her off at her downtown apartment, I'm wound tighter than the stitches in her knitted scarf and more useless than the bits of yarn littering my floor mat. Another round with the heavy bag at Brian's Gym tempts me, but instead, I drive home. Dusk is falling, and my grant proposal needs to take priority. It'll be a late night making up for the hours I lost.

Yet, while my brain should be pondering interstitial neurons and schizophrenia, it's thinking about Fiona's death. I keep seeing her lifeless body crushed inside that antique Murphy bed. Everyone assumes it was a tragic mishap. The police. The neighbors. The coroner. Megan, too, keeps referring to it as an accident, as if foul play isn't even an option. Given she's a pathology resident who wants to go into forensics, that seems rash to me.

"Liza," I imagine my shrink saying, "maybe Megan is too emotionally overwhelmed to think otherwise." I picture him running a hand through his thick hair, a sweet gift for a man in his fifties. "Not everything is a puzzle to be solved."

After a few more minutes of distracted driving, I reach the street of strip malls and residential apartment buildings that includes my own complex. I park my Civic in my assigned spot and head inside toward unit 103, my five-hundred-square-foot studio. As I pass unit 102 on the left, I notice its door is wide open. Curiosity is curiosity, so I glance inside.

A microwave with cracked glass lies toppled on the linoleum floor. To my surprise, so does my middle-aged landlord, Mr. Brent Sinclair. The shortish man with rosacea and a paunch clutches the chest of his polo shirt. Sweat beads on his forehead, and his face contorts in what appears to be pain. When he spots me, his eyes grow wide.

I race into the room and drop to my knees, my satchel falling off my shoulder. This brute and I have had our share of tussles—I pretended to headbutt him once due to his demeaning treatment of my neighbor, April, and another time I cornered him against the wall—but that doesn't mean I want him to die on the floor of one of his rental units.

"Are you hurt? Can you breathe?"

"Chest…pain," he sputters.

I pull my mobile from my satchel and, hardly believing it, dial 911 for the second time today. Once I've given the details to the operator, I place my hand over Mr. Sinclair's, the one still clutching the left side of his chest.

"You're going to be okay," I tell him.

"Getting…unit…new tenant…" His breathing is labored, and his sweaty face is scrunched up in agony.

"Don't try to talk," I say. I can hear the 911 operator on the line, telling me what to do, unaware I'm a doctor. "Focus on breathing."

No sooner have I uttered those words than my landlord stiffens, and a strangled cry squeaks from his throat. He falls limp.

Shit.

I lower my ear to his nose. No breaths. No chest rising. To quote the newly doomsday Megan, his labored breathing is gone "just like that." A check of his carotid pulse confirms that's gone too.

My own heartbeat speeds up. I put the operator on speaker, tell her Sinclair has gone into cardiac arrest, and drop my phone to my side.

Clasping my hands together, one on top of the other, I place the palm of my lower hand over his sternum and start chest compressions.

"One and two and three and…" As I count, my mind flashes back to med school, when I had to perform CPR on a man in the hospital parking lot. I remember how tired my arms got, how exhausted the compressions made me, even with all the boxing and weightlifting I do. I'd like to give Sinclair rescue breaths—there's a mouth covering in my satchel for rare moments like this—but since I'm alone, it's the compressions that are key to keeping him alive until the ambulance arrives. From my phone, I hear the 911 operator tell me the same thing. I nod stupidly as if she can see me and start counting all over again.

"One and two and three and…"

"Does your building have an automated external defibrillator?" the 911 operator asks me.

"No," I puff out.

I think about the times I've told my landlord he should hang an AED on the wall for this very purpose, not knowing, of course, that it might be *him* who needed it. He balked about the expense.

"Eight and nine and ten and…"

Someone plops down next to me. I startle but don't stop CPR. It's my neighbor, April.

"Do you know how to give compressions?" I ask.

She nods, her charcoal-lined eyes as wide as Mr. Sinclair's terrified ones were minutes ago.

"Take over for me."

She does, and, breathless, I dig into my bag and find the plastic face covering. I place it over Sinclair's blue lips, ignoring the foamy saliva that's coating them. In the pallor of his face, the broken capillaries on his nose and cheeks look like tangles of tiny red highways. I signal to April to hold compressions and then blow two steady breaths of air into Sinclair's mouth and, hopefully, into his lungs.

April and I continue like this for a while. Then we switch positions, and I return to the compressions. I'm not sure how many cycles we complete before I hear sirens. I'm aware only of the irony of April giving life-sustaining breaths to a man who has degraded and insulted her, threatened to evict her, and even tried to solicit sex from her in lieu of rent (until I put a stop to it), all because he deemed her less-than because of her sleeve tattoos and her two-year prison stint.

"Mommy?"

April's daughter, Jasmine, is standing just inside the apartment's door, her arms hugging her body. I didn't even notice she came in.

A pounding erupts from the building's main entrance.

"Go let the first responders in, baby," April tells her.

The eleven-year-old girl complies, and within seconds two EMTs enter the unit.

The female EMT immediately cuts open Sinclair's shirt, his torso pale save for where my palms were pummeling him. With the speed of a greyhound, she shaves his chest and applies the AED paddles. After two shocks, between which she took over compressions, the male EMT signals they've got a pulse.

I lean against the kitchen counter. Nearby, April hugs Jasmine and reassures her everything will be okay. April tells me they heard the commotion through the wall. She ran over to see what was wrong. Only now do I notice her apron, the scent of baked bread, the dust of flour on Jasmine's nose.

I wonder if she has also heard that her ex-boyfriend is out of prison, the dirtbag whose past actions and bullying resulted in her paying for his crime, a crime that took a good mom away from her daughter for two years. How would she react to Chopper blackmailing me?

Now is not the time to tell her. Instead, I watch a second body in one day be wheeled out of a residence, this one thankfully still alive.

Even for an unflappable person like me, that's a lot of flapping.

7

———————

At 9:30 a.m. on Tuesday morning, my program director sits behind his desk in his dark-hued office and fixes his gaze on me. His crossed arms and pinched eyebrows confirm what I already know: I'm blowing this presentation.

While my mouth tries to deliver a coherent summary of my planned grant proposal, including a literature search of existing research in my area of study, my brain flashes images of Fiona Carlson's suffocated body in the Murphy bed instead. My landlord's cardiac arrest surfaces too. I have no idea how Mr. Sinclair is doing. Don't know whether he's in the ICU, whether he's had a stent placed, whether he underwent bypass surgery. I only know my forearms still ache from the chest compressions I gave him three days ago.

When I finish babbling, Dr. Darnell Thomas rubs his temples, his ebony hair stippled with gray. In a voice that's as deep as his shoulders are broad, he says, "It seems you need more preparation, Liza."

That's putting it mildly.

"I understand you have performance issues with presentations"—he means my poor eye contact and lack of charisma but is too nice to say—"but your organization of the material is usually excellent. The grant deadline is less than three weeks away, and with Dr. Silverstein facing personal problems, she'll be even more reliant on you to get this proposal rolling."

"Yes," I say.

"Would you care to expound? You had a long weekend to work on it."

I rub my sore arms. "The weekend got away from me. You heard about Megan's aunt, right?"

"I heard the woman died, yes, and that Megan is taking today off to deal with the funeral arrangements. She called my secretary."

I study the in-basket on Dr. Thomas's desk, marvel at how it's stuffed with literal paperwork in this digital age. "Did you hear *how* she died?"

"No. Only that she didn't have any family to rely on beyond Megan. Your colleague has a good heart."

"The woman was crushed to death."

Dr. Thomas gives a start, and his leather chair squeaks.

"Sorry," I say. "I should have phrased that better."

My program director offers a faint smile. No doubt he's wondering why he let such a weirdo into the department.

"She had an antique Murphy bed," I clarify. "Shaped like a piano. The autopsy isn't until tomorrow, but it's assumed she suffocated in the bed. The coroner thinks it snapped shut on her during the night. I'm not so sure about that, so I guess I'm a little distracted this morning."

Dr. Thomas straightens the keyboard on his desk pad. "I don't mean to be rude, but why does it matter to you how it happened? The woman was Megan's aunt, not yours."

"Because Megan and I were the ones to find her."

"Oh my God, why didn't you say so? That's awful."

He appears to want more, so I explain Saturday morning's trip. How we found Fiona's lifeless body. How she'd likely been dead for at least thirty-six hours. How we called 911. If only I had delivered my grant presentation to him this well, we wouldn't be having this conversation.

"That's just awful," he repeats. "No wonder you're preoccupied. That must have been quite an emotional experience."

While he's correct about my preoccupation, he's incorrect about its cause. I feel bad about Fiona's death—of course I do—and I'm sorry Megan lost two loved ones within the span of five months, but my preoccupation stems not from the emotional experience of finding a dead body, but rather from the endless rumination it presents.

Did a malfunctioning Murphy bed really kill Fiona, as Megan and the police seem to think? Or is there more at play? Did the woman have enemies? As a higher-up in her company's HR department, she could have pissed someone off. Or maybe she butted heads with a patient or an employee at the addiction center. Although Megan never mentioned a man in Fiona's life, when it comes to murder motives, a love reaction gone wrong always makes the cut.

All these questions and more have been swarming my brain since Saturday, and the more I try to quiet them, the more they fuss and shout. Dr. Lightfoot has always urged me to schedule extra sessions with him when I'm stressed or troubled, because my mind creates confusing mazes of possibilities during those times. He says what might seem logical to me might not be logical at all. I'm not sure I agree, though, because my conclusions have often been right in the past. Doesn't matter that my convoluted maze might be different from his smooth one. Besides, other than the threat of missing my grant-proposal deadline, I don't feel stressed. Fiona's death merely has me curious.

"…why don't you take another week," Dr. Thomas is saying.

Shoot, I zoned out. My rumination in action.

"We'll meet again next Wednesday," he says. "You can present your plans to me then. Although the research is yours and Dr. Silverstein's, I have to be kept in the loop."

I nod.

"I don't need to tell you how significant this NIH grant could be to your career, not to mention the contribution your research could make to the field of schizophrenia and—" He frowns. "Why do you keep rubbing your arms? Did you hurt yourself?"

I didn't realize I was still rubbing them. I examine my forearms in my short-sleeved blouse. Red streaks ignite my flesh. To avoid looking even more disturbed to my program director, I tell him about finding my landlord in the midst of an acute MI. "He went into cardiac arrest on Saturday. I had to give him chest compressions until the ambulance arrived with an AED."

"Good Lord," Dr. Thomas's deep voice bellows. "You experienced more stress in one day than most people do in a year. Is he all right?"

"Not sure. Haven't heard back. But he had a pulse when they wheeled him out, so that's a good sign."

My program director shakes his head. "You're a remarkable woman, Liza. You saved a man's life but act like it's nothing. You deserve to be proud of that."

I check the time on my phone. "Teaching rounds start in ten. I better go."

"Yes, of course. Roxanne will lead them today. I've got a meeting."

Roxanne is our new chief resident. She's fine, but I miss Martin, last year's chief. For an outsider like me, that's saying a lot. Martin put everyone at ease, and he'd fire off trivia questions when we least expected it. I liked that.

After Dr. Thomas and I part ways, I head down the hallway toward the Death Chamber. It's a drab, windowless room with a long table that holds a microscope system with ten viewing heads and one primary scope, either for our program director or the chief resident. They slip tissue slides onto the microscope stage, and, like good little ducklings, we peer into our eyepieces and prepare for the onslaught of questions. It sometimes gets brutal, hence, the Death Chamber nickname. First-years have teaching rounds at eight thirty. Ours are at ten. Third- and fourth-year residents no longer require them.

When I enter the Death Chamber, Waseem Ahmad is the only other resident in there. His sateen shirt shimmers with high quality, and his face already sports a five-o'clock shadow, even though it's barely midmorning. Coming from the United Arab Emirates, he speaks with a slight accent that's always pleasant to hear. Jen Lopez and John Kim haven't arrived yet, and, of course, Megan won't be here at all.

Waseem greets me while scrolling on his phone. "How's it going, Rocky? Still showing those heavy bags who's boss?"

I give him the expected chuckle and pull out my own phone to check my emails.

Waseem begins telling me about the action movie he saw this weekend. "Too many car chases, not enough character development. I wasn't expecting *Hamlet*, but you would think—"

His voice cuts off abruptly, and I glance up at him across the table. He's usually pretty easy to read. Always smiling, always positive. But of late he's been less…energetic, and his present expression is not unlike Megan's when we found her dead aunt.

"What?" I ask, genuinely worried. When he doesn't answer, just keeps whispering "I can't believe it, I can't believe it" under his breath, I try again. "Waseem? What happened?"

His eyes droop like a basset hound's. "I just…I can't believe someone would be so mean."

"Mean about what?"

He swallows. "You know I like movies, right?"

Everyone in the hospital knows that.

"Well, it's silly, but I'd like to make films someday. Yes, I'm a pathologist, but we only have one life, right?"

"That's not silly."

"Thank you." His voice shakes. "But it appears I'm not meant for it."

"Why's that?"

He holds up his phone. It shows a YouTube video, but I can't see the specifics.

"Don't tell anyone, but I made a short film."

"That's cool," I say, and it is, especially considering it was only a year ago I showed him how to use a video-editing app.

"It's nothing big. Just a fifteen-minute short about a man who steals a winning lottery ticket but then suffers so much guilt he gives the money away."

"Sounds like a good premise. What's the problem?"

"I posted it last week under the name Mad Wasp," Waseem says. "It's a play on my name. Sadly, it hasn't gotten many views."

Oh. No dead aunt then. Just a dead film.

"So I shared it on Instagram, and now…" His shoulders slump. "Now I just got my first review. Well, first comment, anyway, but it's…it's…" He tosses his phone on the table. "I can't read it out loud."

"Want me to take a look?" Dr. Lightfoot would give me points for this social exchange.

Waseem nods, and I reach for his phone.

I note the title of his film, *Losing to Win*, and then read the comment silently:

Just because every Joe Idiot out there can make a movie doesn't mean they should. This guy calls himself a budding filmmaker. Right. And I'm George F*cking Lucas. The angles are sh*t, the dialogue is sh*t, and I've seen less obvious themes on the ad boards in the subway. This guy shouldn't be making compost let alone films. Note to Mad Wasp: Don't quit your day job. You suck.

Jesus. I push the phone back to Waseem. It clinks against his microscope.

Channeling my shrink, only with less eloquent language, I say, "First of all, this guy's an asshole. Don't listen to him. His username is Joe Balls, for God's sake. And second of all, you were brave enough to post your film and share it. That takes a lot of courage."

"You haven't seen the video. What if he's right?" Waseem retrieves his phone. "I'm going to delete it."

"No." My tone is sharper than I intended. "Don't. Not for some dumb troll. That's all he is. Some loser who's pissed you did such a great job straight out of the gate."

"You're just saying that."

I stare hard at my colleague, not an easy feat for someone like me, but for Waseem the prolonged eye contact is worth it. He's one of the good ones, and if I could squeeze Joe Balls's balls, I would squeeze them until they popped. "Listen," I say, "you've known me for over a year. Have I ever been a hand-holder? A sugarcoater?"

This gets a laugh from him. "No."

"Exactly. So I'm telling you like it is. People who trash other people's work with cruel insults are jealous wannabes. It's fine to not like something. Even the best movie in the world has haters. But a negative review is one thing. A mean one that targets the creator is just plain old bullying."

Waseem sits a little straighter.

"You leave that video where it is. Others will watch it and like it. You'll see." I have no idea whether this is true—maybe the film sucks—but giving in to bullies is never okay. At least not in my book. Or in this case, movie.

"Maybe," Waseem says. "Yeah, maybe you're right. Thanks, Liza. But don't tell anyone. It's kind of embarrassing."

I nod, and I'm relieved that when Jen and John arrive, Waseem cracks a joke to them. If I've helped clear some of his hurt, I'm glad.

Now if only I could clear some of Megan's. Then everyone in my circle could get back to themselves, and I could get on with life.

8

―――――

The following afternoon, after reviewing slides from a lung tissue sample, which, unfortunately for the patient, shows the dense blue cells of small cell cancer, I leave my cubicle near the window and grab black tea from the kiosk in the hospital atrium. A shot of caffeine is in order before I return to the residents' lounge, where I plan to work on my grant before I meet Shawna (my one childhood friend) and Tam (her wife) for dinner. Somehow it's become a twice-monthly thing.

Yay me.

Staying focused is difficult, though. Fiona's autopsy was supposed to be performed in Boston today. Megan promised to text me with any updates, but it's almost five, and I've heard nothing.

On my way back from the beverage kiosk, my phone rings in the stairwell. Hoping it's Megan, I yank it out of my back pocket. In my abruptness, hot tea spills out of my cup's sip hole and scorches my hand.

It's not Megan's number. It's April's, my neighbor. She never calls me—knows I prefer texts—so it must be important. News about our landlord, maybe?

"What's going on?" I say in place of a greeting. I trot up the stairs toward the second floor, ignoring the sting on my hand.

The voice that follows is male and most definitely not April's. "Hey, there, Doc."

I screech to a halt in the stairwell.

"You didn't forget about me now, did you? Not after our nice chat the other day."

Chopper.

Shit.

I imagine how horrified April must have been to find her ex-boyfriend on her doorstep. Is she with him now? She must be if he's using her phone. Why didn't I tell her he was out of prison?

Stupid, stupid, stupid.

"You need to leave April and Jasmine alone," I demand. Unlike other emotions, anger comes easily to me.

Chopper laughs, but it isn't a pleasant sound. "I think you've forgotten who's giving the orders here. I did something for you." He lowers his voice. "So now you're going to do something for me. That's how this works. I—"

"Let me talk to April."

"Did you not hear—"

"Now."

A pause, and then a ruffling as the phone changes hands.

"Hi, Liza." April's voice sounds pinched and carries none of its usual buoyancy.

"You okay?" I place my scalding tea on the step.

"Yes, um, Chopper stopped by. He wanted your number. Says you and he have some sort of…agreement."

"Agreement. Right. He's—" I refuse to spill that he's black-mailing me. April doesn't need to be part of this. She'll feel guilty, and I don't want that. She'll worry she's the one who set the ball rolling by overinterpreting my words. That must be what happened, because I didn't ask for it. Not specifically, anyway. Then again, maybe April didn't either. Maybe Chopper heard about the Donovan fiasco from his own prison cell. My name and the surgeon's were all over the news. Maybe he saw an opportunity.

Maybe he knew who I was to April and figured he'd do something big in the form of a shank and cash in on it later, making us think we were the instigators.

The problem is, I don't know which of these possibilities is the truth.

My knuckles tighten around the phone. "Let me talk to Chopper again," I tell April. "I'll explain later."

I won't, of course. This is not a conversation that should see the light of day.

When Chopper is back on the line, I bark, "You leave them alone. Otherwise you'll get nothing from me."

"You give me what I want, and I'll pretend I don't even know them. April and Jasmine who?" he says, chuckling.

If he were in front of me, I'd punch him. Forget breathing exercises and using words instead of fists. I'd punch him in the nose and give him one far more crooked than mine.

A woman in scrubs enters the stairwell. I grab my tea off the step and move out of her way. After she exits on the main floor, I ask Chopper, "How much do you want right now?"

There's no way I'm giving this guy money. It will never end. I have to come up with a plan and quickly. I've been so focused on Megan's aunt that I haven't given this immediate threat the attention it deserves. Chopper is like a scorpion in my path—I sure as shit don't want it there, but I can't move forward until I've squashed it.

"I've got some business to attend to in Boston first," he says, like he's some hotshot CEO, "but I got your digits now, so I'll be in touch. We'll talk numbers again then."

"Fine." I grit my teeth and hang up.

There are a lot of things I hate. Small talk. Parties. Assholes and bullies.

But I really, really, *really* hate not being the one in control.

Since a punch to Chopper's nose wasn't doable through the phone, I fall back on Dr. Lightfoot's breathing exercises. It takes a few rounds before I'm ready to leave the stairwell. By the time I return to the pathology department, my tea is cold.

Outside the residents' room, Megan's and Jen's voices carry from their cubicles into the hallway. Given it's almost six o'clock, I'm surprised Jen is still here. She usually clears out by five thirty to pick up her kids and start dinner. Must be putting together her Ewing's sarcoma presentation for next week's oncology path rounds. How she manages to work full time as a resident and raise three kids is beyond me. I never plan on finding out either. Me as a mother should scare everyone.

I'm about to enter the room but stop short. Jen is crying.

"I'm sorry," she says, presumably to Megan. "You're the last person I should be whining to. You're the one who just lost her aunt."

"Oh, please," Megan says. "You have every right to vent. You've got more going on than any of us."

Though I can't see Megan from my spot in the hallway, I imagine her gently rubbing Jen's back. Megan is good at comforting. I, on the other hand, am not, so I stand outside the room like a dork, sipping my cold Earl Grey tea and wondering if I should work on my grant at home.

Jen's voice hitches. "I just...I get so overwhelmed sometimes. I never get enough sleep. Maybe I'm burned out."

"Who wouldn't be in your shoes? Why don't we make a list, see if there's something you could put on hold or delegate to someone else."

"Gabriel helps as much as he can," Jen says, referring to her husband, who I met last year at their barbecue party, "but he's busy too. There's always some IT emergency his company needs him to manage."

"Your kids will survive if they don't get a home-cooked meal every night," Megan says, "and your house won't explode if it doesn't get vacuumed this week. You put too much pressure on yourself to be perfect. Newsflash, none of us is perfect. Well, except maybe Dr. Thomas. He comes pretty close."

At this, Jen laughs, and I figure that's my cue to enter the room instead of lurking in the hallway like a creeper. Besides, I need my satchel.

I cough to announce my presence and enter the residents' room. Seated in her cubicle, Jen quickly wipes her eyes and smooths her chestnut hair but manages to greet me with a smile. Megan stands at Jen's side with her hand on her back, just as I suspected. She greets me as well.

Pretending I've heard nothing of their conversation, I put my tea on my cubicle desk and nod to Megan. "I didn't expect to see you here."

"Needed a break from funeral talk and executor headaches." Megan rubs her temple as if trying to massage the stress away. "Aunt Fiona left me in charge of everything. I went through her laptop and closed as many accounts as I could. At least she kept her password book up to date, or I would have been in hell. I've also arranged for a funeral service on Saturday. It'll mostly be for work acquaintances who want to pay their final respects. Maybe some of the staff at the addiction center where she volunteered will show up too." She grunts. "And for once my dad and sister will make an appearance. A little late now, if you ask me."

"Any news on her autopsy?" I lean against the window by my cubicle, hoping for a nonchalant tone and not the tone of a woman who's been waiting restlessly all day for an update.

Megan takes a seat in her own workspace, which is one down from Jen's. "Why are you so eager for the results?"

So much for nonchalant.

"I mean, I appreciate you being there for me, Liza, but my aunt got…crushed by a bed." Megan falters for a moment. "What do you expect to learn that we can't already guess?"

"That maybe it was a homicide."

Jen drops the slide case she just picked up. Luckily, it was closed. "Wow, Liza."

"Not everything is a mystery, you know." Megan snatches her

designer bag off her desk and digs around inside it. She jerks the leather fabric this way and that until she plucks out a phone with a purple case. I recognize it as her aunt Fiona's.

"You know what I found in this?" she asks.

I push away from the window with interest. "What?"

"I found funny cat videos, Liza."

I don't much like the way Megan says my name. It carries none of the soothing tones she bestowed on Jen a few minutes ago. Instead, it carries the bite of every mean girl who mocked me during my school years. (Although they each only ever did it once.) Unlike with those kids, though, I deserve Megan's venom. I shouldn't have been so blunt.

"And," she continues, "I found text messages from people thanking her for helping their son, their wife, their boyfriend—or whoever—fight through their addiction."

"Did you go through her whole phone?"

"If you mean did I open every app and see when her next mammogram appointment was and what TV show she last downloaded, of course not. I've been a little busy." Megan tosses the phone back into her purse. "I'm sorry. I don't mean to be irritable. It's just that I've been working nonstop trying to get my aunt's affairs in order, planning her funeral, notifying her contacts, meeting with her lawyer—"

"Of course you have." It's Jen's turn to comfort now, and she reaches over to squeeze Megan's shoulder. "Liza is just curious, that's all. You know she loves a good puzzle, even if it means imagining things that aren't there."

Imagining. That packed word slices through my brain like a scalpel.

I've been around Jen enough to know meanness is not in her makeup. The opposite, in fact. Recently she took the blame for a cytology-smear mix-up when it was actually the intern's mistake, and six weeks ago she made homemade chicken noodle soup for my colleagues and me when we fell ill with a summer virus, each of us dropping one after the other like feverish flies. So I know she's not making fun of me when she says "imagining," as if I'm pulling absurd ideas out of the ether, but that doesn't mean I enjoy her choice of word any better. *Imagining* implies I'm one step away from suffering the same delusions my mother's schizophrenia gives her.

In fact, this whole conversation is making me feel like I'm wrapped up in steel wool. I can barely hold a discussion with one person, let alone two. Too much body language to sort through.

My silence must last too long, because Jen apologizes to me. "I'm sorry, poor choice of words. I'm not implying you make up stories. I just mean you look deeper into an issue than the rest of us. Like you have to solve it before you can move on." Jen smiles at Megan. "Remember that time our reports didn't show up in the EMR? We assumed we forgot to save them and had to read all the slides over again—"

"—and re-dictate our findings," Megan finishes for her. "That was fun."

Jen shakes her head. "Not Liza, though. She said, 'No way am I doing that, peeps,' so she dug in and found the problem."

I shrug. I've never used the word *peeps* in my life, other than for Easter candy. "IT had just done a site update," I say. "Something always goes wonky after that."

"True, and my husband would agree," Jen replies, "but you poked around until you discovered the reports had been saved in the wrong folder. You didn't have to repeat any of your work. The rest of us were sheep who wasted hours of our time." To drive the point home, Jen alters her voice and says, *"Baa baa."*

This gets a laugh from Megan, which is a relief to me. Much better than watching her furiously knit a scarf like she's about to stab someone.

A pop tune warbles from inside Megan's tote bag. She pulls out her cell phone, its case as colorful as her aunt's but with the added accessory of a sparkling Eiffel Tower.

Megan answers the call and sits ramrod straight. "Yes. Uh-huh. I see. That's what I figured." A pause. "Maybe the alcohol contributed then?" She nods at something the caller says. "Okay. Well, thank you for letting me know. I appreciate it."

Megan disconnects and lowers the phone to her lap. Jen and I stare at her.

"That was the fellow working with the ME in Boston. They officially ruled Aunt Fiona's death accidental. Asphyxiation."

My stomach sinks a little. In what? Disappointment?

Not cool, Liza. Not cool.

"They determined she likely died Thursday night, maybe thirty-six to forty hours before Liza and I found her on Saturday. There was alcohol in her system. She usually liked a glass of wine with dinner. No drugs, of course. She helped people stay clean. She didn't join them in using."

Jen shakes her head. "I'm sorry, Megan. That's awful. So tragic."

"Better than getting murdered, I suppose. Or getting killed by a hit-and-run." Megan pushes on the inner folds of her eyes as if physically holding back tears. I assume she's referring to her best friend's death. "Life is so effing random, isn't it?" she says. "You work hard your whole life only to end up like that? Crushed in a bed?" Her face flushes, and her voice grows heated. "The ME better be right, because if my aunt *was* murdered, I'd expect him, the cops, the crime scene investigators, *someone* to scour every inch of Boston to find her killer." She exhales with force, as if blowing out anger. "But they would've found something, right? So it probably was just a tragic, awful, ridiculously random event."

I try to picture it. Fiona sleeping. The bed closing shut on her. Smothering her.

Was it a sudden snap? Bam, just like that? Or was it a slow folding?

I wonder if she was aware it was happening. If so, couldn't she have shifted her position? Pushed the bed open with her legs? Or did the tight space restrict her movement? Maybe she was simply in too deep of a wine-infused sleep to notice.

So many questions, and yet the conclusion of an accidental death answers none of them.

Jen and Megan are still talking, Jen consoling Megan while I stand near the wall and compute the grim algorithm of Fiona's death.

A few minutes later, Megan rises. "I better get going. I need dinner. Haven't eaten since breakfast."

Jen stands too. "Not the best time to ask you, so forgive me, but in case you don't come in tomorrow, can I get your opinion on a tissue sample quick? You're our gross-examination queen, after all. Then we can bolt. My kids' Happy Meals won't buy themselves."

Jen winces as she says this. If I could, I'd make her see what an awesome mom she is, a fact that can't be erased by a night of fast food. But I can't, so I stay silent.

"Sure." Megan follows Jen to the surgical pathology lab. "'Gross-examination queen.' There's a title I never thought I'd hold."

And just like that, the two of them are gone.

Megan's purse, however, remains behind, at least until she returns for it.

I eye it on her cubicle desk, my brain churning.

Might find something interesting. Something that proves Fiona's bed is not a killer but merely an innocent bystander.

I scan the room, confirm I'm alone.

You shouldn't steal.

Not stealing. Borrowing. Just until tomorrow.

I slide closer to Megan's desk.

No, Dr. Lightfoot tells me. *No,* my father echoes.

I open my colleague's Mary Poppins–size purse and push the knitting needles and yarn to the side. At the bottom of the bag I spot the purple phone case against Megan's wallet, next to her aunt's stun gun.

I hesitate.

Don't do it, Liza. It's wrong.

I remove Fiona's phone.

I stuff it into my satchel.

9

———————

When I leave the hospital a short time later, I want nothing more than to race home to my apartment and dig through Fiona's phone. Like a fire burning inside my satchel, it demands immediate attention. Unfortunately, my standing dinner date with Shawna and Tam means the cellular snooping will have to wait, especially since I need to make a quick stop at Home and Hearth Healing to see my mom first. Doesn't matter whether she remembers I'm coming. I stick to my word.

As with many evenings, tonight she's playing guitar outside on her favorite rock, which sits beneath a massive oak tree near the center's back fence. Seeing her there is a good sign. It means she's not having one of her worst days, where she is either a ranting Joan of Arc or a cowering concentration camp survivor named Anna. Those two women have made very few appearances in the last year, and for that I'm grateful, both to Dr. Dhar for his excellent treatment and to the universe for giving my mom's brittle schizophrenia a respite.

The fact she doesn't wave to me in recognition as I approach implies it's also not one of her best (and rarest) days. On those days, she's the energetic and loving mother I once knew, back when she was a popular music teacher with a still-cooperative mind. Regardless, her gifted strumming of "California Dreamin'" tells me she's either still Emily Larkin, just a more withdrawn and quieter version of herself, or she's Meryl Streep.

I lean against the giant boulder that supports her. "Hey, Mom."

Her crossed legs are twigs covered by loose jeans, and a cardigan dwarfs her shoulders. She nods to acknowledge me. When she finishes the song, she says, "I'm glad you came. It's been ages."

I visit three times a week, sometimes more, so this is my first hint she's in a delusional state. "I was just here on—"

"Everything's changed since you were last on set."

Ah. So Meryl Streep it is.

My mother's gaze flits around the well-manicured lawn. Groups of residents and visitors lounge on patio chairs or gather at picnic tables. Some read. Some chat. Some play board games or cornhole. The weather remains mild enough for all.

Emily Larkin / Meryl Streep leans toward me. "That new director has completely changed the script. The writers are furious." Her words rush out in a conspiratorial whisper, and she points her finger to my left. "Cut almost all of Margot's lines. Who does he think he is?"

I look to where she's pointing. Maisy, a gangly woman who's a daughter of one of Dr. Silverstein's friends, sits on a rocking chair and blows bubbles from a wand she dunks in and out of a plastic bottle. Her only audience member is the resident cat named Sonny. The domestic shorthair sits at Maisy's feet and flicks his tail back and forth every time a bubble lands on his head.

"You mean Maisy, Mom?"

"Shh." My mother puts a finger to her lips, her other arm clutching the guitar against her torso. "Margot's in disguise. She doesn't want anyone to recognize her. Whenever fans spot her, chaos breaks out. Last night they chanted 'Robbie, Robbie' so loudly the police came."

Our conversation makes about as much sense as a legal contract written in Klingon, and, although Maisy is no troll, she's certainly no Margot Robbie, who I know of only because of the movie posters Waseem shows me on his phone. But so goes a delusional state.

Regardless, my mom seems to enjoy my company, and as she carries on about the clueless director who thinks he knows everybody's jobs better than they do, I listen and nod at the expected moments or shake my head in shared annoyance, whichever the nonsensical tale requires.

When I prepare to head out, my mother embraces me and thanks me for taking such good care of her. Whether this is Meryl or Emily talking, I'm not sure, but it pleases me to leave her smiling and content.

Unfortunately, my buoyant exit is ruined when I run into Pete Parsons on the way out. Pete is a sadistic orderly I once thought killed his wife. He didn't, but he *did* torment the residents, and now, thanks to me, he's watched so closely by the staff that his twisted tricks are a thing of the past. At least at Home and Hearth Healing.

Needless to say, we're not friends.

Like two alpha wolves, we approach each other in the country-accented lobby, its gingham furniture and spiced-apple air unchanged from the day my mom moved in.

"Hey, Larkin," Pete says with a sneer. "Tattle on anyone today?"

"Hey, Parsons," I respond. "Kill anyone today?"

His shadowy eyes squint. "Watch yourself," he says as I walk past him. "Wouldn't want to get on my bad side. Not with Momma Larkin in here."

I ball my fists and turn around. "If I get wind that you even so much as looked at my mother without a smile, I'll send you to a dentist with all your teeth in a bag."

He shimmies. "Wow, I'm so terrified, I just pissed myself."

It appears I'm no scarier to him than I am to Chopper, but I hold my laser glare a moment longer anyway. Then I nod to Tiana Porter, the receptionist, to buzz me out. If she heard our childish display, I'm sorry for that, but some people are dog crap on your shoe, and Pete Parsons is one of those people. Too meek to draw blood, but cruel enough to scratch the skin.

Once inside my Honda Civic, I drive to Victor's Victuals to

meet Shawna and Tam. New to Morganville, the restaurant is one of those New Agey establishments where the entrées are more visual than filling. But it's Shawna's night to pick, so there you have it.

Shawna Vasquez-Lane, a once-bullied girl I befriended as a child, thereby making my dad sigh in relief that I might not end up a friendless little psychopath after all, is a popular hairstylist in Morganville, her schedule booked further out than a dermatologist's. Tam Vasquez-Lane is her police-officer wife, although she usually just goes by Tam Lane. They've been married four years and have a two-year-old son named Seth.

It would come as no surprise to anyone that our regular dinners on the second and fourth Wednesday of every month were not my idea. After my struggles last year and my failure to discuss my—some might say *questionable*—choices with anyone, Shawna suggested we have more frequent contact. Not surprisingly, my shrink pounced on the idea like a kitten pouncing on catnip. "You'll see me two Fridays a month," he said, jotting it down on his notepad with a pen topped with a tiny globe of the earth, "and your friends two Wednesdays a month. It's a win-win for everyone."

Except me. Four sessions of deep social diving a month, whether I want it or not.

Mostly, I want it. I can't deny it helps me stay centered.

Tonight, I do not.

I only want to hunt through Fiona's phone.

Inside the dimly lit restaurant, I spot Shawna and Tam seated in a circular booth on the left. A modern-art print of geometrical shapes hangs on the wall above them, and a candle encased in frosted glass burns in the center of the table. As I approach their cozy nook, I take a big breath and ready myself for conversation.

Shawna rises and gives me a quick hug. A lavender scent wafts from her long, wavy hair, and her blouse feels silky against my wrists, which hang by my sides. Tam nods and fist-bumps me. Her hair is short like mine, and nothing about her T-shirt and jeans is silky. They ask me how work was, and I give a pat response.

As I slide in next to Shawna, I study their faces. Something isn't right. Normally Shawna sports a wide smile and bright eyes, and

Tam cracks a joke about me having to suffer a meal with conversation, but that she'll "take it easy on me." Tonight, there is none of that. They simply stare at their menus. Even to me, the silence is awkward, and I find myself wishing they'd brought Seth with them instead of dropping him off at their neighbor's. At least the toddler would talk gibberish and break this strange quiet. Even their border collie, Betts, would make for more animated company.

After a long beat, Tam flips her menu toward me and points to a picture next to the starters. "Look at this tiny salad. It's three cherry tomatoes cut in half with a dollop of mozzarella cheese."

"It's a tasting menu," Shawna says, her tone staccato. "Small portions are the whole point."

Tam grimaces at me. "Guess you and I will be making a McDonald's run when we're done."

"Liza recognizes fine food when she sees it," Shawna shoots back.

I mess with the collar of my crew-neck sweater, its tag a wad of sandpaper against my neck. Should I laugh at Tam's joke? Or should I side with Shawna? She and I go way back, so my loyalty should lie with her. Then again, Tam really helped me out with her cop connections last year, so that nets double the points.

The couple must sense my discomfort, because Shawna's posture relaxes. "I'm sorry, Liza. This is the last thing you need after a day at the hospital. It's just…we were…"

"We were in the middle of a fight when you got here," Tam finishes for her. To Shawna, she says, "What? Don't give me that look. Liza appreciates a straight shooter."

An extra point goes to Tam because I do indeed appreciate a straight shooter. No subtext to decipher with straight shots.

"Um, do you want me to leave?" I ask. "I can let you guys get back to it."

Both women chuckle at that, and the temperature at the table drops a few degrees, even if the silence returns. We all peruse the menu, and as my eyes scan the accompanying photographs, I gotta admit I'm with Tam on this one. The portions would barely satisfy Stuart Little.

A waiter with a tight white shirt that shows off his nipples (*yay me*) comes over, and after we order, Shawna picks up where our earlier conversation left off.

"If you're wondering what our fight was about, it was about me wanting another baby and Tam not."

"That's not fair, and you know it," Tam says. "I'd love more kids, but I won't risk your health because of it."

Shawna tilts her wineglass my way. "You're a doctor. Tell Tam I'll be fine. They can put me on a blood thinner if need be."

I scratch harder at the back of my neck. Why do manufacturers put their stupid tags there?

"See, hon?" Tam opens her napkin in her lap. "Even Liza thinks it's a bad idea."

Oh, man. How do I get caught up in these things?

Both women stare at me. Having never seen them fight before, I feel like a child deciding which parent to hug first, knowing whoever I choose, the other will be disappointed.

I clear my throat and address Shawna. "Pregnancy is a hypercoagulable state, and ever since your accident last year, you've had problems with blood clots."

"Just a few small ones in my legs," Shawna counters.

"Yeah, but…" More neck scratching. "Pregnancy can up your risk of more serious clots. You wouldn't want one shooting to your lungs. Or worse, your brain."

"Exactly." Tam smacks the table with her palm, not hard, just enough to show her point has been made.

When Shawna says nothing, just rearranges her water glass, I want to ask the obvious question but don't dare.

Tam goes there for me. "You're probably wondering why I don't have the baby then, right?"

Shawna cuts in before I can say anything. "I'd never ask that of you, you know that."

Tam stares off at a stone fountain in the corner. "I'm thinking of taking hormones, Liza. You know, testosterone. And, well, having a baby doesn't work too well with that." She exhales slowly. "I don't know. Things are complicated in this world."

This conversation has become far too personal for me. I want to grab my satchel and bolt.

"I love kids," Tam says, "and I wouldn't trade Seth for anything, but I've never wanted to carry them. It's not who I am. Shawna knew that from the start."

"I did, and I would never go back on that, I promise. You need to be you."

The two women reach for each other's hand across the table, and although I'm pleased to see them reconcile, I'm still a squirming third wheel in this two-person drama.

"Then I guess we're back to square one," Tam says.

Although the issue seems far from settled, they move on to other topics, and I manage to make it through the first course. When I tell them about Megan's aunt and her death by Murphy bed, they stop munching their tiny meatballs and arugula leaves and instead eat up my words.

Being a cop, Tam is of course fascinated by the thought of a murderous bed, but when I hint that I worry about foul play, she shakes her head.

"Careful, Liza. Just because you caught something once—and Dr. Donovan was a big something, I'll give you that—doesn't mean there's a rotten fish floating everywhere."

Shawna confirms Tam's warning. "Things just got back to normal for you. Don't risk losing ground again by getting involved in something you shouldn't."

I nod to indicate I understand, but inside my bag lies Fiona's pilfered phone, the telltale sign I might very well do something I shouldn't.

I don't tell them about the cell phone, of course. I merely rest my hand on my bag and promise that I'll get to it soon.

10

———

After dinner I return to my apartment complex. I'm worn out from the required conversation and, just as Tam predicted, still hungry after those measly but attractive portions. At least I make it into my unit without having to perform CPR on my landlord or enter another pissing contest with my blackmailer. Unless it's chopped steak to fill my belly, I want nothing more to do with Chopper today.

Fiona's phone practically shouts my name from inside my leather satchel, and as soon as I flip on the lights, I sink down on my bed and retrieve the mobile from my bag.

Sitting cross-legged on the duvet, I'm about to enter the passcode that was mentioned by Megan when we first found Fiona's body. Instead, I hold off and stare at the woman's lock screen. It features a selfie of Fiona and Megan at the New England Aquarium, a giant tank full of colorful sea life behind them and a shark passing above their heads.

I take a moment to reflect on Fiona's passing, a woman who obviously meant a great deal to Megan and no doubt to those she helped in the addiction center. Maybe even those in her company's HR office where she worked. My dad always encouraged me to see people as a whole, not just a label or a one-dimensional being, probably because he worked so hard to get people to not see my mother or me like that. So I offer Fiona a moment of silence. Seems only right before I start snooping around in her phone.

When enough of a moment passes, I enter the four-digit code, 2175, the year Fiona felt would be best suited to her were time travel a reality.

"You might've been right about that," I murmur. "Because it sure wasn't this year."

Fiona's existence, at least her mobile one, flashes to life in front of me, and it's a chaotic existence at that. Pages and pages of apps, some in folders, some loose, some organized in the expected four-by-six grid on her iPhone, others in clusters of only four or five on a page, leaving empty spaces on the pastel screen. Eleven pages of apps in all, but given their seemingly random placement, they could easily be condensed into five or six. I now understand why Megan hasn't had time to look at them all.

I start working my way through. The most traditionally popular apps are located on the first screen. Google, Safari, Maps, Contacts, Weather, Photos, Camera, Mail—all right there on page one. So that part of Fiona's organization system makes sense.

But where to begin?

Perusing Fiona's recent search history seems logical. I open Google to see what Megan's aunt has been up to but don't make it far before my dad's voice intrudes.

What right do you have to go through this woman's private affairs? How would you feel if someone stole your phone and snooped around in it?

I'd be dead, I respond. *Why would I care?*

I know that's not true. I hate people messing with my things.

But it's for Megan, I tell my dad in this mental exchange. *She deserves to know what really happened to her aunt. Besides,* I add, more for myself, *it's not like I'm snooping for voyeuristic reasons. I have a purpose.*

And so I dig in.

Unfortunately, Fiona's search history shows me little beyond the fact that she enjoyed looking at designer handbags as much as Megan does. The fashion apple didn't fall far from the tree. Fiona also excelled at pulling up take-out menus from Boston restaurants. A few political and news pieces here and there. Some articles about drug overdoses, particularly fentanyl. Frequent trips to Amazon Kindle. Several websites with inspirational quotes. Maybe she used the adages in her HR interactions with employees in hopes of boosting morale.

I keep scrolling. Clearly Fiona never heard of deleting her browser history. I'm about to close out the Google app when a website catches my eye: Furries Come Together.

Um…

I may not have an interest in sex—many schizoids don't—but that doesn't mean I know nothing about it. I've tried it a few times, back in college and med school when the fumes of alcohol lulled me into a "Why the hell not?" fog, but the men held little attraction for me, and neither did the act. Nothing I need on a regular basis, anyway, and certainly nothing I desire.

But at the mention of furries, a sexual fetish is the first thing that comes to mind. I could be wrong, of course, so to avoid stereotyping ("Stereotypes are for people with no imagination," Dr. Lightfoot says), I click open the website.

A picture fills the screen. It isn't really sexual. It's simply dozens of adults dressed in full-body animal costumes, clustered together, hugging and cuddling. Cats with aqua-blue eyes, wolves with long snouts, bears with big paws. In the front, positioned on its side, lies a fluffy pink whale. A wide grin lights up its face, and the comedic nature of it makes me snort.

The caption below the photograph mentions a recent convention. Maybe it was a platonic gathering, but a link in the website's lower right corner flashes "Adults Only," and I don't have to click it open to know sex probably plays a role.

I shrug off the website, unsure of its significance. Fiona was probably just curious. Doesn't mean she was a furry. Besides, to each their own. What do I care?

After a couple more scrolls down, I find another unusual website, this one about BDSM. No whiff of ambiguity here. Leather and latex outfits, abundance of skin, whips, sexually suggestive expressions, lewd positions, uncomfortable-looking sex toys of all shapes and sizes.

Gross.

But again, to each their own. I'm the last person who should be passing judgment. At least these people enjoy the company of others. They probably don't snoop around in dead people's phones either.

I scroll through the final month of Fiona's browser history, having only the last ninety days at my disposal. Nothing else suggests she led a secret life. Did she google these sexual lifestyles out of curiosity? Maybe one of her company's employees was involved in something she needed to research before addressing the issue. It seems to me that if she *were* interested in furries or BDSM, there would be far more website visits than the two I found. Unless she deleted them from her history. Maybe she overlooked these two.

I file away the notion of a secret sexual life for now, but as I close out Fiona's browser and open her mail app, I don't dismiss the idea, especially if my goal is to figure out if her death was truly accidental.

Nothing in the email app piques my interest. It does, however, earn my respect. Unlike the phone's general layout, Fiona's email account is organized and tidy, a folder for everything. Despite my own meticulous labels, I could learn a thing or two from her. New email has accumulated since her death, things like newsletters, marketing messages from online shopping sites, and senders who don't know she's dead.

Her email trash is empty, and for some reason the sight of that clean folder puts a squeeze on my throat. I imagine Fiona deleting the trash after work, wanting a clean slate for the next day. Later that night she lay down on her antique Murphy bed and never woke up. Contrary to what my brother insinuates, particularly when he's in one of his dark spells, I *do* have feelings.

When the throat tightness passes, I return to my snooping and switch over to Fiona's work email account. It's as well organized as her personal one, and none of her communications trigger any alarms.

Am I proud of myself for this invasive probe of the woman's private exchanges? Of course not. This is the exact type of situation Dr. Lightfoot advises me to discuss with him first. Personally, I would despise someone snooping through my stuff. Would want to gut punch them across the room—metaphorically, anyway, since I've learned to pocket my fists against people.

But what if I'd died under mysterious circumstances? What if I was murdered and the police didn't conduct an investigation because the medical examiner ruled it accidental, which might be the case in Fiona's death? If that happened, I'd waive my right to privacy, because seeing a killer brought to justice would trump my personal affairs.

I suppose it doesn't matter. There's little for someone to find in my electronic files. Any incriminating secrets have long since been scrubbed away.

Slow down, tiger, my father cautions. *You have no proof Fiona was murdered.*

Maybe so, I think, but I can't forget Megan's own words in the residents' room this afternoon: "The ME better be right, because if my aunt *was* murdered, I'd expect him, the cops, the crime scene investigators, *someone* to scour every inch of Boston to find her killer."

Whether Megan meant me or not, I don't know. I'm not good at subtext. But I'm not hurting anyone with my private inquest, and if I find nothing, I'll slip the phone back into Megan's purse. No harm, no foul.

I slide farther back on my bed and lean against the wall. My eyes burn from the intense scrutiny of Fiona's digital world. To rest them, I stare across the room at my desk, listening to the ambient noise of apartment life—a door slamming somewhere above me, the muted sounds of a television behind me, a friendly shout from the common grounds outside.

When I return to the phone, I open other apps. News, shopping, banking, the latter of which I can't access because a log-in by either face ID or password is required. I doubt Fiona would use her four-digit time-travel code for something so important. Plus, accessing her financial records crosses legal—or at the very least, ethical—boundaries. Although I'm not averse to that (*the greater good, right?*), it seems a step too far for now.

I'm about to flip to the last page of apps when one on the tenth page stands out. *Unite*, it's called, and its logo is an arrow through a heart.

One tap reveals it to be a dating app. Its location on the second-to-last page of the phone suggests Fiona no longer used it. Maybe she downloaded it some time ago and forgot about it. When I open the message tab, however, it's clear her account is still active. The last message she received was less than a week ago.

My senses shift to high alert. I uncross my stiff legs and stretch them over my bed. I may be a crappy subtext reader, but I excel at recognizing suspicious behavior.

And Fiona keeping a dating app hidden all the way back in her phone reeks of suspicious behavior.

Because it means she didn't want anyone to find it.

11

———

Sitting fully upright on my bed now, my fingers pulse against Fiona's phone. I'm convinced I've stumbled upon something crucial. Even the apartment building has fallen eerily silent. Despite my growing hunger, a consequence of my calorie-light dinner with Shawna and Tam, I ignore April's chocolate chip cookies on my kitchenette counter and scroll through Fiona's private dating-app messages instead.

She and a guy named Demetri Pappas communicated frequently. His profile picture shows an attractive man with salt-and-pepper hair, a cleft in his chin, and dark and intense eyes. His name suggests Greek ancestry, and his olive coloring matches mine, a product of my biracial father and fair-complexioned mother. According to Demetri's bio, he's a fifty-five-year-old doctor. Either his photo is a few years old or he keeps in good shape, because he appears to be five to ten years younger.

So what? my dad says in my ear. *Fiona met a good-looking doctor on a dating app. Good for her. Doesn't mean anything.*

I shake my head in disagreement, as if my father were really here. No, I'm not delusional. I know he's not really here, and I know he's not speaking to me. But after having his guidance for so many years, I can't shut it off. Nor do I want to. In this case, I believe he's wrong. Fiona is dead. Fiona was on a dating app. The two things could be connected.

I scan Demetri's most recent messages, two of which are dated after Fiona died.

Why aren't you responding? I miss you.

Hello? Please don't leave me hanging.

I'm dying here, Fee. Text something, anything.

Guess you weren't ready for that place?

I'm sorry if I scared you away. I didn't mean to.

I scroll back even further. Find messages where Demetri says he wants to take Fiona to a special place, that they were far enough along in their relationship for the next step. What that next step was, I don't know, but as I read through more of their messages, I find proof that Fiona, oh she of the HR department and addiction-center volunteer team, did indeed have a spicy side, a side that had no qualms sexting racy exchanges with Demetri Pappas. They discussed their recent dates, recent sex acts (alone or with each other), recent positions they tried, positions they'd *like* to try.

I'm not one to blush, but my cheeks heat with each new discovery. When I learn about how insatiable Demetri is, how aggressive Fiona was, how Demetri wanted to bring in a third party, maybe even a *fourth*, I want to dip both the phone and my eyes in bleach. The only saving grace is that there are no accompanying photos. Thank God for small favors.

I read on. Several emojis make it into their private messages as well. Mostly hearts, eggplants, peaches, sweat droplets, tacos. I'm not sure I grasp them all, but I get the gist. A couple of times, Demetri even slipped in chains and a rope.

I lower the phone and stare at my brain poster across the room. *Shit just got interesting.*

The fact Fiona was on a dating app in itself means nothing. The fact she liked to have a lot of sex means nothing, at least not on its own. She was a forty-six-year-old single woman who could float her boat any way she chose. Whose business is it but her own?

But chains and rope emojis? Her recent search of BDSM and

furries websites? Demetri taking her some place and then worrying her lack of response meant she wasn't ready for it? That could mean a great deal, especially since it appears Fiona ghosted him afterward. Two of Demetri's unanswered messages were sent after Fiona died, but three were sent beforehand. That suggests she probably saw them but chose to ignore them. Why?

I return my attention to Fiona's phone, to the picture of Demetri himself. Rising from my bed, I google "Dr. Demetri Pappas" on the laptop on my desk. Hopefully, that's his real name. Seems like that should be required on a dating app. A person's first name, anyway. Maybe it is—I wouldn't know—but maybe Fiona requested his last name too before she agreed to meet with him.

From Google, I learn it is his real name, but other than discovering he's a pain specialist in Boston, one who matches the photograph and age on the dating app, I find little else. He stays remarkably well off the grid. Then again, he's fifty-five. Maybe that's not so remarkable. Dr. Lightfoot is of a similar age, and he shuns all things social media. Still, I check Facebook anyway. Although several Demetri Pappases pop up on the screen, none match his profile picture.

Back on Fiona's phone, I check her text-messaging app. Nothing from Demetri in those threads, nor is he in her contacts list. Maybe Fiona was cautious. Wanted everything closed loop in the dating app. Wanted her world of kink staying in the world of kink.

Does Megan know about Demetri? Unlikely, since she mentioned nothing about it.

Do I dare bring it up? If I do, she'll know I snooped around her aunt's phone. Not only might that anger her, but it might also embarrass her to know what I found. Could put me on her shit list, and although I might have welcomed that when I first met her last year, I no longer do. Despite her social-butterfly personality—though it's been light on both the social and the butterfly lately—Megan is part of my inner circle now. That means she matters. I don't want to disappoint her. Plus, I still owe her for a solid she did me last year.

On the other hand, I might have discovered something that,

although not proof Fiona was murdered, could raise the curtain of suspicion. Demetri Pappas was into some twisted stuff, and although it appears Fiona could hold her own, maybe the pain doctor took things too far. Maybe he got angry when she rejected him.

Was he responsible for Fiona's death? Were his last two messages—the ones sent after her death—fired off to avoid any doubt cast his way?

Question after question swirls in my head. That rare excitement I get, the kind that comes from discovering a wrong that needs to be righted, sparks a tidal wave of adrenaline in my blood.

I reread Demetri's last message: Why aren't you responding? I miss you.

If he's a good guy, he deserves to know Fiona died. Judging by their communications on the app and the tone of their private conversations, they had strong feelings for each other.

I can't simply message him that she's dead, though, can I? One, he'll wonder why I'm snooping around in her account and might report me. Two, it's cold to announce something like that in a text. Even I know that.

If he's a bad guy, he still deserves a response, mostly so I can find out what he's up to without—hopefully—revealing my suspicion. Otherwise he could cover his tracks. How best to do that?

While I ponder this, I finally grab one of April's cookies and devour it. After a second one, I drop to the ground for ten triceps push-ups followed by twenty regular ones. Exercise always stimulates my brain. Sure enough, during push-up number nineteen, an idea pops into my head.

What harm could come from me contacting Demetri? I'll respond to his last message as Fiona and agree to meet. That's my best chance of getting a read on him. See what he's really like. Then, after forming a judgment, I'll decide how best to proceed. If something seems off, I'll pass it on to Megan. Until then, there's no need to worry her unnecessarily.

Now it's Dr. Lightfoot's turn to speak in my head: *You think you're the best person to get a read on someone, Liza? Really?*

"Yeah, I do," I respond out loud. "Because if he's a psychopath, I'll sniff him out better than a bloodhound."

Using my own phone, I open Google Maps and search for bars near Fiona's Fenway–Kenmore address. Muriel's Irish Pub pops up five blocks away.

Back on the pilfered phone, I return to the dating app's message thread between Demetri and Fiona. After a brief hesitation, long enough to hope I'm doing the right thing but not long enough to fully question it, I type: Meet me at Muriel's Irish Pub on Saturday, one o'clock.

I pause again, my finger hovering over the send button.

Should I or shouldn't I?

If I had listened to caution a year ago, there'd still be a killer loose in Morganville.

That settles it. I push send and shoot the message into the ether.

12

Friday morning I'm alone in the surgical path lab, working at the chrome countertop, shivering in the cold air despite my sweater and protective gown. Although I'm used to the room's formaldehyde scent, it's still not a pleasant one.

For the past ten minutes I've been battling a golf-ball-size liver tumor. Every time I drag my scalpel through the bloody mass to slice off a decent section for microscopic examination, it slips out of my gloved hand. My focus is terrible, and my brain is more scattered than a manic's on crack. Too many thoughts of meeting Demetri Pappas swirl inside it.

Tomorrow the pain specialist will be expecting Fiona Carlson at Muriel's Irish Pub. He'll get me instead. A socially awkward misfit who wonders if he's a murderer.

I squeeze the slippery tumor more firmly and at last slice off a thin portion. I'm about to slice again when the door to the lab flings open. Megan storms in.

She tugs her long blouse over her leggings. "It was you, wasn't it?"

I have a pretty good idea what she's talking about but try to feign innocence. Because, you know, I'm such a great actress. "It was me what?"

"You took my aunt's phone. For the last two days, I've been convinced I lost it. Left it someplace, dropped it out of my purse, whatever. I've been freaking out because I need her contact numbers."

I rest the scalpel on the countertop, wondering how best to play this.

"Luckily, Aunt Fiona's contacts are in her iCloud account, which I got from her Mac, but still, I've been blaming myself for being so careless." Megan encroaches on my three feet of personal space. "And then it dawned on me: Jen and I left you alone in the residents' room on Wednesday. With my purse." Megan plants her hands on her hips. "I don't want to point fingers, and I'm sorry if I'm wrong, but my gut says you took the phone."

As always, nothing gets by her. No sense lying now. Not only will she see through it, but it'll drive a wedge between the two of us I don't want. The question is, how much should I divulge about her aunt's secret life?

"Yes, I took it. I'm sorry."

As if her energy is zapped by my confession, Megan pulls a stool away from the counter and plops down. "Why? And why not just ask me? I would have let you have it. Why be so sneaky about it?"

I'm not sure how to answer. Because I *am* sneaky? Because I sometimes make foolish choices? Because I don't want to worry Megan unnecessarily if it turns out there's nothing to worry about? All of the above are true.

"You're convinced my aunt's death wasn't an accident, aren't you? You thought you might find something on her phone."

At this rate Megan will figure everything out before I have to say a word, but to avoid looking like a mute dolt, I respond, "Convinced, no. Suspicious, yes."

"But why?"

"Because being killed by a bed makes no sense."

"It was an antique bed. Its closing mechanism was ancient."

Megan taps her jeweled ballet flats against the stool's footrest. "Freak accidents happen every day, you know that. Remember the guy who came through the morgue last May? The one with the pole?"

I nod. A steel beam had fallen off the semitruck in front of him. Crashed right through his windshield and skewered him in the heart.

"Or what about that woman who was killed by a piece of a stage set that broke loose and conked her on the head? Or the man we autopsied a couple months ago who got shot by his dog? One wrong step of the paw and bang. Tragic, yes. Bizarre, definitely. But murder? No."

Realizing this conversation could take a while, I remove my gloves, still slick with pinkish foam from the liver tumor, and toss them into the biohazard bin. My protective gown isn't yet soiled, so I leave that on and pull out another stool to sit next to Megan.

"I'm not saying your aunt was murdered," I tell her. "At least not yet. I just wanted to search her phone to make sure the police didn't miss anything. They didn't do much of an investigation."

"Why would they? The ME concluded Aunt Fiona's death was accidental."

"They wouldn't, so I guess...I thought..." The words are paste in my mouth. "I thought if I found something suspicious on her phone, you'd appreciate me looking into it."

Megan studies me, her eyebrows pinched, her lips pressed together in a straight line. Her expression could mean anything.

"And did you?" she asks.

"Did I what?"

She sighs. "Did you find anything on my aunt's phone?" Before I get a chance to answer, she adds, "I thought we trusted each other. We might be night-and-day different, but we've been through a lot together, haven't we?"

I nod.

"And you're not afraid of anything or anyone, so I doubt you were scared to ask me for the phone."

I shake my head. "It wasn't that. You've had a lot going on. I didn't want to make trouble for you if there wasn't any. I figured I'd look at the phone first and then tell you if I found anything."

"The fact you haven't returned it yet tells me you think you've found something."

I fiddle with my protective gown. Should I come clean about the dating app? About the racy texts I read? That I'm keeping the phone in case Demetri Pappas contacts Fiona again? I don't know if he is aware she's dead. That's a crucial bit of knowledge, because if he *is* aware but pretends he isn't, then that stinks of him having played a role in her death.

Megan leans forward. "I know you want the best for me. For all of us. But you don't need to protect me. Yes, I've been…fragile lately, but I won't break." She sits back again and rests her elbow on the countertop.

I decide to tell her. "I found a dating app on your aunt's phone."

"You did? I didn't see anything like that on her Mac."

"It was hidden all the way back in her apps. On the second-to-last page."

Megan frowns but motions for me to go on.

I wonder how best to phrase things. Saying "Hey, fun fact, your aunt was a sex fiend" probably isn't it. "Look, I'm not judging your aunt, but she had some pretty erotic exchanges with a man on there."

"Erotic?"

"Yeah, you know…" The furries and BDSM websites pop into my head. "She was, um, a bit kinky."

Megan laughs, something I wasn't expecting. "Woo-hoo, go, Auntie. Guess she wasn't just a boring HR exec after all."

"No, she wasn't."

"So what're we talking? Did she dress up as a French maid? A truck driver? A cat with a whip?"

After confirming that Megan truly wants the details, I spill what I found, everything from the browser history with the BDSM and furry searches to the private messages with Demetri Pappas on the dating app. When she asks to see the phone, I leave the surgical path lab to retrieve it from my bag in the residents' room. Once I'm back, I pull up the dating app and show it to her.

Before she even looks at it, she peers at me like a parent might a child. "You see how this works, Liza? I ask for something, and you give it to me. I didn't steal it from your purse behind your back."

"Roger that," I say.

Megan scrolls through the messages on the dating app. Although her brow lifts and furrows at various points, I can't interpret what she's thinking.

Finally, she says, "You think this Demetri guy is suspicious because he was into kinky sex with my aunt?"

"Maybe, maybe not, but I thought it was at least worth—"

"Wait, I'm confused." Megan points to the string of messages. "This last one was dated two days ago. My aunt tells Demetri she'll meet him at a pub. But she'd been dead for six days by then. It doesn't make—" Megan flattens her lips. "Oh no, please tell me you didn't message this guy and pretend to be my aunt." She checks the screen again. "Saturday. You're meeting him tomorrow?"

I nod.

"Seriously? You're meeting a complete stranger you think might have had something to do with my aunt's death? *Alone?*"

She's staring at me like I'm a madwoman. Easy enough to pick that expression up.

"Liza, that's insane. You can't go alone. You can't go at all!" She points her finger at me. "If you think this guy is dangerous, you need to call the police."

"I have no evidence he's dangerous. You think I want to accuse an innocent guy? His bio checks out. He's a doctor at a pain clinic. Just because he likes his own pain with sex doesn't make him a killer." This is what I tell Megan, but to be honest, that's exactly what I worry it makes him. "I don't need people thinking I'm delusional. Been there. Done that."

Megan says nothing, but she knows I'm referring to my experience with Dr. Donovan last year. Her stance softens. "I get that. Sorry. I just wish you would've told me about this first. I would've insisted on going with you."

"Then that would make him suspicious of *us*. Besides, you have the funeral tomorrow."

Megan wipes away a smudge on her aunt's purple phone case. "Did it ever occur to you that maybe that's where you should be too? By my side? At a time when I could really use a friend by my side?"

The thought of attending the funeral hadn't even entered my mind. So much for my social training. "This will probably turn out to be nothing. It seemed cruel to involve you if that's the case. You've had enough pain lately."

"Yeah, but meeting him alone? That's not smart."

"It'll be in a public place during the daytime. He's expecting your aunt, sure, but I'll tell him she died. I want to see how he responds to the news, face-to-face."

"No offense, but you think you're the best person for that job?"

"You're right. I suck at reading people. But I'm gifted at sniffing out psychopaths."

Megan seems to consider this and then gives me a slight nod of acknowledgment. "Quite the talent to have."

"I didn't find anything else suspicious on your aunt's phone, so if Demetri seems legit and isn't a psycho, I'll let this go."

Will I? What about Fiona's work at the addiction center? Couldn't there be a suspect or two there? Or a disgruntled employee at the party-supply company?

"You promise?" Megan asks. "I mean, of course I'd want the killer brought to justice if someone *did* murder Aunt Fiona. Losing her and my best friend so close together is messing with my head, not to mention being the executor of her estate."

Megan kneads her hands back and forth. She's probably wishing her knitting needles were in them. If I can answer one question for her—whether or not her aunt's death was an accident—then maybe I can bring her some peace. She's a good person. A little annoying at times, sure, but a good person. She doesn't deserve this much hurt, not when there are millions of assholes out there who deserve it far more.

If I don't try to help her, not only will I let her down, but I'd be letting my dad down too. Doesn't matter that he's no longer breathing my air. I owe him everything. If not for his endless patience and guidance, I'd be in a cell next to Chopper.

I don't know how to convey any of this to Megan, though, so I simply offer a learned response. "Things will smooth out. You'll see."

She stills her hands and, as if not even hearing me, repeats her earlier comment. "If my aunt was murdered, I'd definitely want her killer brought to justice—but not at the expense of my friend. So… just be careful, okay?"

"I always am," I say.

Or at least I try to be.

13

———————

Driving to Boston on a Saturday two weeks in a row is never my idea of fun, especially with a grant proposal looming over my head, but my mind is fixated on Demetri Pappas, and until I answer the question of whether he had anything to do with Fiona Carlson's death, my thoughts won't quiet. I know this about myself, so there's no use fighting it.

As I pass a steady stream of traffic on I-93, I play out other scenarios as well. No sense getting tunnel vision by putting all my chips on the Demetri table. After meeting him at the pub, I plan to visit the addiction center where Fiona volunteered. Maybe someone there wanted her dead. Since it's a weekend, I'll leave her workplace for later, should it become necessary. That's assuming I'd even know how to approach such a thing. I'm no detective.

Don't worry, I silently voice to my dad, who I imagine slouched with exasperation in the passenger seat. *I haven't dived off the self-sabotage board yet.* Case in point: Dr. Thomas expects a more coherent display from me this Wednesday. I spent the last two nights preparing one. In addition to writing an outline for the grant, I put together a PowerPoint presentation summarizing the current literature on white matter interstitial neurons' role in schizophrenia. That should avoid a repeat performance of stumbling idiocy to my program director.

See, Dad? It's all good.

If I had been able to review my grant work with my advisor, I'd feel even better about my progress, but Dr. Silverstein remains preoccupied with her husband and his worsening dementia. I'm sad for her, especially after seeing bruises on her arm. I worry he's growing combative. But I also worry her distraction might blow our chance at a once-in-a-lifetime grant.

Her distraction? my father whispers. I don't miss the irony.

Once I reach Boston proper, the traffic becomes a congested, snorting, honking mess. Cars inch along and stop abruptly. Pedestrians jaywalk and ignore walk signals. A woman flips off a man who just cut her off at the light. Okay, that last one was me. By the time I find a parking spot off Boylston Street within reasonable walking distance from both Muriel's Irish Pub and Fiona's condo building, I'm cursing like a gangster. I could probably kill as ruthlessly as one too.

Fortunately, my temper cools as I stroll down the sidewalk toward the bar. My fashion skills are poor, so I didn't dress to impress. After all, I'm not here to date Demetri. I'm here to sniff him out. For that, my cap-sleeved tee and faded jeans will have to do. But my hair is freshly shampooed and my eyebrows recently shaped. To top things off, I added my mom's necklace, a black-onyx stone in the shape of a treble clef. After giving it to me a few years ago, she made me promise to "keep it safe from the king and his thieves."

As I near Muriel's Irish Pub, I take a deep breath and conjure my years of practice at being someone I'm not. Then I slip off my aviator sunglasses and enter the pub.

As soon as I step inside the bar, the scent of spilled beer and fried food accosts me. Once my eyes adjust to the dim lighting, I scan the place for my prey.

Most every table is filled, patrons chowing down on lunch or sipping an early beer. Knowing Demetri will be looking for Fiona, I ease my way past the hostess stand, currently unattended, and scout each table for a fifty-five-year-old man with salt-and-pepper hair and a cleft in his chin. When I spot him in the far-right corner, I head that way.

A pint of ale sits in front of him, and a strawberry daiquiri, or something like that, awaits his guest. Clearly he knew Fiona well enough to order her preferred drink ahead of time. Too bad it's not a shot of whiskey. I could use one.

I approach the table. "Demetri Pappas?"

"Yes." A frown creases his brow, but despite his obvious confusion, he manages a thorough head-to-toe visual inspection of me nonetheless.

Gross.

I pull a chair out from the scratched wooden table and sit.

He shakes his head. "I'm expecting someone."

"You're expecting me."

The corner of his mouth curls up. "I like your initiative, young lady, but I'm afraid I can't accept it right now." He runs a finger over his glass and stares at my chest, making me wish I'd worn a less formfitting tee. "Although I'd certainly like to."

I snap my fingers, and his attention returns to my eyes. I haven't even introduced myself, and the guy's already coming on to me. Whether or not he's a psychopath, I don't yet know, but he's got predator written all over him. Or, at the very least, oversexed creep. His lewd text messages to Fiona on the dating app and his liberal use of eggplant emojis confirm that.

"I'm Liza." I hold off on my last name for now. "I knew Fiona. Well, I knew *of* her."

Demetri straightens in his chair. "Where is she?" A smile forms on his face. "Wait, did she send you? I was worried my mention of... spicing things up a notch scared her away. Guess I was wrong." He does another head-to-breast assessment of me. "I must admit, she's chosen wisely. I would have never guessed you were her type."

Oh, for fuck's sake.

"Fiona's dead," I say sharply.

Demetri's mouth falls open, almost in a comical fashion. I'm tempted to throw the untouched daiquiri into it, which, for all I know, is spiked with roofies. Instead, I study the man. There's no mistaking his shock. Wide eyes, dropped jaw, forward tilt of his head. Demetri seems genuinely surprised to learn Fiona is dead.

Unless he's a great actor. He's into sexual role-playing, after all. I can't rule anything out yet.

"How? When?" he says.

"Nine days ago. She suffocated in her piano bed."

"Oh my God." Demetri raises his pint glass and then puts it back down without taking a drink. "How is that possible?"

I shrug. I scrutinize his face. Did he really have no idea Fiona died, or is he nailing a well-practiced performance?

"That explains why she didn't respond to me." He finally sips his beer. "Wait, that means you messaged me on the app, not Fiona. Why would you do that? Why not just tell me who you were?"

Because you might have gotten spooked and scurried off.

I don't say that to him, of course. Instead, I ask, "Were you with her two Thursdays ago?"

"I…why? Was that when she died?"

"Yes. At least that's what the ME thinks."

"No, of course I wasn't. If you read my messages, you know she ghosted me before then. That's what it's called these days, right?"

He seems to have calculated the dates rather quickly, at least in my opinion. "Where were you that night?"

"You can't possibly think I had anything to do with her—" His front shirt pocket pings. He pulls out a fancy folding phone, reads the text, and curses. "My son. I have to go."

Before I can confirm Demetri's alibi for the night Fiona died, he stands.

"It's terrible Fiona is dead, shocking, really, but I had nothing to do with it. It hurts that you think I would. Who are you, anyway?"

"I told you. I'm a friend of Fiona's."

"One who snoops through her phone and reads her private messages?" When I don't answer, he says, "You're an intriguing woman, and I suspect there's more you want to say to me. How about we continue this conversation later?"

I consider his suggestion. Is it wise for me to meet him again now that he knows what I'm up to? Probably not, but I can't forcibly keep Demetri here, and I'm no more sure he's a killer than when I first entered the bar. I need more time.

"Okay," I say. "Same place, next Friday night." That'll coincide with my semimonthly appointment with Dr. Lightfoot. Might as well hit two Boston men with one stone. "Eight o'clock, but give me your number in case something changes."

I open my phone. With a grin, he recites his number, and I add it to my contacts.

"It's a date then, Liza… What did you say your last name was?"

"I didn't." I rise and head toward the door. "See you Friday."

Back outside, I'm blinded by sunlight and bulldozed by pedestrians. A car alarm wails from somewhere down the block.

I hope I've made the right choice. I'll be meeting Demetri in a public place. I won't drink anything he buys me, and I won't leave alone with him. Perfectly safe. A second visit will help me figure out why a man so seemingly shocked by Fiona's death would grin and make a date with another woman so quickly.

Is he simply a horndog, looking to get laid?

Fat chance in that.

Or is he a killer who wants to find out what I know and cover his tracks?

14

The Hands of Hope addiction center is less than two miles away from Fenway Park, but in the congested traffic it takes twenty minutes to drive it. I deposit my Civic in the parking deck across the street and trot down a concrete stairwell. A homeless guy sits on the bottom step, his cart nearby. He doesn't ask for anything, but I fish two tens out of my wallet for him anyway. If he were my brother, I hope someone would do the same.

Moving on, I head toward the corner building that houses the addiction center. With its multiple stories and brick and tan siding, it looks more like an apartment complex than a treatment facility. An earlier Google search mentioned it houses both inpatient and outpatient rehab programs, along with post-rehab housing, so it makes sense the place would be big.

Since my truncated meeting with Demetri delivered no answers, this visit to the rehab center where Fiona volunteered seems a sensible next step. I'm already in Boston. What harm can it do? It's not like I'm stalking anyone. If my actions help confirm Fiona's manner of death—whether it be homicide or accident—and bring answers to Megan as a result, then my probing will have been worth it.

You can always be a helper.

I'm not sure my dad's words of advice included pumping employees at an addiction center for information, but so be it. Might as well put the money he spent on my therapy and social training to use.

I step inside the Hands of Hope entryway. It's bland but clean and, for reasons unclear to me, smells like rubber. I make it no farther than the reception window, which is enclosed in glass and manned (womaned?) by a college student wearing a UMass sweatshirt. Beyond her lies a set of double doors, their access most likely blocked.

The young woman yawns, but upon spotting me, she stifles it and replaces it with a smile. Her name tag reads *Shanice*. Behind a metal speak-through box, she says, "Can I help you?"

On my drive over, I rehearsed my spiel. Practice is key for a schizoid.

"Hi, I'm Liza. My friend's aunt, Fiona Carlson, volunteered here."

I'm about to add that Fiona recently passed away, but the receptionist must already know, because she says, "It's so sad. I'm sorry for your friend. We loved Fiona here."

It makes sense Megan would have informed the center of her aunt's death. Trying to make my visit here seem legit will be difficult, but I give it a go anyway. "My friend, Megan, wants to put together a digital scrapbook of her aunt's life. You know, for family and friends, and we were just curious about her work here."

"I'm sorry." Shanice sits fully upright now, and I'm guessing she's about to shut me down instead of buzz me inside. "Everything at the center is confidential."

"Sure, I understand, but we were hoping you could tell us what Fiona did here. You know, in generic terms."

The receptionist adjusts her sweatshirt. "She helped our clients find jobs. Write résumés, set up LinkedIn accounts, that kind of thing."

I nod. "Makes sense given her job in HR."

"Exactly."

"I know Fiona was troubled by the recent death of one of her clients. A fentanyl overdose."

"I'm sorry, who are you again?" Shanice asks me.

Crap. Either she's too sharp or I suck at nonchalant interrogation. Probably both.

"I'm Liza." I don't want to offer my last name, but it'll be suspicious to hold back and even more so if I give a fake one. What if Shanice calls Megan as soon as I walk away, wanting to confirm my identity? I spill it. "Liza Larkin. I'm a pathology resident at Titus McCall Medical Center in Morganville. I work with Megan, Fiona's niece. Megan would have come herself, but Fiona's funeral is today."

"Yeah, I'm bummed I had to work. I would've paid my respects."

Shanice offers nothing more. She's a tight-lipped vault. The center would be proud.

I shift my weight. Speaking through the metal grate is annoying, but I shoot for the net one more time and hope for a basket. "We've seen a lot of fentanyl deaths in the morgue. Fiona and Megan have talked about it, so that's why I asked about her client."

Shanice's phone buzzes on the counter next to her keyboard. She glances at the screen and tosses me an unexpected pass. "It's terrible, that's what it is." She raises her mobile. "Can you believe it? I just got a text that another one of our clients OD'd. Luckily, he got Narcan in time."

"How many deaths have you had? I mean, among your clients, the ones who relapsed."

"I really can't say anything else. I'm not sure what I can give you that would help with the scrapbook. Just know that Fiona was well liked and respected around here."

"So, no enemies?" The question pops out of my mouth before I can stop it.

Stupid, stupid, stupid.

Shanice frowns. "I'm sorry, but I have to get back to work. Give my best to Megan. I've never met her, but Fiona spoke fondly of her."

With that, the receptionist tosses our metaphorical basketball out of the arena, picks up her cell phone, and stabs out a response to whoever texted her.

I've been dismissed.

I wanted to show her a photo of Demetri Pappas. I saved the profile picture from his clinic's website to my phone. Given he works as a pain specialist, I figured maybe Fiona met him at the addiction center or through a shared connection.

Too late now. Not only have I lost the ball, but I've lost the game.

Outside the door, I collide with a stringy man. Stringy hair, stringy build, stringy arms, both of which are covered in scabs. I step back from him and apologize.

He doesn't acknowledge me, just resumes pacing back and forth on the sidewalk near the center's entrance. Maybe he's debating going inside to attend a meeting versus going off somewhere to score some drugs. Either way, I seize the opportunity.

"Are you a client here?" I ask. Not the most subtle question, I know.

"What's it to you?"

"Sorry. I was just wondering if you knew Fiona Carlson. She was a friend of mine." *Well, not really, but close enough.*

"I don't know no Fiona."

He keeps walking back and forth, picking at his arms. I decide to believe him. He doesn't seem rehabilitated enough for job advice from Fiona.

"What about this guy?" I flash Demetri Pappas's picture on my cell phone.

"Who do you think I am? Google?"

"Can you just take a look, please?" I hold the phone out farther.

He stops pacing and stares at it. "I think better with money."

Another extortionist. Just what I need. At least, unlike Chopper, this guy will be a one-hit wonder.

I pluck my wallet out of my satchel and pull out a twenty-dollar bill. I hesitate. He's probably going to spend it on drugs. I shouldn't facilitate that.

It's for a good cause, though—helping Megan. I hand the money over.

The stringy man snatches it away. "Yeah. That's Dr. Demetri."

My pulse ticks up. "How do you know him? Does he volunteer here?"

"Nah. He came by to see Dr. Brad once. He's the one who volunteers on Friday nights. Guess they're partners at a clinic or something."

"Did you talk to him?" I ask. "To Dr. Demetri, I mean?"

"No, but I seen what he did."

"And what was that?"

The man leans against the center's window, his frayed sneakers tapping the concrete and his fingers back to scratching his arms. "That's gonna cost you more."

Maybe I'm being played. A guy looking to score as much cash as he can for a hit. But if he knows something about Demetri, I need to find out what it is.

I grunt and pluck out another twenty. Only thirteen dollars remain in my wallet. "Here. Now, what did you see Dr. Demetri do?"

"He was messin' with some woman here, getting all touchy like. I was comin' down the hallway, saw him talkin' to her. She didn't look too interested. And that's not the worst of it."

"Yeah, what is?"

My extortioner looks both ways down the sidewalk. Passersby pay no attention to us. "I need a little more for groceries, know what I mean?" He holds out his hand.

My cheeks heat with irritation, but I swallow it down. I dig out my remaining thirteen bucks and show him my empty wallet. "This is all I have. See?"

He grabs my cash. "One of the ladies here? A 'client' as you call us? She says she did it with the doc. He paid her."

"Did what?" I ask, but I have a pretty good idea.

"You know." The guy makes a circle with his thumb and index finger and jabs another finger in and out of it. "She says the doctor was kinky. Wanted some dark stuff, if you know what I mean."

I don't know what he means, not entirely, since again, sex isn't my thing, but after seeing Demetri's messages to Fiona, I can only imagine. Fits with what I saw of him. Staring at my body like he owned it. Something is up with this Demetri guy.

"If you ask me," the stringy man says, "Dr. Demetri is the one with an addiction problem. A sex addiction."

Drug-infused brain or not, this guy's take on Demetri seems spot on.

I ask if there's anything else, and my informant shakes his head. He stuffs my money deep into his pocket, as if he's worried I'll yank it back.

I thank him and return to my Civic in the lot across the street. Energy pulses inside me. Excitement is rare for me, so I savor it. Aside from a heart-thumping workout, the only time I feel this juiced up is when I make progress on a challenging problem. Doesn't matter if it's a research question, an unusual-looking cell under my microscope, or a woman mysteriously killed by her Murphy bed. A puzzle is a puzzle, and no drug or drink in the world gets me higher.

Plus, in terms of Fiona's death, unlike the police—or even Megan and the forensic pathologists she emulates—I don't have to follow the rules. I can hunt for the solution in whatever way I want, just like I did with Dr. Donovan.

Climbing into my car, I'm glad I made another "date" with Demetri Pappas for next week. My trip to Boston did nothing to rule him out. On the contrary, he's suspect number one, and if he is behind Fiona's death, I intend to prove it. No way will he get off scot-free. Not on my watch.

I may not be able to help Megan with her grief.

But I *can* help find her aunt's killer.

15

____

My grant presentation to Dr. Thomas in his office on Wednesday goes much better than it did last week. Today I come off as prepared and knowledgeable about my preparatory research. I even spruced up for the occasion: dress pants and a blouse with pearly buttons.

My program director must be pleased because after I finish my PowerPoint, he says, "Nicely done."

"Thank you."

"But it worries me you don't have a completed first draft of your grant proposal yet. Deadlines are like wrinkles. They have a way of creeping up on us, until bam, we're old."

Dr. Thomas smiles, so I assume this is a joke, but despite him being well north of fifty, he doesn't look old to me. Waseem says he has the face of Laurence Fishburne and the voice of James Earl Jones. To Waseem, everyone in the path department has the face or voice of a film star. Except me, apparently. He says my crooked nose makes me an enigma. During our first year of residency, he told me to stand still and then stared at me from all angles, which I didn't much care for. After what felt like a lifetime, he declared, "You're a cross between Zendaya and Gina Gershon, only with short hair and no makeup. Yes, that's it."

Whoever they are.

I close my laptop and say, "I'm waiting to finalize things with Dr. Silverstein. I don't want to write a section only to have her change it up. I've got a solid outline done, though."

Dr. Thomas scratches his neck. "Ah, yes, about that. Dr. Silverstein will be taking more time off to spend with her husband. I wonder if there's someone else you could…"

I know what he's going to say, even if he doesn't finish the sentence. He's going to suggest I find a different preceptor for my research, but we both know that's impossible. Dr. Silverstein is the only neuropathologist at Titus McCall. Moreover, she's the only pathologist who voiced interest in this line of study. There's no time to start over.

"Dr. Silverstein is meeting with me on Monday," I assure my program director. "We had to postpone things because of medical issues with her husband, but she said she'll prepare her findings this weekend. Once she does, I'll pool them with mine and write a complete proposal. Don't worry. We won't miss next Friday's deadline."

Please don't let us miss the deadline.

Dr. Thomas removes a stack of papers from his in-basket. "Well, as long as you make this grant your absolute focus until then—along with your other residency duties, of course—you should be okay. Don't let yourself get distracted with other things." He holds up a finger. "Except for the mini-retreat at my lake house this Sunday. I know how much you love social gatherings." He laughs, and his broad shoulders do a little dance.

Yay me.

Gripping my laptop under my arm, I stand. "It's my number one priority. The grant, I mean. Not the retreat."

Is it, tiger? my father whispers.

Dr. Thomas chuckles again and wishes me a good day.

The following morning I arrive in the residents' room early. Between the grant and my Boston sleuthing, I've fallen behind on reading pathology slides. One and a half days' worth of cytology smears awaits my attention. My goal is to finish before teaching rounds begin at ten.

Thirty minutes later Waseem plops down in his cubicle next to mine. Both his posture and eyes are droopy, and his greeting is about as exuberant as a sloth's.

Uh-oh. The last time my hirsute colleague looked like this he'd just received a nasty comment on his YouTube film.

While he settles in, none of his usual chatter about Netflix series or Oscar predictions bubbles forth. Instead, he leaves the residents' room in a quiet cloud, probably to retrieve his own batch of slides. Keeping an eye out for his return, I pluck my phone from my bag and open up YouTube to search for his short film. If my memory is correct, the title is *Losing to Win*, and his account name is Mad Wasp.

When I find the video, I scroll down to the comments. The original nasty review by Joe Balls remains, stinking up the page with its rot. Three new comments have popped up as well. Two viewers replied in defense of the film. Why you gotta hate, bro? one said. Mad Wasp is just doing his thing. The other wrote, Nice first start. Enjoyed it.

The third new comment, written by someone with the username Mo Bean, must be what turned Waseem into the walking dead. It reads: I'm with Joe Balls. This film makes *Freddy Got Fingered* look like a masterpiece. Save yourself fifteen minutes of pain and shove steak knives in your eyes instead. Trust me, it'll be quicker.

I have no idea what *Freddy Got Fingered* is, but I do know that Mo Bean, a YouTube troll whose bio claims he's a filmmaker and screenwriter, is a shithead who deserves a foot kicked up his ass. Make that an entire leg.

Waseem returns to his desk. Despite the wood divider between us, I push my phone deeper into my cubicle so he won't see what I'm up to. Once he's hunched over his microscope, I sign out of my regular Google account and log back in with a dummy one. I have a couple of them. Not for nefarious purposes, of course. It's not like

I'm stalking people. Not now, anyway. But anonymous email addresses can be useful at times, and this is one of those times.

Choosing my account that carries the name Tyler Pearson, I return to Waseem's YouTube video and log in with my alternate username. After a minute or two of tapping my fingertip over my phone screen while I think, I start typing.

Losing to Win is one of the best short films I've seen on this site. The characters are flawed—

I backspace and change it to The characters are nicely flawed. That makes the hero's decision to give away the money all the more real.

I delete the word real, think a bit more, and change it to touching instead. Then I add Mad Wasp doesn't follow generic film structure. He takes a risk with his story, and it pays off big-time.

I read through my review and hope it makes sense for the film. I haven't watched it yet, but I make a mental note to do so later. Maybe I'll even leave another supportive comment. Waseem deserves to feel as good about his film as he makes everyone around him feel. My colleagues have mentioned they miss his smiles and jokes. Me, too, if I'm being honest. I've kept his confidence, though. Haven't told anyone why he's so down since he asked me not to. Hopefully, my review will bring his cheerful grin back.

Barely have I closed out the YouTube app when Megan slumps into the residents' room with an equally beaten-down demeanor. Even her blouse is gray. Instead of a styled blow-out, her honey locks are pulled back in a messy ponytail. It's been five days since her aunt's funeral, and she appears to have slept little during that time.

Waseem rises to give her a hug. "Sorry you're going through this, Megs. Let me know if I can help. But you've got this. You're tougher than beef turkey."

She smiles at his botched idiom and thanks him. Tells him that means a lot.

"Let me grab you some tea," he says. "You look like you could use a little warmth."

He exits, leaving Megan and me alone in the residents' room.

Still standing, she plops her giant purse on the floor next to her cubicle and sighs. "Munson did another autopsy on a fentanyl overdose yesterday."

Dr. Munson is one of the medical examiners, and also Megan's advisor.

"How old?" I ask.

"Eighteen. Forensics has been finding an animal tranquilizer in some of the tox screens. This guy's is still pending."

"Seriously?"

"Yep." Megan rubs her bloodshot eyes. "As if that wasn't rotten enough, the tranquilizer isn't an opioid, so that means—"

"Naloxone won't reverse it. That's bad."

"Right? That's probably what's causing the uptick in deaths. Munson said traffickers pad their profits by stuffing anything they can in a pill and calling it fentanyl."

Just because I have no desire to form relationships (section 301.20 of the *DSM-5*; I have it memorized) doesn't make me indifferent to young people—any people—dying from opioid addiction and tainted pills. On the contrary. It makes me feel helpless, much like the fire that torched the house of my favorite teacher did. Left her burned and her husband and son dead.

I wanted to heal Mrs. Dixon. Wanted to take away her hurt. Wanted to bring her husband and son back. I could do none of those things. I could only punch my heavy bag in our basement until my knuckles bled. That and investigate the fire on my own. For weeks I was convinced it was arson, tracking down any rumors I could find. Because why would the god Mrs. Dixon believed in, the one she went to church every week to serve, destroy her life so senselessly? I was wrong, though. Fire investigators concluded without a doubt that faulty wiring was the cause.

So, no, beyond voting the right people into office, I can't help these kids dying from opioids now any more than I could help Mrs. Dixon back then, and the reality of that makes me want to beat the drug dealers with the corpses they leave behind.

"…and I'm next in line for autopsy duty," Megan is saying. "Shit."

Megan's words surprise me. One, because she's been swearing a lot lately, something she doesn't typically do, and two, because she usually performs backflips for forensic postmortems.

"Want me to take it?" I offer.

"Thanks, but you don't have to. It's not like I can avoid them. I'm going into forensics." She gives a sharp laugh. "You're the one who should become an ME. A detective, even. Like Jen said, you don't give up until you solve something."

She rests her arms on the wood divider between the cubicles and studies me. Is she sending me a message with those words and that stare? Is she hinting I should keep looking into her aunt's death? Keep looking into Demetri Pappas? Earlier this week, she asked me how my meeting with him went.

"He'd have sex with a potato if he could," I told her. "But as of now, I have no other reason to suspect him."

I left it at that. Didn't mention my planned second "date" with him tomorrow night after my appointment with Dr. Lightfoot. Or my recent visit to Hands of Hope, the addiction-recovery center where Fiona volunteered. Those omissions weren't meant to be deceitful. They were meant to be protective. No need to confuse Megan—or get her hopes up, or whatever her response might be if she learns her aunt was murdered—until I know more.

But if the subtext in her prolonged scrutiny of me now is suggesting I keep looking, then I should do it. Anything to get her out of this funk.

I wish I could say my motives are purely altruistic, but I'd be lying. They're also self-serving, because my colleagues' depressed moods mess with my carefully balanced world. They force me to learn their temperaments and idiosyncrasies all over again, which for a person like me is exhausting. I can't conform myself to my environment if my environment keeps changing.

I realize I've taken too long to respond. When in doubt, offer platitudes. "You'll be a great forensic pathologist," I tell Megan. "You've got better intuition than a psychic."

"Thanks, but there's just so much ugly out there. Being an empath is hard." She pulls out her chair and plops down. "With everything happening at once, I'm a mess."

I hunt for a response. She saves me from finding one by switching gears.

"I have to box up the rest of my aunt's things, but I don't have the energy to drive to Boston yet again and do it. I need some distance. A weekend to catch up on some shows and knit."

More subtext for me? Or am I imagining it?

She twirls in her chair like a sad rag doll. "But I guess I don't have a choice, do I? I'll need to list the condo for sale soon. Can't keep putting it off."

"I'll pack her things for you," I offer. My senses twitter at the thought. This could be exactly what I need. One more trip inside Fiona's condo. A chance to snoop unencumbered and hunt for evidence against Demetri Pappas.

"Oh, I can't ask you to do that," she says.

"It's no problem. Really. I have to go to Boston tomorrow afternoon anyway for my appointment with Dr. Lightfoot."

Megan knows I see a shrink twice a month—given last year's debacle, the whole department likely knows—so I don't bother hiding it. And why should I? The brain is just another body part that sometimes needs a doctor.

"Give me your aunt's keys, and I'll stop by her place when I'm done. Do you have moving boxes or should I bring some?"

"I've got plenty there, but still, it doesn't seem fair to make you—"

"I'm happy to do it."

"Well," she says, drawing out the word, "I've packed up a lot already. Kitchen stuff, living room trinkets, clothes. I plan to give most of it to Goodwill. Some of the furniture I'll sell. I haven't cleared out her bathroom yet or the shelves in her closet. Books, games, wrapping paper, those kinds of things."

"Anything left you want to keep for yourself?"

"No." Megan holds up a finger. "Wait. There is something. Aunt Fiona had an antique jewelry box. Black with sterling silver accents, about the size of a toaster oven. Really gorgeous." At this she straightens in her chair. "I just realized I haven't come across it yet.

That's weird. Must be tucked away in her closet. Somehow I missed it."

"Is it valuable?"

"Who knows? Maybe. My guess is it's worth more than the jewelry inside it. The jewelry can go, but I want the box as a keepsake."

I nod. "What about your dad or sister? Anything they'd want that I should pack separately?"

"The only thing my dad wants is a framed photograph of their family when they were kids. Why, I don't know, since they never got along, but I've already grabbed that for him. My sister wants nothing." This last is said with a bite, and color returns to Megan's cheeks.

"Then it'll be easy for me." My mind is already lost in what I might find in Fiona's closet. "I'll pack up whatever is left—other than the jewelry box—and label it, so you'll know what to give away or junk."

"Are you sure? I mean—"

Waseem returns with Megan's tea. "Sorry it took so long. Bumped into a friend in the cafeteria."

I wonder if the friend is Jackson, an internal medicine resident Waseem sometimes hangs out with. Megan long ago surmised Waseem is more interested in the Jacksons of the world than the Jessicas, but the fact his homeland outlaws such things keeps him from acknowledging it, either to himself or to others. I might not be an empath, but that makes me sad. Maybe I'll have to leave his film another review.

I stand and finish my conversation with Megan. "Seriously. I'm happy to do it."

She wraps her hands around the paper cup as if siphoning its heat. "That's incredibly kind of you, Liza. Thank you. But don't feel like you have—"

"It's no problem."

My heart dances a beat of anticipation.

No problem at all.

16

Brian's Gym is small, utilitarian, and well suited to committed exercisers who mind their own business and don't make conversation. In other words, my dream gym. I've been coming here since I moved to Morganville from Boston four years ago.

Thirty minutes of pounding the heavy bag followed by an hour of weightlifting helps me mentally prepare for my meeting with Demetri tomorrow night. When I finish, I nod to the two other people in the weight room and head out into the dusky evening, my stomach growling for the late dinner I'm about to have.

While I'm driving home, skirting the bulk of Morganville and its historic downtown, my phone buzzes. Not having a death wish, I wait until a red light to check it. It's a text from Chopper, my black-mailer. No words. Only a GIF of an hourglass with sand running out of it and emojis of a knife and a clock. Chopper's a freaking poet now.

I toss the phone onto the passenger seat. Just because I don't want to deal with the ex-con doesn't mean I can keep ignoring him. Clearly he's not going away.

Also clearly, I'm not going to pay him. Anything he spews about me would hurt him just as much as it would me. I'm not the one who put a shank in Sam Donovan's side.

Still, with as focused as I've been on Fiona, I've given him little thought. My brain doesn't enjoy multitasking. Aside from my job, it prefers a singular obsession, and that obsession is currently Fiona, not Chopper. Regardless, I'm going to have to stretch my cerebral capacity and allow him to share the spotlight.

A few blocks from my apartment complex, I pull into a Chipotle at the same strip mall that houses my dentist and hair salon. It's about time for an appointment for both. While I wait for the teenage employee to pile my burrito bowl high with chicken, beans, and rice, I shoot Chopper a text back: **Tied up with some things. Need another week. Will be in touch.**

Hoping that will do for the time being, I carry my spicy meal to my car and drive the short distance home. With the leaves starting to turn, New England will be a cornucopia of fall foliage in a few weeks. I welcome it. Nothing quiets my restless brain better than an autumn run in a wooded neighborhood. Not even a tussle with Brian's heavy bags has that calming power.

Any serenity my drive home has offered gets snuffed out the moment I step into my apartment building and spot Mr. Sinclair. He's standing in the open doorframe of the same unit where I pounded on his chest two weeks ago. Although it's good he's recovered enough from his heart attack to be here—not counting his pasty complexion and obvious weight loss—my flesh boils when I see who's with him.

Pete Parsons. The sadistic orderly from my mom's mental-health facility. The one I asked Dr. Dhar, the center's director, to keep a close eye on. The one who despises me.

What the hell is he doing here?

If I'd had proof of the pranks he played on the patients, Dr. Dhar would have fired him, but I didn't. That's unfortunate, because the residents at Home and Hearth Healing deserve better than his sorry ass.

He must've snagged my address from my mom's file. I'm her

main contact person. Does he intend to move into my building now? A "you messed with me so I'll mess with you" sort of thing?

Super.

At least Mr. Sinclair, who normally occupies the top tier of my shit list, seems less bullish tonight. If I'm reading his downcast eyes and closed-lip smile correctly, he seems almost contrite. Or maybe he's simply annoyed to owe me one.

"Hey," he says.

I nod in greeting, and then, because I've been well trained, ask, "How are you feeling?"

"Pretty good, thanks to you. Starting to get back out there."

"Just glad you're better. They put in a stent?"

"Yep. Only had one bad artery. They tell me everything looks good now."

My gaze shifts to Pete. I try not to scowl but am not sure I succeed.

Like an innocent child, the orderly grins at me, wide-eyed. "Wow, Liza, I didn't know you lived here."

Given that psychopaths are easy for me to read—my own twisted version of Megan's empath curse—I don't miss the smirk on Pete's face and the unspoken *gotcha!* it conveys.

To Sinclair, I say, "You might want to rethink renting to this guy. He's not stable."

"*I'm* not stable?" Pete says. "Choice words coming from you."

I ignore him. "He works at my mom's center. Has a history of tormenting patients."

Sinclair's nostrils twitch. Whether I saved his life or not, his underlying feelings for me probably remain the same. Our contentious run-ins over the past couple of years can't be erased by a few chest compressions and rescue breaths.

"I check references," my landlord says. "How about you let me decide who I should and shouldn't rent to." With a wave of his arm, he ushers Pete Parsons into the apartment.

Pete throws a final glance my way. "Wouldn't it be cool if we were neighbors?"

I shoot him the best death stare in my arsenal, but it doesn't seem to intimidate him like it has Sinclair in the past.

My landlord closes the door, and the two men disappear, leaving me saddled with one more problem I don't need.

17

———————

A redbrick row house in the coveted Beacon Hill neighborhood of Boston serves as both Dr. Lightfoot's home and his psychiatry office. On this Friday afternoon, the brown-accented den in which I divulge my secrets—some of them, anyway—is as sequestered from the world as ever, save for an occasional passing car outside the bay windows.

A coffee table separates our leather wingback chairs, its coasters absorbing the condensation from our glasses of ice water. Usually it's tea, but today I requested something cold. Soft music of flutes and violins plays in the background. The legs of a clock shaped like a male doctor in a white coat swing back and forth hypnotically.

As usual, I worry the sensory comforts of the room will lull me to sleep.

As usual, my shrink's prodding will keep that from happening.

"Thanks for always staying late for me," I tell him. "I wouldn't feel right leaving work any earlier than four fifteen."

"I'm happy to do it. Sorry I had to cancel our last appointment." He smooths his dark blazer over his jeans. "Why don't you fill me in on your past month? Anything we should work through?"

While I ruminate on how much to share, knowing that revealing too little does me no good mental health–wise, but revealing too much risks unraveling the Fiona investigation I have no wish to walk away from, I stare at the doctor clock. Is there a female equivalent? Is she dressed in a skirt instead of pants? I hope not. Other than back when I was too young to choose, I've never worn a dress in my life.

"Let's try that again," Dr. Lightfoot says after my lack of response. "That was too open-ended of a question. Any interesting cases this past month?"

"A lot of fentanyl overdoses."

My psychiatrist shakes his head. "That drug is everywhere. Counterfeit pills get smuggled across the border, laced with potent drugs, ripe for overdoses. One tablet can kill you because you don't know what's in it. I've lost more than a few patients to ODs." He points a thumb behind him toward his desk. "I keep naloxone in my office now. My car too. Never know when it might be needed."

Dr. Lightfoot seldom veers off the topic of me, and that, combined with his stony glare, tells me this issue is a raw one for him.

"They come in fun colors too," I say. "Pink, purple, turquoise. Looks like harmless candy to teenagers."

My shrink nods. "Rainbow fentanyl. Hundreds of potential overdoses in each bag."

We sip our water and ponder the situation, him having lost patients to the drug, me having to cut their dead bodies open on the table.

Finally, I say, "There is something I'd like to run past you."

"Shoot."

"One of my colleagues wants to make movies someday."

"As a pathologist?"

"People can do more than one thing in life. You like to restore old furniture, don't you?"

"Touché," Dr. Lightfoot says, bowing slightly.

"I'm not sure pathology is the career he really wants. He's from the UAE, and his family is packed with doctors and very conventional. His true calling seems to be film. That's all he talks about.

Not superficially either. He reads lots of books on the craft. Screen-writing, directing, producing, you name it."

"I see. So what's your question?"

"He recently made a short film and posted it on YouTube. Social media being the cesspool that it is left him with a couple hurtful comments from trolls." I unzip my hoodie, the room feeling warm. "So I posted a couple reviews of my own, using aliases. Praised the film, pumped it up, that kind of thing. Wanted to make him feel better about it. He seems down lately. Sad, even, and if *I'm* picking up on that, you know he must be. Am I wrong to leave fake reviews? Or is it okay to lie in a situation like that?"

Dr. Lightfoot grins at me, the lines around his eyes crinkling.

"What's so funny?" I ask, defensive.

"Nothing's funny. In fact, your words warm me. They show me how far you've come over the years."

"How so?"

"Your empathy skills have matured a lot since I first met you. Don't get me wrong. You've never been as soulless as you claim to be. You've always looked out for the underdog. But your ability to pick up on the less-obvious hurts, the more subtle emotions, has evolved. Do you think the Liza of five years ago would have sussed out why one of her colleagues was depressed? Would she even have been interested?"

I say nothing, but the answer is no.

Dr. Lightfoot leans forward. "It's like this: had someone beaten your colleague up, I have no doubt you would have avenged him." He holds up a finger. "I'm not saying you would've chosen the best way to do it—that's a whole other avenue of discussion—but you would have done something to defend him."

"Of course I would've."

"A physical beating is an obvious hurt. Your colleague sporting a black eye or a bruised arm is easily seen. But your friend showing only emotional wounds? You picking up on his depressed mood, whether from him not smiling as much or not laughing anymore? Those are nuances you wouldn't have noticed before, and as a result your empathy wouldn't have been roused."

I frown. "People are either empathetic or they're not. They don't suddenly become it."

"Not true, Liza. Not true at all. It can be taught. Your dad knew that. That's why he worked so hard with you. Your mother, too, before she got ill."

"And you," I add, not wanting my shrink to underestimate his own contribution.

"See? You being concerned about leaving me out? That's empathy right there."

"I…"

"Just because empathy didn't come naturally to you doesn't mean you couldn't learn it." Dr. Lightfoot crosses an ankle over his knee. "And now you're surmising people's pain purely from their body language. That's huge, Liza."

"But…how is that possible?" The human mind never ceases to fascinate me.

"You're getting older. Your brain has matured. It's created new pathways from both learned and lived experiences. Neural connections form throughout our lifetimes. You know that."

I play with my hoodie's zipper and think about the people in my life. Dr. Silverstein's troubles with her husband and his dementia. Waseem and his dejectedness. Megan's recent personal losses. Jen feeling overwhelmed.

I lower my voice. "If that's the case, I'm not sure I want to have empathy. It's hard seeing people struggle. Makes me want to fix everything for them."

"That's a heavy burden and not at all what I'm implying. You can be there for people, sure, but you don't have to fix them. You *can't* fix them."

Dr. Lightfoot's words make sense, and they echo the words of my father, but they don't lighten the responsibility I feel.

"You've let more people into your life this past year—or your inner circle, as you call it. Back in med school you were able to disappear into the crowd of students, but in residency, you and the other residents are forced into more intimacy. You can't slip away from them so easily."

What he says is true, although it wasn't exactly done willingly. With a colleague like Megan, a woman who takes the word *team* to an almost spiritual level, you get sucked into the cyclone whether you want to or not.

"Plus," Dr. Lightfoot continues, "you'll be thirty in a couple years. People your age start reevaluating their lives. Start seeing things differently."

I squirm in my seat. No doubt he wants me to explore this concept, hear my reaction to his remark, but for the moment it's too abstract for me to absorb. Self-examination doesn't suit me.

I revert back to my earlier question. "Is it wrong to post those reviews for my colleague? Should I take them down?"

"Hmm," my shrink says. "White lies to make people feel better —are they right or wrong? That's the age-old question."

"And what's your age-old answer?"

Dr. Lightfoot chuckles. "Was the film good?"

I shrug. "I'm no critic, but it seemed fine to me. Has a good message. Maybe a bit predictable, but some people like that."

"Then my advice is to leave your reviews where they are. It's a gray zone, really, but it would be cruel to delete them now. I wouldn't post any more, though. It's not honest, is it?"

I shake my head to his rhetorical question. At least I hope it was rhetorical. I'm not so daft that I can't figure out leaving fake reviews is dishonest.

"A more honest thing to do would be to tell your friend you watched his film and enjoyed it. Give him a few specifics on why. Coming from a person he trusts, your opinion will carry more weight than that of an online troll's, or at least it should."

"I did that already."

"Excellent," Dr. Lightfoot says.

We pause for another water break. A glance at the doctor clock confirms we've spent a lot of time discussing Waseem. Good. Less time to talk about my plans for tonight.

Still, I know I need to bring the Fiona issue up, both for my mental health and to not waste Dr. Lightfoot's time. For the next five minutes, I tell him about Fiona's bizarre death in her antique

Murphy bed and how I'm convinced it wasn't an accident, despite the medical examiner's conclusion. I also come clean about finding the dating app, visiting the addiction center where Fiona volunteered, and meeting with Demetri Pappas last weekend (although I don't mention his name). I'm reluctant to divulge all of this, and I don't want to be thwarted in my search for answers, but I've learned lying to my shrink does me no good. Maturing brain, right?

When Dr. Lightfoot stiffens and spends too much time adjusting his watch, I worry I've revealed too much. His face sobers into an expression I've seen many times from him in this room.

After a long pause, he says, "It can be difficult to wrap our heads around senseless deaths. Suffocating in a Murphy bed is certainly senseless. But, while I commend you for wanting to help your friend Megan, you've seen before how dangerous running blindly down the wrong track can be."

"I may have run blindly, but I wasn't wrong about Dr. Donovan."

My psychiatrist shifts in his chair. "Well, yes, but we both agreed you didn't choose the best paths to prove it."

I didn't agree to anything of the sort, I want to say but manage to bite my tongue.

"You've got a vivid imagination, Liza." Dr. Lightfoot angles his head. "No, I'm sorry. That's condescending and not what I meant. It's more that you have an actively deductive brain. You search for logic in everything."

"And that's a problem?"

"Not in and of itself, of course not, but the problem occurs when your logic leads you down the wrong road. Once you're on that road, you struggle to find the exit ramp. This risks you heading in the wrong—or worse, dangerous—direction."

"You're saying my choices are terrible."

Dr. Lightfoot clears his throat. "I'm saying your brain doesn't always process things the same way other people's do. This isn't a new revelation. You're well aware of it."

"I know, but you said my brain is maturing. Maybe my choices are too."

Dr. Lightfoot opens his mouth, then closes it without saying a word. It appears I've stumped him.

"The fact I'm telling you what I've done so far, looking into Fiona's death, proves my brain—and my choices—have matured, doesn't it?" I ask.

He hesitates but then smiles. "I believe you've walked me into a trap." He tips a pretend hat to me. "I do appreciate you showing me your cards. That's remarkable progress, especially since I didn't have to dig it out of you with a pick and shovel. Just be careful with your sleuthing. Run it by me first. Or Megan. Or your friend, the police officer. You can text me anytime, you know that. We can work through your thought processes, make sure you're taking the best actions. Like we just did with your colleague, the budding filmmaker."

I nod. Dr. Lightfoot is a wonderful man and a great doctor. I don't need my late father to tell me that. Contrary to popular belief, there are plenty of good men out there, and over the years, my psychiatrist has helped me a great deal.

And yet, while I disclose to him that I'm going to Fiona's condo after our session to pack up the remaining items for Megan, I leave out the part about wanting to snoop around and see if there's something that proves Fiona was murdered. I also don't mention my plans to meet Demetri again afterward to see if I can uncover what, if anything, he's hiding about Fiona. Like whether he killed her.

Needless to say, I also don't tell my shrink about Chopper.

Why not?

It's simple.

Good guys like Dr. Lightfoot, like my dad, like Dr. Thomas and Waseem—they believe goodness resides in everyone, or at least most everyone. They believe most people have the best of intentions and those who don't can be reasoned with by socially acceptable means, for example, the court system.

But I know better. The world of psychopaths functions differently. No amount of shrink training or parental guidance or brain maturation can wire that knowledge out of me. Tackling psychopaths requires outside-the-box measures. One dark mind to another. It's just the way things are.

So for now, my second "date" with Demetri will remain private, as will my negotiations with Chopper.

Because in this instance, people like me, people with darkly wired brains, simply know better than their shrinks.

18

As I drive through Boston toward Fiona Carlson's condo to pack her remaining items, I feel good about my appointment with Dr. Lightfoot. Sure, I withheld some information, but not much. In fact, I disclosed more details about my investigation than I thought I would.

Maybe he's right. Maybe I *am* maturing. Maybe I'm becoming more empathetic, more willing to let people in. Maybe one day I'll even get better at navigating social etiquettes and norms.

It's past six thirty, and the evening traffic remains heavy. The setting sun peeks out between buildings and blinds me, making the drive even more difficult. When I reach Fiona's complex, I struggle to find a parking spot. An underground lot for tenants probably exists, but I forgot to ask Megan for access. Eventually, after what feels like an hour but is probably only ten minutes, I find a spot three blocks away. Satchel over my shoulder, I lock the car and trot toward Fiona's eight-story building.

Before I left Dr. Lightfoot's office, I texted Demetri Pappas and told him I had to push tonight's meeting back to nine thirty. Although he gave me his number the last time we met, I'm not thrilled he now has mine. That leaves me less than three hours to box up Fiona's bathroom and closet. Not to mention to snoop around. Megan said there wasn't much left to pack, so hopefully I'll finish in time.

Outside the building's front doors, I type in her access code—the ever-dependable 2175—and step into the lobby. When I reach the gold-accented elevator, I'm not alone. A squat, muscular guy steps into the lift with me. I recognize him from the day Megan and I found her aunt's body. He was the one who barreled through the gathering crowd outside, seemingly oblivious to the fact that a dead woman had been found in the building. Like before, he doesn't make small talk, just stares at his phone until I exit on the fourth floor. For that I'm grateful.

As I near Fiona's unit, number 405, I run into another resident leaving his condo.

He peers at me through his wire-rimmed glasses. "Oh, hi, Liza, isn't it?"

"Um, yeah." Like with the guy in the elevator, I recognize this egg-shaped man with wispy hair from the crowd of spectators two weeks ago. I also recognize I won't be escaping small talk after all.

"You probably don't remember me," he says. "Why would you? Finding Fiona's body must have been traumatizing."

He extends his hand, and I reluctantly shake it.

"I'm Chuck. We met outside the building. Megan introduced us."

Aside from recognizing his face, I don't remember much about him, so I offer what I hope is a polite nod and withdraw Fiona's key from my pocket. "I'm just here to pack up a few things. Megan needed some help." Maybe he'll take that as his cue to mosey on down the hallway and leave me be.

"I'm the one who brought Fiona meals," he says. "She was so busy, and I always made too much food for one person. It was no problem."

Now it comes to me. Megan mentioned how much her aunt appreciated the dinners. I also remember thinking he probably hoped to be more to Fiona than a meal-delivery service but that he never stood a chance. An unfair judgment on my part, but hey, it's the world we live in. Pretty people like other pretty people. Fiona was pretty. This man is not. I may be a schizoid, but I'm not blind. Demetri, with his confidence, dark eyes, and cleft chin fits more in Fiona's league.

Thinking of Demetri, I want to hurry and get on with my task. He's enemy number one on my list until proven otherwise.

Chuck is chattering on about Fiona's preference for romaine lettuce over spring mix, and I realize I've tuned him out. Can you blame me?

"Sorry," I say. "I have to be somewhere soon." Recognizing that my interruption might be rude, I add, "But thank you for your kindness to Fiona. She and Megan spoke highly of you." I have no idea whether they did, but it seems to have been the right thing to say, because Chuck smiles.

"Oh sure, I was happy to help out. Fiona meant the world to me. Sorry, I don't want to hold you up." He lifts the empty cloth bag in his hand. "I have an errand to run, but I'll be back shortly. Let me know if you need anything."

I assure him I will. Once he's tottering toward the elevator, I close the short distance to Fiona's door and unlock her dead bolt.

Inside the studio I drop my satchel on the floor and take in my surroundings. Enough daylight remains to see by, but I flip on the lights anyway. Across the room, the piano-shaped Murphy bed mocks me. "Go ahead," it says. "Try to prove I *didn't* snap shut and suffocate the life out of Fiona."

Then again, why am I villainizing it? The antique bed could just as easily be saying, "Please, Liza. Prove that I'm not a murderer."

But if not you, I silently reply, *then who?*

Realizing that having a conversation with a piece of furniture could grant me a bed next to my schizophrenic mom, I get to the task at hand.

As promised, Megan already packed up the combined living area and kitchen. Boxes stacked two to three high stand neatly on the floor. All that remains are the larger items, including the killer bed, a sofa, a rolled-up area rug, and a breakfast table. A stack of flattened boxes leans against the wall, and a roll of packing tape lies next to them.

If only Fiona's laptop were still here. I'd love to browse through it, but Megan mentioned she took it back to her place. She plans to reset it to factory settings because Fiona used it for work issues as well as personal. Since it's off limits to me, short of breaking into my friend's apartment—a line I wouldn't cross, not for something like this, anyway—I'll have to make like an old-time detective and gumshoe things. At least Fiona's phone gave me a solid lead in Demetri.

Having only the walk-in closet and bathroom to box up, I start toward the back of the condo. After three steps, a ping from inside the closet makes me freeze. Although I can't see the interior of the walk-in from my position, its door is open.

Another noise follows. A grating sound this time, like two objects sliding against each other.

Someone is in there.

Megan? Did she feel guilty about me packing up the rest of her aunt's things and decide to stop by? That'll put a crimp in my snooping plans, for sure.

I'm about to say her name but hold back. Call it paranoia or call it instinct, but something doesn't feel right.

If Megan were in the closet, she would turn on the light. Yes, there's a window in there, but if memory serves me correctly, the storage space is pretty dark. The fire escape outside blocks much of the natural light.

Thump!

My nerve endings prickle with tension. I force myself to think through the rational choices, just as Dr. Lightfoot has asked me to do. Confront the person? Leave? Call the police? Text Megan to see if it's her?

What if I'm overreacting? It could simply be a pigeon who nosed its way in. How stupid would I look if I called the police over a pigeon?

I decide to check it out, but cautiously.

Tiptoeing over Fiona's hardwood floor, I reach the wall that fronts the closet and peer around the corner to look inside.

A man blinks back at me.

19

W e stare at each other, this man in the shadowy closet and me wondering who the hell he is. He's thin and has thick eyebrows, that much I can see. He also clutches a small chest.

"Hey." My tone is sharp. "What're you—"

The man lobs the chest at me. It cracks me on the forehead, and I stumble back, grabbing on to the open closet door to keep from falling. The box crashes onto the floor, and its contents spill out in a jangling chaos.

The intruder scurries out of the window and onto the fire escape. I swear I hear him say, "Be smart and mind your busy," but in my dazed state I can't be sure, and the words make no sense. He descends the fire escape and disappears from view. By the time my feet move again and take me to the open window, he's almost all the way down. He leaps off the last few metal rungs to the ground and tears off down the alley.

With my head outside the window and my palms resting on the ledge for support, I inhale deep breaths of city air. The sulfur of pollution mingles with the scent of fried food from an adjacent window and trash from the dumpsters below, but I don't care. I need to breathe to clear the pounding in my head. Dusk has fallen, and lights from the building across the street flicker inside small apartments.

As my dizziness clears, I realize this is the second time I've seen a skinny guy fly down this fire escape.

Slowly, so as not to ignite more vertigo, I rise to a full stand. Is the man who clobbered me with the chest the same guy who was on the fire escape two weeks ago? Seems too much of a coincidence to be otherwise. What was he doing inside Fiona's condo? He must have sneaked in through the window. There was no sign of forced entry at the front door.

I blink and study the window, a single-hung model with a vertical slider. The wood near its latch is splintered. I lower the glass pane and find it smudged with grime and fingerprints. When I slide the brass arc over to the locked position, the splintered wood prevents it from doing its job. The window opens regardless of whether or not the brass piece is locked.

That's not good. Especially given that a woman was found dead in this condo two weeks ago.

I sway on my feet. My skull feels like a crowbar cracked it open. I rub my forehead, and my fingers return sticky.

After wobbling to the bathroom, I look in the mirror. An inch-long cut and a grade-A goose egg decorate the right side of my forehead—parting gifts from the box-throwing stickman.

Since the bathroom isn't yet packed up, I'm able to find a clean washcloth in a wicker cabinet. Next to it sits a basket of Fiona's healing crystals. I skip the crystals and start cleaning my laceration.

Fortunately, the cut is not deep, and a rummage through Fiona's medicine cabinet nets me a box of wound-closure strips. I also find a bottle of sleeping pills. Did Fiona take them for general insomnia? Stress from her job? Uncertainty about Demetri? Worry about fentanyl use in the people she helped at the addiction center?

Whatever the reason for their use, the unused pills shouldn't be thrown in the trash. I pocket them and make plans to drop them off at the Morganville Police Department, where they can be disposed of safely.

Once my wound is cleaned and closed, I lower my lips to the

sink faucet and gulp several mouthfuls of metallic-tasting water. The building's pipes are probably older than dirt.

Feeling back to myself, the dizziness mostly passed and the adrenaline rush of surprise gone, I return to the closet and flip on the light. I glance down at the chest that clobbered me. Must be Fiona's antique jewelry box. Just as Megan mentioned, it's black with silver accents and is about the size of a toaster oven. The chest yawns open on the floor. The closet's carpet runner likely cushioned its fall. Earrings, necklaces, and bracelets lay strewn about it.

I'm about to reach for the box but withdraw my hand. I know what my father would say. He'd tell me not to touch anything and to call the police.

I lower my butt to the floor and draw my knees to my chest. Whether I want to or not, calling the police is the logical next step.

Three reasons hold me back. One is obvious: I don't like talking to people and just want to be left alone. Two is practical: It'll delay me. I'm supposed to meet Demetri in two and a half hours at Muriel's Irish Pub. Then again, if the guy who attacked me minutes ago also killed Fiona, what's the point of meeting Demetri again? The two men may have thick eyebrows in common, but the guy who decked me was definitely not Demetri. Too thin, too young.

Reason number three why I don't want to call the police is more personal. It's a reason that could make me look unstable: Once the police are involved, my own investigation might have to end.

If Fiona was killed, her murderer needs to be brought to justice —it doesn't have to be at my hand. But if the cops assume this was a random break-in, they'll claim there's no evidence it has anything to do with Fiona's death. Then I'm back to square one. I'll still need to find out what happened to her, but now I'll have the restrictive noose of the Boston PD on me as well. Once I make that call, give my name, blah blah blah, I'm on the record, and that's a place I don't want to be. The best scenario would be to find proof on my own first, so that they don't brush me off. Bringing them in too soon could muddy the situation.

Regardless of how I proceed, something isn't right. Why was the guy in Fiona's place tonight? Is he her killer? Did he stuff her in the

Murphy bed to make it look like an accident? If so, why would he come back to steal the jewelry box? You'd think he'd want to stay as far away as possible. Its contents can't be worth that much. Or maybe he was there for another reason and just happened to pick up the box when I walked into the closet. Did he tamper with the window so he could crawl in and out, or was it simply worn from age? Assuming it was him I saw scurrying down the fire escape the day Megan and I found Fiona, maybe he's broken into other units in the building as well.

In that case, he might have had nothing to do with Fiona's death. He might simply be a thief.

And if that's true, meeting with Demetri remains necessary.

Something else occurs to me. Didn't Megan tell me she couldn't find her aunt's jewelry box? Seems unlikely it would have been so well hidden in the closet that Megan would have missed it but a thief wouldn't.

Too many questions, too much confusion, especially with my headache. I'll have to ponder things later. For now it's back to the issue of reporting a break-in. I know what I need to do.

Shit.

Rising from the closet floor, I trudge to the front door and fish my cell phone out of my bag to call the police. When I finish reporting the incident, the woman informs me an officer will be by shortly. Next, I dial Megan. Reluctantly. But she deserves to know. I don't need Dr. Lightfoot to tell me that.

"Oh my God," she says when I relay the details of the break-in. "Are you okay?"

"I'm fine. Just a little goose egg."

"I'm so sorry. I should have packed up her things myself."

"Why? So you could've gotten whacked by her jewelry box instead?"

"I'll drive over," she offers.

"No need for that. You've had enough stress. I'll fill the police in and let them take it from here."

Well, mostly.

"What would I do without you, Liza?"

Does Megan really mean that, or is it just something people say? An automatic phrase that floats effortlessly out of normal people's mouths, but from mine would sound insincere. Or is it yet another veiled way of telling me she's glad I'm on her aunt's case? If so, I don't want to disappoint her by failing.

"How did he know about my aunt's jewelry box?" Megan asks. "I can't believe I missed it. Maybe it was just a lucky find for him."

"I don't know, but the closet window doesn't lock. Maybe he's done this with other units too."

I don't mention I think I saw the same guy tear down the fire escape two weeks ago, nor that I wonder if he had something to do with Fiona's death. If he did, maybe he was actually returning the jewelry box, not stealing it. Maybe he didn't want anyone to find it on him because it might link him to Fiona's death.

It's all speculation on my part, and it seems unfair—cruel, even —to worry Megan prematurely.

"Did you find anything on your aunt's laptop?" I ask.

"Her laptop? No, not really, why?"

"Just wondering."

"She searched a lot of websites about overdoses and counterfeit fentanyl. Bookmarked articles on the dangers of tainted pills, including the uptick in Massachusetts cases. That makes sense given her volunteer work, don't you think?"

With this information, my mind wanders down a new track. Did Fiona find out someone at the addiction center was selling drugs? Namely bad fentanyl, given her online research? Did that discovery put her at risk? From the skinny man in her closet?

I close my eyes and try to recall what he said to me, something about being smart and minding my *busy*. My business? Was it *business* he said, but in my groggy state, I heard *busy*?

Jesus.

That could imply he knew I visited the addiction center and was asking questions about Fiona.

My mouth dries up at the thought, and I crave another drink of water, even the gross-tasting liquid from those ancient bathroom pipes.

"Liza?"

But wait. Demetri is a specialist in a pain clinic. Maybe Fiona discovered something about him. Who better to sell pills on the side than a pain doctor?

"Liza? Are you there?" Megan asks.

"Yeah, sorry." I force myself to focus. My foggy head is jumping to too many conclusions. I need more measured thought.

"You sure you're okay?"

"I'm good." I check the time on my phone. My meeting with Demetri is coming fast, and I still need to snoop around the condo. "I'm sorry, but it doesn't look like I'll be able to finish packing up your aunt's things. When I'm done with the police, I should probably head home." Lying to the people in my life isn't enjoyable, but it always comes easily.

"Don't worry about that," Megan says. "I'll take care of the rest of her things. I'm just relieved you're okay." Her voice falters on the phone. "I don't know what I'd do if something happened to yet another person in my life."

I say nothing because I don't know what to say, but something tightens in my chest at her words.

I suppose that would be empathy.

20
____

By the time I approach Muriel's Irish Pub it's nearly 10:00 p.m. The interaction with the police at Fiona's condo took longer than I thought it would, so I had to text Demetri I'd be late.

The police asked detailed questions about the guy who attacked me with the jewelry box, but when I told them I worried the intruder might be Fiona's killer, the younger of the two cops stared at me like I was an alien. The older one cleared his throat and said, "When someone dies tragically in a freak accident, we often spin the events into something that makes more sense. Sadly, though, creating a mystery where there isn't one keeps the dead from resting in peace."

He meant well, I suppose, but his condescending psychoanalysis and philosophizing irked me. Then again, there's no proof to suggest I'm right, and I can't yet rule out Demetri. None of us want cops accusing people of murder without evidence to back it up. The last time I pointed a finger at someone before having proof, I was labeled delusional. A suspension from my internship soon followed. No way am I going through that again.

So, biting back my irritation at the shrink-in-a-box cop, I

thanked the officers for their time and silently vowed that if we crossed paths again, I'd have some proof to offer them.

Unfortunately, a snoop around Fiona's condo after they left delivered none of that proof, unless one counts two vibrators, one set of fluffy handcuffs, and a plastic tub of other sex toys hidden away in her closet as proof. Not exactly items you donate to Goodwill. Now I'll have to hope my encounter with Demetri Pappas coughs something up.

Outside the pub I ready myself. This is far too much social interaction for a Friday. For any day. I step inside and, once my eyes adjust, spot Demetri at a table near the mahogany bar. Smoothing my short hair and brushing imaginary lint off my dark jeans, I approach him. Although nothing says sexy about my ribbed turtleneck sweater, his gaze is already on my chest.

Swallowing my revulsion, I sit. Two frosty pints sweat on the table, his nearly gone, the other still full.

"Sorry I'm late." I push the untouched beer aside. "And I don't accept drinks from men unless it's been in my sight the whole time."

Demetri frowns but then chuckles. "That's quite the greeting you have." He points to my bandaged forehead. "What happened?"

Before I can answer, he waves down the freckled barmaid and nods toward me.

"Whatever lager you've got on tap is fine," I tell her. To Demetri, I say, "Ran into a door."

He looks askance at me, like maybe he doesn't believe me, but he doesn't ask anything more about my injury.

Taking in the man across from me, I imagine Fiona would have been attracted to him, even if I'm not. His button-down shirt looks expensive, and he wears a gold class ring. A doctor like him could afford fine things, but whether or not he makes extra money off the books—namely by being a high-class drug dealer—is a thought that repeats in my mind. Given Fiona was forty-six and I'm twenty-eight, the age of his female companions is clearly a nonissue for him.

He winks. "I've been looking forward to this all week."

Me too, I think. *But for different reasons.*

"Did you ever meet Fiona here?" I ask. The waitress returns with my beer.

"Fiona?" Demetri scrunches his face, as if he's already forgotten the woman. "No, I don't think so. Why?"

"Just wondering how well you knew her, that's all."

"Again, why?"

"Did you meet her on the dating app? Or did you already know her, like professionally from your pain clinic or her volunteer work at the addiction center?"

"What's with the third degree? I thought you were a medical resident, not a cop." Demetri laughs, but I don't know if it's a genuine laugh or the nervous laugh of a man who has something to hide.

"Fiona was my friend's aunt," I say. "Megan's been having a hard time dealing with it. I'm just trying to find something that might make her feel better."

Demetri drains the last of his beer and flags the barmaid down. "Another pint, and two shots of Johnnie Walker." When she leaves, he says, "I feel bad for your friend. For her aunt's death."

Do you? I wonder.

"I didn't know Fiona from work or from the addiction center. My partner volunteers there, not me." Demetri sighs. "I guess I'm not the most altruistic person. I could be better. But to answer your question, I met Fiona on the dating app. The fact we both work with addiction in one fashion or another was pure serendipity."

I take my first sip of beer, its foam now dissolved. "That's quite the coincidence."

"Life works out that way sometimes, doesn't it?" He crosses his arms. "Here's what you can tell your friend. Tell her that her aunt was a wonderful woman. Smart, funny, attractive." He winks for the second time and says, "She was also…adventurous, if you know what I mean, but maybe leave that part out."

The waitress returns with Demetri's second beer and the two shots of Johnnie Walker. He swigs one of the whiskeys and pushes the other toward me. His voice grows husky. "What about you, Liza? Are you adventurous too?"

Ugh. What a dog.

But to get entry into his world I need to play his game, so I drain the whiskey shot and don a crooked smile. Hopefully it looks alluring and not like a post-Novocain droop. "I *can* be," I say.

This isn't a lie. I have been adventurous. Just not the kind of adventurous Demetri has in mind.

"Wonderful to hear." Demetri leans closer to me over the table. "Because I'd like to invite you to a party tonight and—"

"A party?" Few words scare me more than that one. "What kind of party?"

Demetri clinks his pint glass against mine. "A very special party, I promise you."

I don't like the sound of that.

Maybe he interprets my discomfort as fear, because he adds, "Don't worry. It's nothing dangerous. It's more…" He stares off at a nearby table, where a couple shares a giant mound of cheesy fries. "It's a party for people who enjoy…stepping outside of conventional boundaries." His gaze returns to me. "And you, Liza, seem like a woman who defies conventional boundaries. Very much so."

I hesitate, enjoying even less the direction this conversation is taking. "Depends on what type of boundaries we're talking about."

"I'll make a deal with you. You come to this party with me, and I'll tell you whatever you want to know about Fiona. In fact, I'll do even better than that. I'll *show* you who Fiona was." For the third skin-crawling time, he winks. "At least who she was after dark."

If this were any other man, I'd race home to wash off the stench of hyperactive hormones. But Demetri is not any other man. He's the man who was dating Fiona around the time she died, a woman I now know was a crystal-loving professional by day and a dating-app kink by night. No judgment, but a deviant lifestyle gives more credence to her being murdered, at least in my opinion. If I'm determined to find an answer for Megan, one that helps her make sense of this world—or, at the very least, makes her still want to be a part of it—I need to continue this two-step with a man almost twice my age and a hundred times my sexual drive, no matter how much the moves repel me.

"So, if I go with you, you'll tell me more about Fiona?" I say. "About her work at the addiction center, her interest in fentanyl overdoses, that kind of thing?" I worry I've revealed too much with this last piece of information. If he was involved in her death, it might scare him away.

Stupid.

It appears I needn't have worried. Demetri's face droops, and, if I'm reading him right—which is a fifty-fifty shot at best—he seems to show real remorse.

"Far too many people are dying from opioid overdoses," he says. "I'm in a real catch-22. I need to treat their pain, but I don't want to get them hooked on drugs. Fiona understood that. It was a subject we talked about."

I didn't expect this detour into seriousness. If Demetri is being sincere, it cuts a hole in my theory about him being a drug dealer. I'd need Megan's people-reading superpower to help me determine if it's the truth. The guy could be lying. Could be as skilled in the craft as me. And if he did kill Fiona because she discovered he was selling drugs on the side, my investigation of him becomes even more important: Stopping him means future lives will be saved.

On the other hand, maybe his motive wasn't drug related. Maybe it came down to sex. He wanted something too perverse, and when Fiona didn't comply, he killed her. Or maybe she *did* comply, and it went too far. Autoasphyxiation comes to mind. Jen assisted in an autopsy of just such a case.

If that's what went down, then it's not Demetri's work in the pain clinic that implicates him. It's the kinky part of his life that does.

And now he wants to invite me into that kink.

Is it worth it?

I ponder this. If it helps get a murderer off the streets, then yes, suffering through a weird party is worth it. Even my father and Dr. Lightfoot couldn't argue against that. Besides, I can take care of myself.

"Okay," I say to the mysterious, hyper-sexed pain doctor across from me. "Lead the way."

I rise from the table and down the rest of my beer.
Looks like I'm going to need it.

21

———

On the outside, the private club resembles an abandoned waste of space, accessible only by an alleyway. On the inside, its darkness swallows Demetri and me until we reach a concealed door, behind which hums a muted rhythm.

Demetri raps out a bizarre knock. The peephole darkens momentarily, and an eyeball peers back at us. Demetri raises a glossy black business card, and the door swings open. Allowing myself no time to change my mind (*What are you doing, tiger?*), I follow Demetri inside.

Soft lighting, musky scents, and a seductive jazz beat greet us. Before I can absorb anything else, I do a double take. Less than ten feet away, a furry treks across the floor. A giant panda bear, to be exact. The bear is being led on a chain by a woman in thigh-high leather boots and a skintight black unitard that exposes the fleshy mounds of her breasts. A whip dangles from her other hand.

It takes a lot to get a reaction out of me.

This visual oddity succeeds.

The dominatrix notices my surprise and smiles. As if putting on a show for me, she tugs the panda bear's chain, which is attached to a padlocked collar around his neck. He stumbles forward. They pass by and head down a darkened hallway.

When they disappear from view, I return my craned neck to midline and take in the rest of the surroundings. The intimate space, dimly lit with wall sconces and overhead chandeliers that emit a golden hue, boasts a spattering of central tables, half of which are occupied by patrons in various stages of undress. An ornate bar with a brass runner lies on the right. Bottles of booze crowd a mirrored wall behind a shirtless bartender, his abs putting even those of Brian's Gym–goers to shame. Private booths flanked by velvet curtains line two of the walls. Some of those drapes remain open. Others are drawn closed. I try not to picture what's happening behind them.

Beside me, Demetri laughs. "Sorry. This must be a bit…startling at first." He places an arm around my shoulder. "Your expression tells me you need a drink. Immediately."

Finding my voice, I shake his arm off. "What's this place called?"

"Oh, it has many names, but let's call it the Wicked Wonderland for tonight."

"Then call me Alice because…uh…this is weird."

A large man approaches us. Demetri shakes his hand. Judging by the guy's size and demeanor, he might be the bouncer. His shirt sticks to him like cellophane, and his shorts expose every nook and cranny. He palms something to Demetri. Before I can see what it is, Demetri slips it into his pocket. The pain specialist then leads me deeper into the surreal room toward the bar.

At the counter I glance back at the entryway and the nearby hallway that swallowed the dominatrix and her panda prey. They haven't reappeared.

Not knowing what I've gotten myself into but realizing I need to play it smart, I tell Demetri, "I texted my friend on the way over. Gave her the address of this place and your name. You know, in case you're thinking of abducting me, which I'd highly recommend you don't. Not if you want to keep breathing."

This is a lie, of course. I've sent Megan nothing. She doesn't need to know I'm still looking into Demetri, not until I find something.

"You don't know the address of this place," Demetri points out. "We parked four blocks away and came in from the alley."

"I'm aware of the general vicinity."

He grins his grin, which is the same grin you might see on a wolf who's just eaten a rabbit. "Your friend is welcome to join us. The more the merrier. But for the record, I'm not in the habit of abducting anyone. You can leave any time you like." He licks his lips. "But I don't think you'll want to."

From the bare-chested bartender, who Demetri greets as Killian, my "date" orders two bourbon shots. This time I don't hesitate in drinking one. The alcohol burns my throat, but I welcome it. I'm not scared to be here. Not shy either. I'm rarely either of those two things. What I am, however, is at the helm of a ship I have no idea how to navigate. Therapy hasn't trained me for half-naked people doused in eau de sex.

"What else would you like?" Demetri asks as I take a seat on a stool.

I order another whiskey, but with Coke this time. While the booze takes effect, I study the overhead bar lights, unsurprised to find nude forms etched in their glass. After a few gulps, I'm almost ready to communicate with this stranger by my side. It's important to rein in my natural antagonism. Giving him attitude will only push him away, and I need answers before I do that. A seductress I am not, so reasonably likable will have to suffice.

If Demetri is growing impatient with my silence, he doesn't show it. He merely peruses the club-goers around him. A goth woman in a see-through dress. A man wearing only a neon-pink thong. A couple sharing one suit. The man wears the pants, and the woman dons the unbuttoned blazer, her satin underwear on full display. With them is a naked guy, his buttocks and back visible to me. When he turns around, I notice he's not actually fully nude. He wears a velvet sock on his penis, and a padlock hangs from a chain around his neck. It's the same kind of padlock the panda bear wore on his collar. Looking around the room, I spot other padlocks as well, attached to whatever skimpy part of clothing they can find.

After I've drained my whiskey Coke and a buzz dulls my hyped-up senses enough that I can speak without scorn, I turn to the strange, uninhibited doctor who thinks bringing a woman he doesn't know to a place like this is acceptable. "So this is where you brought Fiona, huh?"

Demetri places a warm hand over my cheek. I fight the urge to swat it away.

"Such a beautiful complexion you have." His thumb strokes the underside of my chin. "Not Mediterranean roots like mine, though, is it?"

When I don't answer, wanting him to respond to my question about Fiona instead, he flags down the bartender and orders two more drinks. I don't object.

With his hand still on my face, he says, "Be cagey, I don't care. We're all a big, beautiful melting pot, and you, my pretty lady, are a dish of perfection."

The alcohol must be affecting his vision. I'm no ogre, but I'm no cover model either.

The music changes from a jazz number to a techno beat. Colorful strobe lights flicker over an empty dance floor in the corner.

"Fiona," I say flatly, my antagonism rearing its head despite my best efforts. I'm tired of his facial strokes and compliments. "Did you bring her here? Is that why she pulled away from you? Did you freak her out with your"—I scan the room again, take in the couple sharing one suit, their lips locked on each other and their hands roaming the buttocks of their padlocked naked man—"extracurricular interests?"

Demetri's palm finally releases my face. He picks up the fresh drink the chiseled bartender delivered. "Are you always this much fun?"

"Yes."

He laughs, but then his smile fades. "I brought Fiona here." He raises a thick eyebrow. "Believe me, she had her wild side. She may have been all power suits and sensible heels by day, but at night, well, she enjoyed this place. At least at first."

"What changed?"

"I must've pushed things too far."

I sip my third drink, wondering what he did to turn the sexually adventurous Fiona Carlson away. A dominatrix leading a man (woman?) in a panda suit on a leash into a back room might be risqué to me, but to Demetri it might simply be a Monday. My mind tries to conjure more sexually deviant acts. Doesn't want to.

"Was it something dangerous?" I ask.

Demetri leans back on his barstool and digs around in his pocket. "Dangerous? No. Not in the hands of someone experienced. As long as you have safe words, it's perfectly harmless. A…stress reliever I enjoy. I work hard, Liza. I need to relax, blow off steam. Surely as a doctor you understand that."

I can't see what Demetri has plucked from his pocket—it's cupped in his hand—but it makes me wonder what else he's hiding. A wife? Was he worried Fiona would report this potentially dangerous "stress reliever" to his spouse? He wears no wedding ring, but that means nothing. Or maybe some other woman was harmed by his "blowing off steam." Maybe Fiona found out and Demetri killed her to keep her quiet.

Demetri seems to read my mind. "You look like you think I had something to do with Fiona's death."

"Did you?"

He frowns. "You told me Fiona's death was a tragic accident. That she suffocated in her bed."

"I never said it was an accident."

Demetri's head jerks up. "It's been ruled a homicide?"

"No, but that doesn't mean it wasn't one."

He swirls his glass, the ice clinking inside it. "I haven't seen Fiona in weeks. The last time we met was here, in this place. We went back there." He points to the hallway that swallowed the dominatrix and her pet. "When she saw what I had in mind, she left. Simple as that. She stopped returning my messages shortly after. If you're looking for a mystery in her death, you won't find it with me."

I examine his features. I have no idea whether he's lying.

"Besides," he continues, "you told me she died on September third. I was at an auction that night, at the art museum. Bought a sculpture."

"So you say."

"I have the damn receipt if you'd like to see it. I would never hurt Fiona—or anyone else for that matter. Yes, Fiona was a fun and remarkable woman, but there are other cats in the barn, so I moved on. If the only reason you came here was to prove I killed her, you'll be disappointed."

"Why else would you think I'd come here?" I ask, genuinely curious.

He shrugs. "When I first met you in Muriel's Pub, I could tell you're a different type of woman."

"I am."

"So I thought maybe you'd be into different kinds of things. Hey, you can't blame a man for trying." He opens his palm and reveals what's cupped inside it. A small key. "So are you?" he asks.

"Am I what?" I stare at the key and wonder if it's what the bouncer gave him when we arrived.

"Are you into trying different things?"

"What's the key for?"

He flips it between his fingers. "I'd rather show you."

"I'd rather you tell me."

He waves his arm around the room. During our conversation, the place has grown more populous with scantily clad guests. Another furry, too, this one a puppy. Like the panda bear earlier and the nude man with a velvet sock on his penis, the puppy sports a padlock around its neck. Another scan of the club reveals at least every third person wears a similar padlock.

"Let's just say the key unlocks a special plaything for the night," Demetri replies.

I stare at him, unsure how to respond, dumbfounded that people like him exist. People so uninhibited that they venture into twisted territory with complete strangers.

In my ongoing bewilderment, I don't notice until too late that the dominatrix has approached the bar, her panda pet nowhere to be seen. Worse, she seems to be here for Demetri and me.

I brace myself for what's about to come.

Yay. Effing. Me.

22

Trying to look nonchalant, I glance away from the dominatrix. Maybe she'll move on.

She doesn't.

She greets Demetri but calls him Tony, which makes sense because who wouldn't use an alias in this place? Then she takes a seat on the barstool next to me.

The bulk of her breasts poke uncaged from her leather unitard. When she catches me staring at them, she winks, much like Demetri has done all night. Nowhere on her body is a padlock. No surprise there. This woman is not a lock wearer. She, like Demetri, is an opener.

"A glass of white wine please, Killian," the dominatrix says to the bartender. To Demetri, she asks, "Hey, Tony, who's your friend?" Her eyes sweep my body. Maybe she's searching for *my* padlock.

Demetri—aka Tony—aka padlock opener—squeezes my shoulder. "This is Liza. Liza, this is Nyx."

"Nix?" I ask. "Like the lice treatment?"

The dominatrix lets forth a throaty laugh. When Killian hands her a glass of wine, she raises it my way. "Sexy *and* funny," she says.

Anyone who's met me knows I'm neither of those things.

"Not Nix, N-I-X," Demetri clarifies. "Nyx, N-Y-X. After the goddess of night, a child of chaos and darkness and one you don't want to mess with. Even Zeus feared her."

"That's me," Nyx says.

She sips her wine and eyes me in what looks like hunger. I can't be sure. Dr. Lightfoot's expression cards didn't include lusty sex drives. Thank God for small favors.

Nyx touches the bandage on my forehead and murmurs words of sympathy. "Should've let me bandage you up. I need the practice."

"Nyx is going to nursing school," Demetri says.

"Soon anyway. Hopefully. Need the dollars first." Staring at me, she licks her fingertips and rubs them over her voluminous breasts, her nipples dangerously close to popping out. "A girl can't do this forever."

I'm not gonna lie, my cheeks flush in fervent desire, but that desire is not for Nyx. Nor is it for Demetri. It's an urgent desire to be anywhere but here. Nyx has catapulted me onto Planet Awkward like I've never been catapulted before.

She smiles, no doubt at my reaction. "If you ever need Nyxie for a job, you let me know. I'm a freelancer. Always looking for a finan- cial transaction." She leans toward me and whispers, "Of any kind."

I say nothing because I have nothing to say. In what world would I need to hire her services?

She runs her black fingernails through my pixie cut and asks Demetri, "Are we going to have fun with this one tonight?"

Demetri studies me, his expression equally hungry but somehow more disturbing. "That's my utmost hope. How to categorize her is the question, though."

They continue to examine me as if I'm a liver cell under a microscope. "She's kind of doe-eyed," Nyx says, still dragging her nails through my hair. "There's an innocence to her."

"Oh, but she's got a toughness too," Demetri counters. "It's not so obvious here—she's out of her realm—but believe me, it's there."

Nyx slowly lowers her hand, brushing against my own breast as she makes her way to my biceps. She strokes the muscle through my turtleneck sweater.

I should do something, say something, run the fuck out of here, and yet I'm paralyzed. Paralyzed not only by an acutely painful unfamiliarity, but also by the need to find out what happened to Fiona. How can her death not be related to this shit show? Then again, Demetri has an alibi, and if it's true, it's a good one.

Nyx removes her hand from my arm. "She's as fit as an Olympic athlete inside her shell. Be careful. She could fool us. There might be more giver in her than receiver."

Okay. That's it. I'm about to show them exactly what I *can* give— my jaw hard, my fists clenched—when Nyx nods.

"Oh yeah," she says. "Right there. See it? She's got a wildcat inside her. Luscious Liza is no one's receiver. You're going to love it here," she tells me. She tips her drink toward Demetri. "Excellent find, Tony."

Demetri finishes his drink. "Let's hope so. After the week I've had, I need it."

Nyx rises from her stool and massages his shoulders. "Aww, poor baby. Your son again?"

Where the hell am I?

Demetri leans into her touch. "Theo is still using, still stealing. Maybe even selling now too. We cut him off for good last month. No more staying at my place or his mom's."

"That must be difficult for you," says the dominatrix slash sex-capader slash nurse-to-be.

Have I gone mad? Maybe I really am Alice, lost in a wonderland where fetishes, padlocks, and worries over sons collide, as if it's perfectly normal to talk about one with the other.

"Last I heard, he's crashing at a friend's," Demetri says. "I'm surprised he has any left. Probably some guy from the skateboard park near Fenway. Never does any real work beyond that and getting high." Demetri snaps his fingers, as if snapping all the stress away. "But tonight is about escape, not my problems. What do you say, Liza?" His hunger is back, though maybe less intensely. "Have I chosen wisely by picking you? Or are you going to let Nyx and me down?"

Is he genuinely attracted to me, or am I merely a pawn in their sick game? Like one of those nerd parties where guests compete at bringing the best dork. Waseem mentioned a movie about that once. I wasn't paying attention. Now I wish I had.

Either way, just like Fiona, I'm out. I'd rather attend Dr. Thomas's resident retreat this Sunday five times over than endure another minute of this. There's nothing more Demetri will tell me about Fiona, at least not tonight, and I have no interest in sex with either him or Nyx. They're wasting their time. Then again, maybe that's part of the fun at the Wicked Wonderland. Who doesn't like a challenge?

I stand, wobbly from both the booze and the weird exchange. "Sorry. Not sure what vibe I gave off that said this was my type of thing, but I'm about to let you down."

Nyx makes an exaggerated pout. "That's a shame. We could've had some fun."

Demetri rises from his barstool, his face unreadable to me. "Please. Reconsider."

I step back, worried they won't let me go.

I take another step back. When neither one comes at me, I turn and falter to the door, a little tipsy, a lot disturbed. The bouncer blocks my exit and points behind me. I turn around and see Nyx slinking over. She grabs my hand, and for a moment I think she's going to force me back.

Let her try, I think. *Let her try.*

Instead, she slips a card into my back pocket, her hand cupping my butt for too long. "If you change your mind, Luscious Liza, you give me a call." Her husky tone deepens. "I think I might do just about anything for you."

23

With a breeze lifting my hair and the sun warming my face, I'm seated on a deck chair behind Tam and Shawna's ranch home on Waverly Boulevard. Around me birds chirp, and the smell of grilled meat fuses with the crisp scent of approaching autumn.

As I polish off the rest of my chicken kebab, I wait for the wives to stop laughing. I've just relayed last night's experience at the sex club to them, and neither one can catch their breath. They sit on a porch swing, their border collie, Betts, curled up by their feet.

"Wait, wait." Tam wipes her eyes. "He brought you along as a prize?"

I lick barbecue sauce off my lips. It's not as good as the sauce my dad made for his food truck—during the two years he was able to live out his dream before he died—but it's close. "I don't know if I was a prize exactly. It just felt that way. Like they were sizing me up or something."

Shawna, still laughing, presses into Tam. Although I wasn't in the mood to socialize (*Am I ever?*), especially with Dr. Thomas's resident retreat tomorrow, I'm happy to see my two friends enjoying each other's company, even if it's at my expense. The last time I saw them they were arguing over the logistics of having another baby, something they both want but something neither one of their bodies is prepared to offer, Shawna's because of injuries sustained after a severe accident and Tam's because of potential hormone therapy.

Their two-year-old, Seth, waddles up and hands me a fistful of dirt. Cupping it, I wonder what he expects from me. After a beat, I thank him and dump it into my napkin, hoping I've responded appropriately. He nods and prances back to his bucket, where he's tossing in all sorts of outdoor terrain. His "soup," he calls it, and other than referring to me as Lie-Lie, unable to pronounce my name, his vocabulary is excellent.

I thought about keeping Demetri a secret from Shawna and Tam. A lie of omission, my shrink calls it. But if I learned anything from last year's traumatic ordeal, it was to be more transparent with them when something suspect is on my mind. Aside from Dr. Lightfoot, these are the two people who know the real me, as well as anyone can know me anyway—Shawna as my childhood friend and Tam through Shawna.

So before we ate, I came clean about my ongoing suspicion that Fiona's death wasn't an accident. Told them about finding the dating app on her phone, tracking down Demetri, getting clobbered by a jewelry box in Fiona's apartment, and reporting it to the police. They got quiet and exchanged a look with each other, a look whose subtext was easy to read because I've seen it before. It was a look that said: *Is Liza going off the deep end again?*

Fortunately, my story about last night's kink-fest lightened the mood by a thousand degrees.

Tam finally corrals her laughter. "Sorry. We're only laughing because the thought of you in a club like that is the stuff of reality TV shows. Liza Larkin? The woman who sent a surgery resident running away in terror when he tried to date her? It's too funny."

It wasn't me who sent Trey Washington running. Okay, maybe it was a little, but mostly it was his desire to cover up his own mistakes.

"Do you still see him around the hospital?" Shawna asks.

"Sure. We say hi, but that's about it."

"I bet it is." Tam extends her arms and crosses her index fingers, as if warding off a demon. I assume I'm the demon. Then she stops the bench's swinging, and her humor fades. "We're poking fun at the sex-club thing, sure, but you thinking Fiona Carlson was murdered is serious business. You understand that, right?"

Sometimes Tam talks to me like I'm dense, or at least that's my perception, but I know it comes from a place of concern, and I don't blame her. I've done dense things in the past. Besides, she's a cop. It's probably in her nature.

"Yes," I say. "I do understand. That's why I'm telling you. To get your opinion in case I…go down the wrong path."

The wives stare at me. Shawna puts a hand over her heart. "Who are you, and what have you done with my friend?" Her lips curl up, so I know she's kidding.

Tam nods. "That's good, Liza. That's real good, and I appreciate it. If you talk to me about things, maybe we can avoid you ending up at any more sex clubs. Deal?"

"Deal."

"So you now believe this Demetri guy didn't have anything to do with Fiona Carlson's death?" Shawna asks.

"Last night I wasn't so sure. It was all so creepy. But I started to think about it more. He has a solid alibi. He was at an auction the night she died. Claims he has a receipt for what he bought, and there were probably a lot of witnesses. Plus, I'm no longer sure about his motive. He pushed things too far with Fiona by taking her to that weird place, true, and she walked away, but judging by what I saw last night, he has plenty of other options to keep him entertained."

Shawna accepts a handful of leaves from Seth, leaves that didn't make it into his nature soup. "Is there anyone else at the club who might have wanted her gone?"

I think of Nyx. Can't imagine why she might want to hurt Fiona, beyond the typical BDSM stuff. Nyx doesn't carry the stench of a psychopath, and if she killed Fiona, would she really give me her phone number? Seems unlikely. When I got home from the club, I tossed her card in the loose-change basket on my kitchenette counter. You never know when something might come in handy. Already a plan is swishing around in my brain.

"Maybe a sex act gone too far?" Shawna says, interrupting my thoughts.

Tam turns to her. "Look at you, getting all *Law & Order: SVU* on us." To me, Tam says, "Fiona suffocated in her bed, right?"

"Yes. She died by asphyxiation."

Tam leaves the porch swing and grabs another hot dog off the grill. "I suppose it's possible she could have died by some weird sex act, but Boston PD is good. If they had found her death suspicious, they would have investigated it. The ME officially ruled it as accidental?"

"Yes."

The conversation pauses, and I know what Tam and Shawna are thinking: *Then why are you still looking into it?*

Tam points to the bandage on my forehead. "What about that guy who clocked you? Think he could be up to something?"

Her question surprises me. It implies she doesn't think I'm conjuring fantasies, not completely, anyway.

"I'm proud of you for reporting that," Shawna says. "It's probably the last thing you wanted to do, but it had to be done."

I nod, accepting her praise.

She and Tam smile at each other.

"Our little Liza is growing up," Tam says.

Once again, their shared humor at my expense doesn't bother me. On the contrary. Dr. Lightfoot's theory about my brain maturing resurfaces. Maybe there is some truth to it, after all.

I accept another handful of dirt from Seth. When he's not looking, I dump it again in my napkin. "I'm not sure what the fire-escape guy's story is. Is he a random thief, or did he know Fiona? That's the question."

"You did what you could," Tam says. "You reported it. Let the police take it from there."

"They dusted for prints. Not sure if they found anything. I'm not in their loop." I stare pointedly at Tam.

She shakes her head, clearly picking up on my unspoken words. "I'm a Morganville cop, not a Boston one. I helped you here with Dr. Donovan, but I don't have sway there." She holds up a hand. "I'm not saying I'm discrediting you—believe me, I learned not to do that last year—but there's not enough juice in your theory for me to start poking around in someone else's department."

"Couldn't you ask Kenny?" Shawna says. "Or what about Miranda?"

"Sure, I know a few cops there, but not in the precinct near Fiona Carlson's place. I doubt a condo break-in will be high on the information chain. Why would Kenny or Miranda know about it?"

Tam polishes off the rest of the hot dog. My pleading eyes never leave her.

"Fine." She sighs. "I'll see what I can find out."

"Thank you," I say.

Shawna unwinds her ponytail elastic, tames her loose hair, and secures it back in place. "What about Megan?"

"What about her?" I ask.

"Does she know about last night? Does she know you're still looking into things?"

"I didn't tell her about the club. She's got a lot going on." I watch Seth fill his bucket with water from a watering can.

"You might want to be transparent with her too," Shawna says.

"I'm trying to be, but what's the point of misleading her until I know something for certain?"

"What do you mean, until you 'know something for certain'?" I don't miss the wariness in Shawna's tone. "You said you'd let the police handle it."

Tam's words, not mine, I think but don't say.

I shrug. "I don't know. Right now I'm at a standstill. Maybe I've been wasting my time driving back and forth to Boston. I'll focus on work for a while. My grant won't write itself."

My own words leave me feeling oddly dejected, like a fisherman convinced he's got the catch of the day on his line, only to reel in an old boot instead. I wanted to have an answer for Megan. Wanted to be able to say, "I know who killed your aunt."

Instead, I have nothing.

Nothing but the phone number of a dominatrix and a goose egg on my forehead.

24

Back in my apartment, with a half dozen of April's freshly baked sugar cookies, I still harbor a sense of defeat. I'm not sure why.

Is it because of all the time I wasted looking into Demetri, convinced he had something to do with Fiona's death? Or is it because accepting her death as a freak accident underscores how pointless life is? Knowing that any of us can exit the world that senselessly (*Smothered by a Murphy bed? Really?*) makes going through the motions of everyday life seem absurd.

I stuff a cookie into my mouth. Then another.

Maybe it's far simpler than that. Maybe I'm disappointed because the puzzle I had hoped to solve, a puzzle that juiced me up the same way bringing Dr. Donovan down juiced me up, might not be a puzzle at all.

I push away from the kitchenette counter and pace my small studio. Is it time to put this whole Fiona thing to rest? Time to admit I have no proof her death was anything but an accident?

Yes, my father and shrink say in my head.

My NIH grant application needs to be my priority. Getting

through residency needs to be my priority. Surviving the second-year resident retreat tomorrow needs to be my priority.

Equally important, despite how victorious exposing Dr. Donovan made me feel, it needs to be a one-off. Seeking to replicate that sense of power, that satisfaction, can lead only to bad things.

I plop down on my bed, exhausted by this mental reflection. If this is what a maturing brain has to offer, Dr. Lightfoot can have it back. I want no part of it.

Staring up at my ceiling, my eyes start to close, and my mind drifts off. Just as I'm about to fall asleep, my phone buzzes in my pocket and startles me back awake.

When I see who's texting, my heart rate climbs. I prop myself up on the pillow.

Demetri.

Why?

Maybe he refuses to take no for an answer. Maybe that's what happened with Fiona. She said no, and he said yes. A yes in the form of a pillow to her face and suffocation. Then he folded her up in her bed like she was nothing. Nothing more than a padlocked receiver to his key-wielding giver.

And just like that, my mind plunges back into the dark puzzle.

I read his text: Hope you'll reconsider. Everyone loved you last night.

Everyone? I met one person. Nyx. Two if you count the bartender, Killian. Hardly meets the definition of *everyone*.

My thumbs hover over the screen. How best to respond?

You need to shut this down, my father tells me. *Demetri didn't kill Fiona. He has an alibi. His only crime is being an attractive and wealthy man who is used to getting what he wants.*

Before I can counter with, *Yeah, but what if...* and drag myself deeper into the darkness, I make a decision my father would applaud. I respond to Demetri with: Sorry. Not interested.

Is it the age difference? he texts. Because I'm healthy and young at heart. This is followed by a smiley-face emoji.

It's not your age, I type. I'm not into dating anyone. I—

A picture comes through before I finish typing. Curious, I click it open.

It's Demetri at the beach. He's dressed in colorful swim trunks and holds a surfboard. A few other men surround him. The image doesn't appear to be from that long ago, and his toned body does indeed belie his age.

I start typing that he's riding the wrong wave with me but then pause.

Wait. Who's that guy in the back, the one with the thick eyebrows?

I zoom in on the young man standing behind Demetri and bolt upright on the bed.

Feverishly, I text: Who is that guy in the picture with you?

Which one?

The one behind you. His shoulder is blocked by your surfboard.

He's nothing but a disappointment, that's who he is.

I enlarge the guy's face as much as I can. Recognition slams me again. Those dark eyebrows. That skinny frame.

I've seen this man before. At least I think I have. Last night in Fiona's closet, just before a jewelry box smashed into my head.

Who is he? I stab out again.

Demetri types back: He didn't get his work ethic from me, I'll tell you that.

I wait for the next text bubble, my heart pounding, adrenaline once again flooding my arteries. I know what he's about to say.

Finally, it comes.

That's Theo.

That's my deadbeat son.

25

———

On Sunday, at an oak table inside Dr. Thomas's lake cabin, I'm forced to participate in ridiculous team-building exercises with my fellow second-years. My mind focuses only on Demetri's son.

During a game of Newly-Res—an activity designed by Waseem in which we ask each other questions à la *The Newlywed Game* (*shoot me now*)—I steal glances at my phone and study the beach picture Demetri sent me. I mentally compare his son, Theo, to the guy in Fiona's walk-in closet two nights ago. The lighting was poor in the small room, and I didn't get a great look before the jewelry box conked me in the head, but I think the two men are one and the same.

Which means Demetri's son is the thief who broke into Fiona's condo.

If only I could be sure.

Earlier this morning, when my colleagues and I arrived at this cedar-scented cabin, they asked about the bandage on my forehead. I told them I injured myself at the gym. The wound is better but still ugly. I cleaned it again and applied a fresh dressing. Now I just need a fresh look at the guy who inflicted it.

Is he really Demetri's son? Or am I making connections where there are none? Based on the beach picture on my phone, Theo shares the same thin body habitus as the guy who attacked me in the closet, but so do lots of men. Many men have thick eyebrows too. Imagine what might happen if I march into the Boston Police Department and report that the son of a man I visited a sex club with might be the same guy who broke into Fiona's place—maybe even killed her—based on nothing but a questionable photograph. The hypothetical conversation plays in my mind:

What makes you think the two men are the same person? the cop asks.

Because both guys are slim and have thick eyebrows, I respond.

The squad room erupts into laughter.

Someone at the table flicks my head and drags me out of my rumination. It's Megan on my left. She's smiling and saying something, but I don't catch it.

To my right, Jen laughs. "Liza. Base camp to Liza."

Waseem flashes that grin that's been AWOL for a while. "I think we lost her somewhere back at the Compliment Circle."

My mind flounders back to the task at hand—a retreat with my colleagues. In other words, torture time. From around the table, their smirks and raised eyebrows make me wonder how long I was daydreaming. Shadows from lack of sleep still darken Jen's eyes, but she seems in better spirits than a couple of weeks ago when she was crying in the residents' room, burned out from her duties as a working mom. John offers his usual shy smile, but even he maintains lengthy eye contact that leaves me unsettled. Dr. Thomas, who's in the kitchen preparing a meat-and-cheese tray, doesn't laugh, but he also doesn't mention my mind wandering and poor participation. He knows me well enough by now and is probably just grateful I showed up.

My program director brings the charcuterie board to the table. It looks like a work of art. Then he retreats to a recliner near the fireplace and scoops up a pathology journal, no doubt to give us our space.

Waseem digs into the sausage and cheddar, cracking a joke about his coronary arteries being eager for an onslaught.

"You're in a good mood lately," Megan says to him, biting into a cracker topped with pepper jack. "You've got your spark back. Glad to see it."

Waseem waves her off as if it's nothing, but his body wiggling suggests he's excited about something.

"Spill," John says. "What's got you as hyper as a schoolboy off his Ritalin?"

Because John is often silent like me, his comment gets a round of laughs, including from Dr. Thomas across the room.

Waseem's gaze flickers between Megan and John. "It's dumb. Don't worry about it."

"What's dumb?" Megan asks.

Waseem shrugs. "It's just that I got some great reviews on a short film I made. It's no *Indiana Jones* or *Star Wars*, but it feels good to know people enjoyed it."

"Not dumb at all," Jen pipes in. "I can't believe you made a movie. That's really cool."

Megan nods her agreement. "What did they say?"

Waseem summarizes the reviews, and since I'm the one who posted them, I hear my own words spoken back to me. *Characters are nicely flawed. Takes a risk with his story. Pays off big-time.* Next comes my brother's review. I texted him a link to the YouTube video the other day and asked him to leave a comment under a fake name. Ned's words are glowing but not over the top, and I'm glad he came through.

At our last session, Dr. Lightfoot said posting fake reviews in order to make Waseem feel better was a gray zone. I understand my shrink's point, but Waseem's joy and buoyed confidence seem anything but gray. To me they're the exact shade of right.

While the rest of my colleagues eat cheese cubes and salami slices, I excuse myself by saying I have to make a call. It's a lie, of course, but this retreat is taxing my social limits. A few minutes of solitude on Dr. Thomas's deck is needed.

Outside, I take a seat on a porch swing. It's similar to Shawna and Tam's, only with no dog at my feet. Zipping up my hoodie, I inhale the early autumn air and admire the cabin's surroundings.

Dense woods fall on either side, and in front of me a rocky shore separates the lawn from the lake. The water ripples and sparkles peacefully.

I rest my head against the swing. For the first time in a long time, my mind escapes its endless rumination, and I simply absorb the nature around me. Dr. Lightfoot should bottle this. A spritz or two of my program director's lakefront property would quell my angry outbursts better than any breathing exercise.

Minutes pass—maybe five, maybe fifteen—and I'm so deep in my restive trance that when a voice speaks on my right, I jump and almost fly off the swing.

"Oh, sorry." John pushes a clump of hair off his forehead. "Didn't mean to sneak up on you. Was just wondering how things are going."

"Um…okay." Why is he out here?

He studies the lake, his hands slipping into his jeans pockets. Soon after, he pulls them back out, as if not sure what to do with them. A scar blemishes the inside of his wrist. It's round and deep, like an old burn. I've never noticed it before.

"It's nice out here," he says.

"It is."

"Not too cold yet either."

Okay, now he's creeping me out. The one person I can rely on to bypass pointless chitchat is my colleague John Kim. What, exactly, is going on?

He points to the swing. "Mind if I sit?"

I must hesitate too long, because a pink blush creeps into his face.

"Sorry," he says. "I was just wondering how your grant was going, but I'll leave you alone."

He turns to retreat, his sneakers thumping a loose board on the deck. At the same time, my dad's face pops into my head. *Liza, don't be rude.*

With a sigh, I slide over on the swing to make room for John. "It's going okay." Another lie. My grant situation is not going okay.

John seems to be aware of this. He sits and says, "Really? Everything's good? I heard Dr. Silverstein was taking a leave of absence."

"Well, yeah, her husband's dementia has gotten worse. She might need to put him in a facility."

"That must be hard," John says. He pauses. "Like what you had to do with your mom."

I shift around on the swing's cushion, having no desire to discuss my mother. "It's a tough thing for Dr. Silverstein—or anyone—to do, but sometimes it's for the best." I think of the bruises I saw on my advisor's arm.

John nods. "But it's left you in a bind, hasn't it? Or did she already sign off on your grant application?"

"No, not yet." Any calm the lake oasis gave me is gone. With Dr. Silverstein's focus on her husband, I'm rudderless. "I don't want to pester her, but at the same time I'm worried…"

"Worried you'll miss the deadline?" John finishes for me.

"Yeah, that."

We sit there in silence, and even though I'm confused by John's presence, I can't deny it feels good to have someone who understands what's at stake with my research grant. Of the second-year residents, John and I are the most academic.

He rubs his palm. "Liza, I was wondering if you might want to, well, go—"

"Hey, you two introverts." Jen opens the screen door and steps out. "You can't escape that easily. This is a team retreat, you know."

She's smiling as she says it, so I know she's kidding, but John and I both rise and follow her back inside.

Waseem and Megan are still seated at the table. The charcuterie board has been joined by a tray of brownies, and our glasses of lemonade have been topped off. Dr. Thomas is quite the host.

I retake my chair at the table. Before I can ponder what John was about to ask me, Megan says something that grabs my attention.

"Duante, the forensics fellow, told me there's been another fentanyl death."

"How old?" Jen asks.

"Young kid. Seventeen." Megan sweeps cracker crumbs off the table with her napkin. "It's awful out there. Cases are increasing all over Massachusetts, especially around Boston. Their MEs have found the same animal tranquilizer in tox screens that we have. Tainted pills, most likely being sold in the city. Duante said the Boston police managed to get their hands on a couple pills but haven't found the dealer yet."

Beyond my short exchange with John outside, this is the first conversation of the day that interests me. By way of Megan, the forensics fellow has given me more information than Tam was able to. Like before, I wonder about Fiona and her work at the addiction center.

As always, Megan seems to read my mind. "Liza thinks fentanyl might tie into my aunt's death. At least that's one of her theories."

Everyone looks at me.

"How so?" Jen asks.

Waseem grabs a handful of salted almonds from the charcuterie board. "I thought your aunt's death was ruled an accident."

"It was," Megan confirms. "Probably just a horrible accident, but since she helped out at an addiction center, Liza made that connection."

"You've got good instincts, Liza," Jen says, "but that's kind of a stretch, don't you think?"

Megan answers for me. "It is, but on the other hand, if Fiona discovered something about these pills, something that got her"—Megan clears her throat—"got her killed, then someone needs to find out what it was."

Once again I wonder if she is trying to tell me something. Signaling me to keep looking. I don't know. Maybe I'm seeing fumes that aren't there. But I do know that Megan did me a solid last year. She didn't speak up about something that could have sunk me. I owe her, and since I don't like owing people, I intend to pay her back. If her aunt was murdered and the guy in Fiona's closet was her killer, then I intend to find out.

Demetri Pappas said his son, Theo, has a drug problem. The guy in Fiona's closet looked like Theo Pappas. That's an angle that needs to be followed up on, especially after learning that someone's selling tainted drugs in Boston. Fiona was researching the subject before she died. Maybe she did discover something that got her killed, and maybe it has nothing to do with a sex club.

Answering that question will require yet another trip to Beantown, but so be it. Next weekend I'll visit the skate park where Theo hangs out. Find out once and for all if he was the guy trolling around in Fiona's closet. If so, he might be her killer.

A new wave of adrenaline hits me. My nerve cells tingle in anticipation.

26

I don't panic much. Once, as a kid when I got locked in an old steamer trunk. Once, when I thought my mother got abducted from Home and Hearth Healing. (She didn't. She hid under a blanket in a storage closet for twelve hours to protect herself from "Hitler's men.") And once, when I got caught inside a house I entered illegally. That was only a year ago.

But as I sit here Sunday morning on a bench in a skate park near the Charles River, waiting for Theo Pappas to make his appearance—if he even will—that acidic taste of dread still coats my tongue.

It's not because I'm worried about my safety when it comes to Theo. Nor is it because of Chopper, who's been gracing my cellular airwaves again with his ticking clock of blackmail. His last text warned that if I don't get my ass moving and fork over what he's "owed," he's going to pay another visit to April and Jasmine.

Okay, maybe Chopper is partly responsible for my recent panic, but I'll deal with him tonight. I press my satchel against me and feel the heft of money inside.

The *real* source of my panic, however, involves my NIH grant, namely its 5:00 p.m. deadline this past Friday.

See, Dad? I do *have my priorities straight.*

It wasn't my fault. It was Dr. Silverstein's delay that pushed my catecholamines into overdrive.

After the resident retreat at Dr. Thomas's cabin a week ago, I polished off my portion of the grant. Stayed up until 2:00 a.m. editing the written parts and creating pie charts and tables to support my request for funding. On Monday night, I skipped Brian's Gym, a rarity for me, and reviewed every word, punctuation mark, and table again. Then I waited for Dr. Silverstein to look it over, add her portions, and give it the final finger-kiss of perfection. She'd emailed me with a promise that despite her leave of absence, her additions would be ready on Tuesday by five.

Tuesday by five came. No grant.

Wednesday by five came. No grant.

Thursday by five came. No grant.

By 7:00 p.m. Thursday evening, I was pounding the heavy bag at Brian's Gym so hard I worried my hands would break, protective gloves or not.

At nine o'clock Thursday night, Dr. Silverstein called me in tears. I don't do well with tears. They make me want to solve whatever problem triggered them, and the impossibility of that makes my throat tight.

Dr. Silverstein told me her husband wandered out of their house Tuesday afternoon. He wasn't found until the next day, holed up in a neighbor's shed, weeping and disoriented, much like my mother had been in her closet of terror. My advisor's swallowed sobs and halting speech set off that familiar throat squeeze. If I could have absorbed her pain, I would have. Aside from Shawna, Dr. Silverstein is the nicest person I know. The kind who looks out for others, even before themselves. The kind who magically soothes other people's heartache. The kind I'll never be.

To top it off, my advisor lamented the challenges of growing old. "It's better than the alternative, of course," she said, her voice quavering on the phone, "but it's not for the faint of heart. Everything is behind me now. My husband's mind, my kids needing me, skin that doesn't sag."

She said the last with a quiet laugh, and that allowed my windpipe to relax enough for air to enter my lungs.

"I've seen your smartwatch," I told her. "You take more steps a day than a college track team. Young people have nothing on you."

That netted a more robust laugh, and relief crept over me. I didn't care about my grant just then. I only cared about easing Dr. Silverstein's hurt, which of course I never could. Investigating whether Megan's aunt was murdered or not I can do. Curing Mr. Silverstein's dementia, I cannot. No being "a helper" there.

At that point, Dr. Silverstein apologized for being so morose. "Don't worry, Liza. I promise I'll get the grant back to you tomorrow morning. My husband is in the facility now. It was the right thing to do." A pause, as if the words were still too difficult to say. "He's safe there. I'm heading home and will finish my part of the proposal tonight."

The thought of my advisor having to pull an all-nighter to finalize a grant after admitting her husband to a center, especially a grant that has far more implications for my career than hers, only fueled my guilt and frustration.

But Friday morning came and still no email. I checked my inbox constantly, my foot tapping the floor like a jackhammer and my fingers picking at a thread in my sweater until a hole formed. All the while, I racked my brain for another research project I could start this late in the game, certainly none that carried the same prestige nor interest for me.

At four fifteen, forty-five minutes before the Friday afternoon deadline, Dr. Silverstein's email came, the grant attached. I speed-read through her additions and checked for errors. Nothing obvious jumped from the pages, but I couldn't give the changes the deeper attention they deserved.

"Perfect is the enemy of done," my dad always said.

So, with ten minutes to spare, I submitted our NIH grant. Two days later, my heart rate has yet to normalize.

From my bench I stare out at the concrete curves and dips of the skate park. As I watch a handful of young men and one woman ride colorful boards along its contours, I force myself to quit ruminating about the grant. It's over. It's in. It's done. Now it's time to focus on what brought me here.

A cool breeze ruffles the oaks and maples surrounding the park, but under the cloudless sky, my hoodie and jeans are all that's required to keep me warm. Just like at Dr. Thomas's cabin last week, the autumn nature soothes me. It's good Theo isn't here yet. Gives me time to collect myself.

Of course, there's no guarantee he'll come. This might not even be the right place. Demetri mentioned a skate park near Fenway, and this is the closest one I found. It's not far from Fiona's condo building either. Coincidence or something more?

The strap of my satchel scratches my neck. I loosen my death grip but don't remove the bag from my body. Not with that much cash inside.

Yesterday morning I went to the bank and withdrew $13,000. Pretty much my entire savings. The teller eyed me for a long beat, as if I were up to suspicious business. I suppose, technically, I am.

Technically? my dad whispers.

My salary is decent, and I spend little, so the amount isn't the problem. My savings will fill up again. The problem lies in what I'm going to do with it.

After I withdrew the money, I made a phone call and then texted Chopper: Meet me here at eight Sunday night. You can park in the alley behind the bar. Then I texted him the address.

You want me to come to fucking Boston? he responded.

You want your fucking money? I shot back.

Three middle-finger emojis followed. I took this as assent.

Like I did with my grant a few minutes ago, I shove Chopper out of my mind and check the time on my phone. Not quite 11:00 a.m. Plenty of time to spy on Theo should he arrive. With the day free until eight o'clock and my grant submitted, I have all the time in the world.

Fortunately, I don't need it. Forty minutes later, a skinny guy with a head of dark hair and a skateboard under his arm material-izes from between two massive trees and saunters into the park. Whether he came by car or foot, I don't know. I raise my phone, zoom in, and snap a photo. Studying the image, I find the same thick eyebrows and jawline as Demetri's. Based on the beach picture Demetri sent me, this skateboarder is definitely his son.

But is he also the guy who broke into Fiona's place to steal her jewelry box? And before that, maybe to kill her?

I straighten on the bench and crack my knuckles. That's what I intend to find out.

27

Theo has skills with a skateboard, I'll give him that.

For an hour I watch him, along with three other guys and the lone girl, shoot down the ramp and whip in and out of the concrete bowl. Their bodies—and sometimes their heads too—disappear in the deeper slopes and then pop back up seconds later. Even covered in Bubble Wrap, I'd be in the hospital with a skull fracture if I tried those moves.

How long Theo will keep at these aeronautics is anyone's guess, but I've got snacks and water in my bag, and I don't have to deal with Chopper until tonight. A number of Sunday strollers populate the green areas of the park. That offers plenty of camouflage should Theo recognize me from Fiona's closet. Assuming he *is* the man who clobbered me. As to my plan once he leaves, well, that's a play-it-by-ear kind of thing.

My phone buzzes in my back pocket. The relentless vibration tells me it's a phone call, not a text. I'd prefer to send it to voicemail, but it could be Home and Hearth Healing calling about my mom, and I can't ignore that. Nor should I ignore Megan if it's her.

I'm startled to find the caller is Brent Sinclair, my landlord. I answer with a cautious, "Yeah?"

"Hey, Liza, glad I caught you."

Sinclair's voice carries only a smidgen of his usual hostility toward me. Guess that's the perk of saving someone's life. Having not seen him since he showed the apartment to Pete Parsons, I don't yet know if the orderly signed a lease. I hope a million times over he didn't.

Sinclair clears his throat. "Just wanted to thank you again for, you know, keeping me from joining the angels."

"You're welcome." *Is this a trick?* I wonder. His being nice to me is as unlikely as him *becoming* an angel. Not with his earthly dirty deeds, anyway.

"To show my appreciation, I'm going to waive your rent for the next month."

I sit up straighter on the park bench. That's *definitely* not the Brent Sinclair I know.

"You don't have to do that," I say, but then a thought occurs. "Waive April's instead."

"April?" Sinclair replies, as if she's some stranger and not the woman he sexually harassed in the past.

"Yes. April. She helped you too, and she needs it more than me."

A pause. "Okay then. You've got a deal."

We say our goodbyes and hang up. His act of kindness surprises me. Maybe people *can* change. Maybe, like me, he's building new neural connections as a result of his lived experiences. Nearly dying is a pretty big lived experience.

I chew on this for a bit and then return my attention to Theo in the skate park. Thirty minutes later, he flips his flame-painted board up with his foot, catches it in his hands, and sticks it under his arm. After high-fiving his buddies, he trots over to a big oak tree not far from me. Plopping down in front of it, he pulls a vaping device from his jeans and starts puffing away.

I study him, his limbs lanky, his relaxed posture that of a carefree child. Could he really be a killer? He doesn't look like one. Then again, I have learned firsthand that killers can put on a good show. Or is he simply an aimless young man hoping to score a few bucks by breaking into people's apartments?

Worried he might recognize me if he looks my way, I pull my hood up. Moments later, he pockets his vaping device and rises. Without glancing in my direction, he slips away between the same grove of trees he appeared from a couple of hours ago. Where he's off to, I don't know, but I intend to find out.

We go by foot, me a good distance behind him. Theo struts with his head lowered and his skateboard hugged close to his side. He passes between pedestrians without acknowledgment. Soon the two of us are hoofing it down Boylston Street, where delivery trucks snort their exhaust fumes and pollute the air.

Where is he going? It's not lost on me that his general direction is toward Fiona Carlson's building. Sure enough, a few blocks later, he turns onto the same narrow street that houses her condo.

A shiver of electricity dances down my spine. This is progressing far better than I dared hope.

If what Demetri told Nyx about his son being a deadbeat is true, and that he and his ex-wife cut their son off, then there's no way Theo could live in this area. Unless he's a skateboarding pro who wins big bucks in competitions, Fiona's place would cost more than he could afford. Doesn't matter that it's a studio apartment not much bigger than my own. Boston property in a neighborhood like this doesn't come cheap.

And yet, as we approach the eight-story building with ecru siding and bay windows, he's clearly headed in that direction.

Fewer people dot the sidewalk on this residential street off Boylston. Theo will notice me if he turns around. Only an elderly couple walking a chubby pug and a mother pushing a stroller separate us. He doesn't turn around, though. Instead, he veers off into the alley on Fiona's side of the building. It's the same alley he scurried out of before, right after he lobbed a jewelry box at my head.

Before turning down the alley myself, I pause. What if this is a trap? What if Theo is aware I'm following him? He could be waiting for me to round the corner. Waiting to whack me on the skull again, only this time with his skateboard.

I rub the lingering bruise on my forehead, the wound scabbed over but still tender.

Deciding to play it safe, I jog across the street, slink behind a parked SUV, and glance down the alleyway.

Theo is not waiting to jump me. He's climbing up the rungs of the same fire escape he shinnied his skinny butt down twice before. The question is, why?

He bypasses Fiona's closet window on the fourth floor. It appears her condo isn't his destination. When he reaches the seventh floor, he scans the alleyway in both directions and the sidewalk I just vacated. I duck down behind the SUV, hoping he hasn't seen me. My satchel, still slung around my neck and shoulder, digs into my hip.

I watch him through the car's windows. As if satisfied the coast is clear, he resumes climbing, stopping at the eighth and final floor. He lifts the window and, like a man who's done this many times before, swiftly enters the unit, skateboard and all. Within seconds, he's gone.

Whether there's anyone inside that condo, I don't know, but one thing is for sure: my suspicion that Theo Pappas is the same guy who broke into Fiona's apartment and bonked me in the head with her jewelry box is now confirmed.

I rise from my hiding spot behind the parked SUV and cross the street toward the alley. An open dumpster spews its rank odor my way, but other than a stray cat digging around in its offerings, I'm alone.

I grab the fire escape's handrails. One peek. That's all I need. A quick peek to see what Theo is up to. Maybe I'll find something solid to report to the police, and then they can handle it. I'll do things right this time around.

After adjusting my bag, I begin my ascent, my sneakers quiet on the metal rungs. When I pass Fiona's window, I see the shadowy outlines of her empty closet. Megan mentioned she'd stopped by yesterday to pack up the remaining items. Once she clears out the furniture, she'll list the place. Minus the killer bed. That she plans on destroying, antique or no antique. Guess I can't blame her.

Before I reach the eighth-floor window, I pause. I have no idea if there's a closet on the other side of it or if the place has a different floor plan than Fiona's. Hers was a studio apartment. Others are likely bigger, especially the penthouse units.

Gripping the rails more tightly, I climb the last diagonal flight of steps and crouch low on the grated platform, just beneath the window. A scan of the alleyway below makes my stomach flip. Eight stories up feels like skyscraper height when the only thing supporting you is a thin metal grate. After confirming the cat remains my only witness, I slowly rise and look inside the window Theo disappeared into.

The first thing I notice is that Theo has wedged a wooden bar inside the top window frame so that the riser can't be raised. A homemade locking device, I suppose. Looking deeper into the room, my eyes need a moment to adjust. The inside lighting is dimmer than the outside natural light, but soon I discern contours.

Unlike Fiona's place, the escape window doesn't dump into a closet. Rather, it appears to be a bedroom, one that's under major renovation. Wood planks lie everywhere. Sheets of drywall hang haphazardly. Worktables hold piles of tools.

I startle and jerk back. My heart leaps to my throat.

I just spotted Theo.

He was right there, not far from the window, sitting on a mattress against an unfinished wall. Thankfully, his body was shifted away from the window. He didn't see me.

For a long spell, I stand frozen on the metal grate, wondering how best to proceed. I've come this far. It would be stupid to back out now. This guy is up to something, and I need to get an idea of what.

Removing my phone from my back pocket, I edge forward to spy on him again. It's now clear the mattress is a piece of foam, its yellow coloring visible beneath the lone blanket. A duffel bag and loose clothing lie scattered nearby, as do bags of potato chips and boxes of crackers. Demetri said his son was crashing at a friend's. More like squatting. If it were a friend's place, Theo would use the front door. I picture the condo owner, out of town or holed up at another residence, unaware a drug-using skateboarder is making himself at home in the place.

Theo, still not spotting me, removes something from the duffel bag. It's a gallon-size plastic bag filled with—

I catch my breath. Inside the bag are hundreds, maybe thousands, of pills. Even with the subpar lighting, the rainbow of pastel colors is obvious. Like thousands of miniature Easter eggs.

Holy shit.

Theo removes a handful of pills, counts some out, and dumps them into a tiny plastic bag. He does this twice more.

Is he selling them? My God, have I found the guy behind the tainted fentanyl?

I swallow. Blink a few times. Make sure I'm seeing what I think I'm seeing.

Did Fiona discover the same thing? Did she encounter Theo at the addiction center, maybe as a former client? Maybe she caught him squatting in her building. Maybe she found his drugs, and he killed her to silence her.

In my mind I hear Dr. Lightfoot warning me that I'm jumping to conclusions. He'd be justified, but I can't lose my chance at proof if I'm right. Raising my phone, I snap three quick photos of Theo and his bag of goodies. My mobile is in silent mode, but something must catch his attention—a shift in the light, my body movement, an ambient noise—because he jerks his head over his shoulder and spots me.

I ram my phone back into my pocket, grab the thin handrails, and fly down the stairs. My satchel swings at my side, the money inside it smacking against the metal bars. If only I could have left the bag in my car at the park, but I couldn't risk someone stealing it.

Above me the window opens.

"Hey," Theo shouts.

Shuffling follows. He's probably lunging out of the window to get me, but I don't look up to confirm. Instead, I fly downward, my pulse pounding.

"Should've stayed out of it," Theo yells. "You're a dead woman now."

I near the bottom and leap off the remaining three steps, just like Theo did after I caught him in Fiona's closet nine days ago. I sprint off down the alleyway.

When I reach the sidewalk, I pivot left and keep running, startling a couple on their Sunday stroll. A few blocks later, on the much busier Boylston Street, I merge into groups of pedestrians. Once enough people surround me, I shift from running to a speed walk. No need to draw more attention to myself. At a crosswalk, I finally risk a glance behind me. If Theo is still following, I don't see him.

Maintaining a trot, I cross at the light and keep going. Once I reach the skate park, I return to a run and hustle to my car. After confirming Theo is nowhere nearby, I stab Google Maps open on my phone and search for the nearest police department. I set the GPS to start, rev my engine, and head that way.

It takes six blocks of driving before I breathe normally again. My shoulders start to relax, and I give myself a mental pat on the back. I'm doing things right this time around. No *craziest of the crazy train* here.

I chew on those words, words the psychopath surgeon tossed my way when he caught me doing something I shouldn't have been doing. "The craziest of the crazy train," he'd called me.

Not this time. This time I'm on a luxury line. This time I have proof.

And soon the police will too.

28

———————

Outside the police department, I maneuver my Civic into a tight spot, pulling as close to the curb as I can without nicking the Corolla in front of me or the BMW behind. The building is gray in color, with dozens of symmetrically square windows from which I imagine the cops already scrutinizing me, running my plates, checking me for priors. Such is my paranoia.

Before I go in, I need to make a couple of phone calls. If I'm going to do this right, then I need to do it right.

The first call goes to Megan. Wanting to get this over with, I talk fast and come clean about being in Boston and spying on Theo.

She cuts me off. "Wait. I don't understand. Who's Theo? What do you mean a condo under renovation?"

"Listen, I'll give you the full details later, but right now I need to talk to the police."

The dashboard clock reads almost three. My meeting with Chopper is at eight, and I'll need a half hour before that to set up plan B.

I really hope I won't need plan B.

Continuing with Megan, I say, "The guy who attacked me in your aunt's place, the one who was stealing her jewelry box—or returning it, I'm still not clear about that—is the son of the man she met on the dating app. His name is Theo, and he's squatting in a top-floor unit, a bigger one that's under renovation. He has a bunch of pills in there. I don't know what it all means, but that's for the police to figure out."

After a few more questions from Megan and a promise from me to explain everything in more detail later, I end the call.

Spent already, I call Tam next. Maybe she can get ahold of someone at this precinct to tip them off before I go in. Let them know I'm not some random nutcase. I stare up at the imposing building on my right and try not to look guilty.

My conversation with Tam unfolds much the same as it did with Megan, followed by the expected berating for acting like a "vigilante sleuth." At least my cop friend commends me for driving straight to the police station.

"I'd call that progress, wouldn't you?" she says.

"Sorry. Didn't realize I was talking to my shrink."

Tam snorts. "Just head to the front desk. Tell them you'd like to speak to an officer on duty about something you saw. They'll write up a report and get it to the right person."

I scratch my neck and then my forearms, every part of my body itchy. I just want to go home. Play a couple of video games. Disappear into the void. I've had enough excitement for the day.

If you want the thrill of the race, my father says in my head, *you better be prepared for the pit stops.*

"Look," Tam says, maybe sensing my reluctance. "I'll call the department and vouch for you."

Relieved, I thank her and hang up. After allowing a few minutes for her to notify them, I grab my satchel and climb out of the car. Just as quickly, I duck back in. I stare at my bag. What if they run it through a machine and discover its contents? How am I going to explain having $13,000 on me?

With sweat dotting my forehead, I exit the vehicle, pop the trunk, and drop my bag inside. Leaving that much cash in the car disturbs me to no end, but if there's any place it should be safe, it's outside of a police department.

Wiping my brow, I lock the vehicle and head inside.

Officer Doris Cho is nice. She doesn't mock me. Doesn't ask whether I'm creating excitement out of nothing. Doesn't make me repeat the same thing over and over. She simply sits at her cluttered desk, swivels her chair back and forth, and listens, jotting a note now and then. I mention Fiona's odd death by Murphy bed, the dating app, my encounter with Demetri (minus the specifics of the sex club, since I don't want to get anyone who works there in trouble), and identifying Demetri's son as the guy who attacked me in Fiona's closet.

When I finish, Officer Cho studies her notes. "So you think Theo Pappas killed your friend's aunt? A woman whose death was ruled accidental?"

"Maybe," I reply. "I mean, I don't know for sure. Someone else could have done it. But he *was* in her condo—likely more than once given the broken window latch—and he's now squatting on the top floor."

"Squatting doesn't mean you're a murderer. It usually means you're homeless."

I nod because she's right. A worrisome thought pecks at me. What if I'm implicating an innocent man? What if Theo is just a guy going through a rough patch, and I'm about to make his life hell?

But I saw those pills.

I relay this to Officer Cho, who has asked me to call her Doris. "As I said, he had a huge stash of colorful pills and was divvying them up into small bags. At the very least, he's selling drugs, drugs people are dying from. If Fiona Carlson found out, he might also have killed her. She was researching fentanyl overdoses before she died, especially the local cases."

The officer's gaze focuses somewhere above my head. She rubs the knuckles of one hand, as if deep in thought. If only I could read her mind.

"We've had an uptick in ODs, no lie there," she says. "We can't keep up with the counterfeits. But here's the thing. I only have your word about Theo and his bag of drugs. While I don't have any reason to doubt you, a defense lawyer would."

A warmth of satisfaction stirs in my belly. I pluck my phone from my pocket. "I have proof. I took a picture of him with the pills." As soon as I open my photo app, my satisfaction turns cold. The quality of all three photos is poor, the window's glass obscuring the details. Not only is Theo in shadow, with his profile mostly obscured, but a beam of sunlight distorts the bag of pills. They could be pills, they could be marbles.

I curse under my breath but show Doris the photos nonetheless.

"Looks like a bag of sweets," she says. "Candy. At least that's what his lawyer will say. And a definitive ID on the guy would be impossible. Most of his face is turned, not to mention blurred."

I sink down on my chair, the hood of my sweatshirt bunching up against my neck. My confidence deflates, and a heavy dose of fatigue replaces it. The proof I thought was proof might be no proof at all.

"Your police friend from Morganville told me you helped catch that surgeon who was killing his patients."

The officer's change in subject throws me. "Yes."

She twirls her pen. "That's pretty cool. You kind of like this amateur sleuthing, do you?"

I can't read anything into her tone, but I worry she's pegged me as a bored Avenger wannabe.

Are you, tiger?

"No," I respond, maybe as much to my father as to Doris. "I just 'kind of like' making sure bad guys don't get away with murder."

Her pen stops twirling. I apologize for my snark, but she cuts me off. "I meant no offense," she says. "I agree, this whole thing is strange."

My fangs retreat.

"The son of Fiona Carlson's boyfriend broke into her apartment and might also be squatting in her building? Yes, that's strange," Doris repeats. "Strange enough to talk to both father and son about.

But talk is all we can do, and only if they're willing, because we don't have anything on them to do more than that." She pauses, as if reconsidering what she's just said. "Well, we have your eyewitness account that a man who looks like Theo Pappas broke into Ms. Carlson's place and might have a bag of illegal drugs in his possession, so that's more solid, and based on what you've told me, the doctor sent racy messages to the woman, creepy stalkerish stuff, even. But again, her death was ruled accidental. At most we're dealing with a break-in of her place."

I pocket my phone. "That's up to you—or the detective, or whoever—to decide. I'm only telling you these things because Fiona's death hasn't sat right with me."

I realize I should tell her about Demetri's alibi, a solid one at that. It's not because I have special feelings for the guy—I don't—or that I want to protect him. I just don't want an innocent man to be suspected of murder.

When I tell Doris about the auction Demetri attended the night Fiona died, making it unlikely he killed her, she bites her lower lip and studies me. "Who needs a detective with you around?"

I can't tell whether she's joking, so I say nothing, but I'm now even more relieved that Tam called in to vouch for me.

"You need to be careful," Doris says. "This Theo guy threatened you, chased you." She points to the faded bruise on my forehead. "Attacked you. From now on, you leave the police work to us, okay?"

"That's why I'm here," I reply.

The officer tilts her head. "Why are you doing this? Why is it so important to you?"

I examine the frayed shoelace of my right Converse and shrug. "I want to help my friend."

What more is there to say? People like Officer Cho, or my colleagues, or Shawna and Tam don't understand that for social illiterates like me, help is the only thing we have to offer.

You can always help them, Liza.

You can always be a helper.

29

———

After meeting with Officer Cho, it feels as though a huge weight has been lifted off me. Intense one-on-one conversations with cops, especially where I feel like an alien on display, are not my thing. After two such exchanges in as many weeks, first after getting clobbered by a jewelry box in Fiona's closet, and then today, I've had enough police encounters to last a lifetime.

To reward myself, I stop at one of Boston's pubs for a beer and a pulled-pork sandwich. Tuning out the well-dressed couple arguing at the table next to me, I snarf down my dinner, guzzle my beer, and give myself another self-congratulatory kudos.

I did things right. Even though it was harder than chewing rocks, I fessed up to Officer Cho about the prying I've done on my own. As Tam said earlier, that's progress. Dr. Lightfoot would agree. And now Fiona's killer will be caught, and I can get back to my life.

Well, almost.

In a couple of hours, I'm going to do something most people—normal people—would not consider the right thing. It's my move to make, though, and in my opinion, a necessary one. We're not talking about a case of someone needing to be caught and dealt with by the police, like Theo Pappas. We're talking about someone needing to be silenced.

That would probably cancel out any progress points I've made with Tam and Dr. Lightfoot, but it has to be done. Not only for my sake, but for April's and Jasmine's too. My cookie-baking neighbor and her giggling sous-chef daughter deserve to be free of the Chopper anchor around their necks. In two hours I hope to accomplish that.

To pass the time, I scroll through news headlines on my phone, check for emails about my NIH grant submission—which is pointless because it's Sunday, and I just submitted it Friday—and play *Hearthstone*. No more beer, though. I order a diet soda from the waitress instead. I need to be alert.

At seven o'clock, I pay my tab and drive to the Wicked Wonderland, a place I never thought I'd visit again. I park two blocks away and hustle to the alleyway that hides the private club. Once inside the building but outside the concealed door, I rap the strange knock that was sent to me via an audio text earlier. Hopefully I've been cleared to enter. My contact, a certain buxom dominatrix, assured me it would be no problem.

As before, an eyeball appears in the peephole. Seconds later the door swings open.

"She'll meet you at the bar," the bouncer says in lieu of a greeting. He nods toward the ornate counter with the brass runner and mirrored wall. His tone is as emotionless as mine, and although he's not the same bouncer who handed Demetri the key during my last visit—a key that presumably unlocks the padlock of a submissive receiver—his burly build and skintight clothing are so similar to the other guy's he might as well be.

I wind my way through the intimate space, but unlike before when sultry music and walking sex paved my way, nothing but silence ushers me in now. Nyx told me the action doesn't kick off until 9:00 p.m., and given the empty tables and curtain-lined booths, she wasn't kidding. Probably doesn't help that it's Sunday night. No furries or half-naked people parading around yet. Even the bartender, who's stacking glasses behind the counter, still wears his shirt. I'll consider that a win.

I sip the club soda he pours for me and ready myself to meet Nyx, which, to be honest, requires something stiffer than club soda. Yesterday morning, after I withdrew money from the bank, I dug Nyx's business card out of my catch-all kitchen basket and called her. Following that, I texted Chopper to meet me here tonight. I wasn't thrilled Nyx's skills might be necessary, but if plan A doesn't work in ixnaying Chopper, then I'm going to need plan B.

In plan B, Nyx is the ixnayer.

It doesn't take long before she appears. This time around, her breasts are better contained in a black bra with metal studs, partially covered by a blazer, but her skirt is short, and her boots remain thigh high. A posh ponytail secures her long hair, and her made-up face glows with a healthy sheen. Next to her, my jeans and hoodie probably scream *receiver*.

Approaching me, she says nothing. She simply wags her finger in a follow-me gesture and leads me to a secluded corner booth. Once we're seated, her lip curls up on one side, and she appraises me through her false lashes. "When I gave you my number, this wasn't exactly what I had in mind."

"Sorry to disappoint you."

"My disappointment in one area is my pleasure in another. I'm always happy for a cash payout."

"You don't have to do anything too terrible. I just need a few… compromising photos."

"Compromising I can do. Illegal, I won't. Well…sometimes that's a shade of gray."

My own lip curls up at that. "You're singing my tune now."

She taps a bloodred fingernail on the glossy table. "I knew you had a wildcat side. Saw it the second I laid eyes on you. Probably more than a little."

"A lot more than a little," I say. "Just not the kind you're used to. But let's hope no shades of gray are needed. If plan A works—just a normal conversation—then I'll kiss plan B goodbye."

Nyx gives me the side-eye. "I still get paid, though, right?"

"Of course. Nursing school isn't cheap."

She smiles and winks. "I like you, Liza. Sure you don't want to stick around when you're done?"

"I'm sure." I reach into my satchel and, like a spy in a rotten B movie, pull out an envelope stuffed with twenty Benjamins. It's a lot, I know, but if she has to do what I might need her to do, then she'll have earned it. "Here's the first two K," I say, handing the envelope to her. "The third comes when we're done, or, if I don't need you, when I leave."

"You don't trust me?"

"Not really."

Nyx bursts out laughing. "I do like people who speak their minds." She rises from the table. "Your man has been cleared to enter. Jason will let him in."

I assume Jason is the bouncer.

Nyx crosses to my side and leans over to plant a kiss on my cheek, her lashes tickling my skin. Then she flutters her fingers under my jaw.

"Text if you need me, Luscious Liza."

Moments later she disappears into the dark hallway that swallowed the furry nine days ago.

As I watch her leave, I wonder how much of her seductress persona is an act. Probably most of it. Which is good, because she's not going to need it for starting IVs and inserting urinary catheters. Hopefully.

I turn and eye the door.

Chopper should be here soon.

30

———

At eight twenty and as promised by Nyx, the bouncer in the cellophane-tight shirt opens the door of the Wicked Wonderland to let Chopper in. I'm relieved my nemesis found the concealed entrance. My directions must have been good. Now I just have to hope he listened like a good boy and parked nearby in the alleyway. That's a critical element for plan B, should it come into play.

At first Chopper saunters into the club like he's the bad-ass white supremacist he resembles, wearing yet another black metal T-shirt and displaying arms full of sinister-looking tattoos. As he takes in the bar's erotic artwork and sexual atmosphere, however, his gait falters.

I wave him over to my corner booth, one of only two tables occupied at this early hour. He looks my way but doesn't acknowledge me. Instead, as if trying to hide his uncool misstep, he takes his sweet time checking out the bottles behind the bar and places an order with the bartender.

Chopper wants to show me who's in charge, I guess.

We'll see about that.

When he finally sits down across from me with his amber-colored booze on the rocks, I say, "You're late."

"And you're lucky."

"How's that?"

"Because I've been generous in my patience with you, more than you deserve." He holds his thumb and index finger a few millimeters apart. "I was this close to snitching."

"If you really wanted to implicate me, you'd have done it by now."

"Is that right?" He downs his drink in one swallow and then, as if he's some elite VIP, snaps his fingers at a fleshy barmaid in tight shorts and demands another whiskey Coke. As he stares at her departing backside, he says, "What the hell kind of place did you drag me to?"

I ignore the question. "Anyone you spew your fiction to, your made-up story that April or I had anything to do with Sam Donovan's death, will see it for what it is: the words of an ex-con trying to blackmail two innocent women for cash."

"Ha. Innocent?"

I worry he sees right through me, but I can't yet read his psychopathic face well enough to be certain. I don't know if April put the bug in his ear before he—or whoever he got to do it—shanked the surgeon. April and I never talked about it. But I do know I vented my frustration to her about Donovan possibly getting off for his crimes. I remember how hot my cheeks got, how murderous I felt, how I seethed through gritted teeth that he'd be better off dead.

Seeing my rage, did April initiate what happened next? Did she feel she owed me for the things I've done for her? Paying her rent a couple of times. Getting Sinclair off her back. Watching Jasmine while she worked an extra shift at the diner. I hope not. April is a good person. She doesn't deserve to go back into the system and lose Jasmine again, especially not on my account. The thought alone makes me want to punch my own face.

Regardless, whether I was the instigator of that shank in the surgeon's side or not, the satisfaction I derived from his death left me content to let his murder ride without questions.

It's also highly possible Chopper is a lying jackass. Maybe he heard about my takedown of Dr. Donovan, knew of my connection to April, and then, when someone else stabbed the surgeon for whatever reason, Chopper used it as a get-rich scheme for himself. Once his own time was served, he looked me up, confessed to killing Donovan on my behalf, and then demanded payoff for his silence.

The barmaid delivers Chopper's drink, and as he studies her ample bosom, I study him. His buzz-cut hair, his prison-sculpted guns, his scowling lips that require no emotion card to decipher. Does he really have four aces in his hand? Or is he bluffing with pocket deuces? Because it's hard to believe April had anything to do with Donovan's death. She'd never risk her new life with Jasmine, not even for me. Nor would I want her to.

Even though Chopper hasn't said anything, I nod. I'm pretty sure plan A is all I'll need to end this.

Getting on with it, I reach into my leather bag and pull out a thick manila envelope. I plop it on the table. "Here."

Chopper chews an ice cube from his drink. "How much?"

"Ten K, but once it's yours, this ends here and now. Got it?"

Chopper spits the ice cube back into his glass. "You suck at math, Doc. I asked for fifty."

"You're getting ten."

"Then you're getting time. April too."

He's bluffing. I'm sure he is. There's no way April would have asked him to kill someone. He simply put two and two together in hopes of making fifty grand.

"You're full of shit," I tell him. "April would never get involved in this."

"Oh no?"

"No. She wouldn't risk Jasmine going to foster care again."

Chopper smiles like a man who takes pleasure in drowning kittens. "Hey, Daddy's out now. She can live with me."

I assume he's being sarcastic. He wants to take care of Jasmine about as much as I want to spend the rest of my life in the Wicked Wonderland. No sooner have I thought it than a man with clamps on his nipples wanders by. Fortunately, Chopper seems not to notice.

"Right," I scoff. "Like the court would ever hand Jasmine over to the king of deadbeat dads, not to mention an abuser and a drug dealer."

But would they? I have no idea. If Chopper has truly left his drug days behind him and paid his debt to society, who knows?

A wave of nausea washes over me. "No," I repeat. "April had nothing to do with this."

"Hmm...you sure about that?" Chopper swallows a mouthful of alcohol and leans over the table toward me. His whiskey breath stinks up the air. "Did you know April came to see me in prison?"

"Bullshit. After you went away and she got out, she wanted nothing more to do with you. All you gave her were black eyes and grief."

"You keep telling yourself she's innocent, Butch." Chopper was no doubt one of those punk-ass middle-schoolers who called everyone homophobic names while he bullied them. "She came to see me a few days before your surgeon got the old—" He mimes a stabbing motion with his hand. "Bet they catch those family visits on camera. They're always watching us. Leaves a nice record to back me up."

I sense his threat but don't respond.

"Suit yourself." He grabs the envelope of cash and turns his body in the booth as if to leave. "But if you don't cough up another forty grand, I'll tell my tale to the piggies. Then they'll blow April's precious little home down."

A swirl of pinpricks dances in my gut. I don't have $50,000 to give him. Ten alone was a kick to the teeth. Even if I could afford it, there's no guarantee Chopper won't come sniffing around for more.

I relay my suspicion to him. "If I did have the money—which I don't—how do I know three months from now you won't ask for more? Three years from now?"

He grins, flashing an eyetooth with brown discoloration. "Guess you'll just have to trust me. Then again, running a business is awfully expensive, and in a couple years when you graduate from pathology preschool, you'll be making plenty of cash. Enough to share, for sure."

His words confirm my fear. He'll never let this go. Whether

April really asked him to kill Sam Donovan or not, Chopper will continue to extort me, expecting a constant replenishing of his bank account in exchange for his silence.

I remain convinced he's bluffing about April. Maybe she stopped by the prison to have him sign something for child support. Or maybe it was the opposite. Maybe she asked him to relinquish all parental rights. Still, with her visit caught on camera, Chopper can spin it any way he wants.

Looks like plan A—giving him ten grand and telling him to jump off Prudential Tower and leave us the hell alone—isn't going to work.

That leaves plan B. It better do the trick. April's future depends on it. Mine too.

Just as Chopper rises from the booth, I grab his tattooed forearm. "Wait."

He lifts an eyebrow.

"Hold on a minute." I try to sound contrite, even a little desperate. I suppose in a way I am. "Let me get you another drink. We'll figure this out."

"Now you're talking, Doc." He sits back down and appraises me. "You know, despite that butch hair, you're kind of a looker."

His eyes travel down my chest, and his lewd assessment is somehow a hundred times worse than Demetri's.

"Not all payment has to be in the form of green, you know." His tongue darts between his lips.

Because his request for sexual payment works in my favor, I resist the urge to rip the golden sconce off the wall and ram it down his throat. Instead, I leave the booth and head to the bar. It's not quite nine o'clock, and the place is still dead. Nipple-clamp guy is nowhere to be seen.

I order another whiskey Coke for Chopper but ask for a double. When the bartender delivers it, I request a beer for myself, one from the tap on the far end of the bar. As he leaves to pour it, I remove my tiny plan B bag from my pocket and dump its powdery fragments into the whiskey Coke. With a swizzle stick from the bartender's fruit tray, I give it a good stir.

As I wait for my change, I shoot off a text to Nyx: Plan B is a go. She texts back: I'll be out in ten.

Is that enough time, I wonder? How long before the sleeping pills I pilfered from Fiona's medicine cabinet (but hadn't yet dropped off for proper disposal) mix with the alcohol and make Chopper sleepy enough to go with Nyx, but not so comatose that we have to carry him?

Make it twenty, I type back. Better yet, wait for my text.

I return to the velvet-lined booth with our drinks and slide in next to Chopper. When I put my hand on his thigh, his brow lifts, and he smirks.

Don't barf, don't barf, don't barf.

"Let's see if we can make this work," I say. I don't even try to sound coy or sexy, because I'd fail at both.

He slings an arm around me and yanks me against him, his chest a granite slab.

"Smart decision, Butch. Even though you suck at math."

"I'm only doing this to protect April and Jasmine."

"The reason doesn't matter to me."

He swallows half of his drink. When he places the glass back on the table, he rubs my breast with the back of his hand.

"Was kind of lonely in prison, if you get my drift." He breathes his drugged, whiskey breath in my face. "So, you know, there's no guarantee *this* is a one-time thing between us either."

Every cell in my body wants to bolt from the booth, but I force myself to play along.

We drink—me sipping, him swigging. Words come out of my mouth to pass the time. Words like *payment schedule, ground rules,* April and Jasmine being *off the table.* He smirks and drinks, brushes against my breast, feels up my thigh. I constantly check the time on my phone. Why hasn't he conked out yet?

"Let's take this somewhere private," he says.

Sweat dampens my armpits. His ongoing lucidity stresses me out. Maybe I didn't crush enough pills.

Finally, he yawns. Then again, bigger this time. Soon he's a wide-mouth, yawping macaque.

He shakes his head. "Whoa. Guess I drank a little too much." He holds up his empty glass. "Wuz…wuz this a triple?" he slurs.

My fingers fly over my phone screen. Now! I text Nyx.

I pry myself away from Chopper's weighty arm and stand. I hold out my hand. "Come on. The women's bathroom is a single. It locks."

He's obviously coherent enough to catch my meaning, because he slides out of the booth. Or tries to, anyway.

"Whoa," he says again, reaching for me.

I put his arm over my shoulders and allow him to use me for support. We head to the back hallway that leads to…well, leads to whatever it is Nyx does. If the bartender wonders what we're up to, or if he even cares, he doesn't show it. He simply leans against the counter and scrolls through his phone. I imagine keeping your mouth shut in a place like this is part of the job requirement.

Halfway down the Wicked Wonderland's shadowy corridor, Nyx appears from a room. She smooths her sleek ponytail, removes her blazer, and stands there, imposing and provocative in her short skirt, thigh-high boots, and studded bra. A leather domino mask covers her upper face, maybe as a means of disguise.

"I do this all the time," she told me yesterday when I called her, "and I'm happy to make extra cash, but your request is a little out there." After I explained who Chopper was, how he was a violent ex-con trying to extort me and, more importantly, was threatening his ex-girlfriend and daughter, who want nothing to do with him, Nyx cursed into the phone. "I've known men like him. Cruel bastards every one of them. So, yeah, I'm in for whatever you've got, Luscious Liza."

Now, to Chopper, she says, "Hello, handsome. Heard you're up for some fun."

"Fug yeah," Chopper slurs. "I like fon."

Nyx waves us into the back room, presumably the same room she dragged a leashed panda into on my first visit. Never did I imagine I'd be venturing in there too.

Chopper is an anchor on my shoulders, but we get him inside. Like the rest of the private club, the lighting is soft, but not so dim that it obscures the room's erotic accessories and pseudo-torture devices, including a pillory. Ropes and hooks hang from the ceiling, and black candles line every surface. Gloves with claws sit on a side table, along with whips and chains. Several pairs of handcuffs too.

Trying not to conjure the macabre uses of these unpleasant devices, I concentrate instead on getting the sluggish Chopper to the center table, which, creepily enough, resembles one of Titus McCall's autopsy tables—only ours don't have black padding and restraints. They don't fold into various positions for perverse and sadistic acts either.

Chopper doesn't resist lying down. In fact, he seems relieved. Once he's fully supine, Nyx approaches him with a leather whip in her hand. I scan the room and spot the wheelchair I requested she bring. It's a lightweight number her grandmother uses at airports and malls and is waiting for us in the corner. Even for me, this is messed up.

Before I have time for second thoughts, or to question whether I'm doing the right thing, I open the camera on my phone.

Nyx and I get to work.

31

———

Monday and Tuesday pass slowly at work, my mind spiraling between Theo Pappas and Trevor "Chopper" Jones. I view pathological tissue slides and submit my impressions into the electronic system. I attend lectures given by various attendings. I make frequent trips to the hospital's beverage kiosk for Earl Grey tea.

On one of those trips, I stopped in a restroom and ran into Jen. She'd just popped a pill into her mouth and was using tap water to swallow it down. She jumped when she saw me, and I couldn't help but wonder what she took.

"Fancy meeting you here," she said.

Circles of fatigue rimmed her eyes. When I performed my social duty and asked how she was doing, she waved me off and said, "I'm handling the shitstorm that is life." Then she left without saying another word. The encounter has gnawed at me since.

My mind flits often to Dr. Silverstein too. I hope she's adjusting to her husband no longer being at home. Four years ago, when I admitted my mom to Home and Hearth Healing, I felt like a traitor, even though everyone knew it had to be done. So I understand my advisor's hurt. Even when you know it's for the best—and in the situation where your husband's dementia is so bad he leaves bruises on your arms and gets lost in a shed overnight, it's definitely for the best—admitting them is still torture.

On Wednesday, as I slip my laptop into my bag and tidy my cubicle desk to head home, I wonder why Chopper hasn't contacted me yet. I keep waiting for the next bomb to drop. If he's wondering why he woke up hungover and funky in the front seat of his Subaru in a Boston alley last Sunday, he hasn't texted me to ask why.

I replay the lurid events of that night in my mind. When Nyx and I finished with Chopper, I rolled him out to the alleyway in the wheelchair Nyx had pilfered from her grandma and stuffed him into his car. I was surprised to find an old Subaru. I had Chopper pegged as a pickup or Camaro kind of guy.

Given how much I strained to transfer his sleeping body from wheelchair to car, it was lucky he wasn't a pickup-truck kind of guy after all. Otherwise I would've needed Nyx's help hoisting him in. I'd already pushed the adventurous woman to her limits. I didn't want to involve her further. As it was, I forked over an extra three hundred bucks for her troubles, hoping it would sweeten the deal for her silence. She seemed to enjoy herself, though. Maybe her moral boundaries are as fluid as mine.

Now, on Wednesday night, after two hours at Brian's Gym and a stop at a gyro place not far from my apartment building, I can't take the rumination any longer. Too many loose ends, from Theo and Demetri to Chopper. As soon as I enter my studio and toss my bag on the counter, I pull out my phone and call Tam. I prefer texting, but if she has any information on Theo, this could take a while.

"I know why you're calling," she says.

"You do?"

"Yes, and I doubt it's to ask about Seth biting one of the other kids at Mommy and Me class or to hear about the client who went off on Shawna. You're calling to find out if I heard anything back from Doris Cho."

"Wait…what?" A fire sparks in my gut. "What happened to Shawna? What do you mean a client went off on her? If someone's picking on her again, I'll—"

"Whoa, don't go into Rottweiler mode. That's my job now,

although we both know Shawna's not that shy, overweight girl anymore. One of her high-maintenance clients threw a hissy fit. Claims Shawna used the wrong color on her hair, but of course Shawna didn't. She used the exact color the woman insisted on, even though Shawna had told her it wasn't the best choice, that color comes out differently on different hair types. She recommended a softer red instead, but the client insisted on 'intense cherry.' She got intense cherry all right. Then she blamed Shawna for the results."

"What did she do? The client, I mean."

"She started shrieking like a crazy woman and… Oh, sorry."

Even though Tam can't see me through the phone, I wave the comment away. "It's fine. I know what you meant. Not everything is about my mom, and you don't have to strike a perfectly good word from your vocabulary on my account."

"Well, anyway, the client started screaming at Shawna, grabbed a can of hair spray, and doused her in the eyes with it."

"That's assault!" I take a seat at my desk. How can Tam be so calm?

Because she doesn't have anger issues like you, my brain replies.

"Yep. Shawna's eyes were red and teary for two days. Had to go to the doctor for some drops. She refuses to press charges, though, even though I told her she should. She says the woman has suffered enough. Guess her husband is going through chemo for colon cancer." Tam grunts. "Doesn't make nearly blinding my wife with hair spray right, though."

"No, it doesn't."

"But you know Shawna," Tam says. "Always forgiving. The client apologized. Profusely. Sent Shawna flowers—which, honestly, I would've thrown out—and offered to cover the doctor's visit. So Shawna isn't pressing charges. She even told the woman she'd help tone down the color if she wants."

"Shawna's a way better person than me."

"Ditto. I was pretty pissed, to say the least. So yeah, that's what's going on, and as if that isn't enough, Seth is biting other kids. Not sure if that's a sign we should have another kid to keep him company or give up fighting about it and close the subject for good."

"Sorry to hear about Seth." I mentally dust off my scariest and most awkward rotation in med school—pediatrics—and try to offer something that helps. "Biting isn't uncommon for a two-year-old. Usually it can be extinguished quickly with—"

"Yeah, we handled it. Thank you, though. I appreciate you letting me blow off steam."

Realizing Tam has a lot going on, I'm about to apologize for bugging her with my own issues and end the call. She starts talking again before I can.

"Okay, getting back to your unasked question. Yes, I heard back from Doris Cho today. Was going to call you earlier, but it's been a day." Tam exhales, and I imagine her sinking down on her couch and plopping her feet on the coffee table.

"That's okay. I appreciate you contacting her for me at all. Really."

"Ah, it's no problem. You know Shawna and I are always here for you." Tam laughs and adds, "Even when you don't want us to be."

I laugh politely because this is what people are expected to do.

"So I told Doris you wanted to know what they found out about the guy squatting in that building near Fenway Park," Tam says.

"Yes. The same guy who broke into Fiona Carlson's condo and cracked me on the head."

"Doris claims they contacted the owner of that top-floor condo. It's being renovated, just like you thought. The owner has been staying somewhere else in Boston until the unit's finished, but he gave them permission to look around with him. Neither he nor the police found any evidence of squatting."

I kick my scuffed loafers off and lean back in the desk chair. "Theo must have cleared his stuff out. I saw a foam mattress and a duffel bag. Some clothes and food on the ground too."

"Yeah, he probably scrammed when you busted him. But hey, there's something I need to tell—"

"Did the cops check for fingerprints? DNA?"

"It's not a crime scene, Liza. They're not going to run a forensics analysis on a condo being renovated just because some guy might have snuck in there. Besides, the owner wasn't too concerned."

"And if that squatter is the guy who killed Fiona?"

"There's no proof of that," Tam says. "And it's a moot point now because—"

"A moot point?" My voice rises. "He had a bag of pills. He might be selling bad drugs. Maybe Fiona found out, and he killed her." I take a deep breath and slow down, not wanting to sound unhinged like I did last year. "I'm not saying it's for sure. I'm just saying it's worth looking into. Why are people blowing me off?"

"Fiona's death was ruled accidental," Tam says. "Even if this guy—"

"Theo Pappas."

"Even if this guy you think is Theo Pappas broke into Fiona Carlson's apartment, there's no evidence he—or anyone else—killed her. But what I'm trying to tell you is—"

"Even with those pills he was selling? That had to be what he was doing. His dad thought so too. He—"

"Will you let me finish what I'm trying to say?"

I squeeze the desk chair's armrest, forcing my frustration into it. "Sorry."

"Look, I don't know if Theo Pappas was squatting in that condo. I don't know if he was selling drugs. I don't even know if what he had in the bag you saw *were* drugs. But..." Tam pauses. "I do know that he was *personally* using drugs because..."

"Because what?"

"Because Theo Pappas is dead. That's what I've been trying to tell you."

32

I bolt up from my desk. "Dead? How? What do you—"

Now it's Tam's turn to interrupt me. "Despite what you think, Doris Cho isn't blowing you off. She followed up on Theo Pappas. They tracked him down yesterday and found him dead. Overdosed, most likely. Probably another victim of this opioid nightmare. His body was nowhere near Fiona Carlson's condo building. It was in an old warehouse in South Boston, a junkie hangout from the sounds of it. He was probably a regular there."

I put the phone on speaker and pace my studio. It's impossible to absorb this news. Four days ago I watched Theo Pappas sail through the air on his skateboard like a pro. Then he yelled down the fire escape that I was a dead woman. Sure didn't look like a "regular" junkie to me.

And now he's dead.

Does Demetri know? The man means nothing to me, but I still feel bad for his loss. Even after five years, my father's death leaves an ache in my chest, and losing a child has to be worse. Demetri will blame himself. He'll think cutting his son off the dole led to his death.

Even though Tam can't see me, I shake my head and stare out

the window at the playground behind the apartment complex. Theo overdosing doesn't add up. He was involved in something. I caught him in the act, and now he's dead. That can't be a coincidence.

Tam is saying something about Theo's toxicology results taking a while to come back, but I cut in. "Do you think it's my fault?"

"Why would it be your fault?"

"Because I outed him as the squatter who robbed Fiona's place. I thought he killed Fiona, but what if it was someone else? Someone Theo knew? Maybe I made him a liability. Made him a target of whoever killed Fiona in order to keep him quiet. Theo threatened me. Said I was a dead woman. That implies I was on to something. What if I'm next?"

Silence floats from Tam's end of the phone, punctuated only by her dog barking in the background and a door closing. Is she contemplating my theory? Or does she think I'm bonkers?

In case it's the latter, I say, "I'm spitballing here. I'm not delusional. But you have to admit it's weird that a guy with ties to Fiona is now dead."

"Sure, it's weird," Tam agrees. "But a guy with a substance-abuse problem breaking into people's homes for drug money is not. That's the only thing linking Fiona to Theo. The police aren't exactly playing board games and singing camp songs, you know. They've got tons of cases to deal with, and before they can close a fraction of them, more come in. So without Fiona's death being labeled a homicide—or even a suspicious death—and without any evidence that she knew Theo or that he was selling drugs, what exactly should the police look into?"

"But—"

"Theo Pappas is dead," Tam repeats. "Overdosed. He doesn't have a home they can search. They found no bag of pills on him. Just a needle sticking out of his arm and his lips crusted with vomit. Didn't find anything at his parents' houses either."

I leave the window and sink down on my bed. I ball up the duvet in my fist.

Tam must sense my frustration. "Sorry," she says. "I know that's not what you wanted to hear, and I know you just want to get justice for your friend's aunt if she really was murdered. That's good of you, for sure, but until there's something else to investigate, the Boston PD has a silo of other crap to deal with, including trying to bust whoever is selling those toxic pills."

I hear her words, understand them even, but I can't get past the image of Theo lying dead of an overdose in a scuzzy drug den, his skateboard by his side. What if I'm responsible for his death? What if my snooping got the guy killed?

"His dad must be in shock," I say. "They had a falling-out. No parent wants that to be the last time they saw their kid."

Tam's voice softens. "That's…thoughtful of you to say."

I imagine she wanted to add the word "surprisingly" but held back.

"Theo Pappas's death isn't on you," she says. "Did you force him to take drugs?"

"No."

"Were you there to physically render aid but withheld it?"

"Of course not."

"Then his death isn't on you." More barking from Betts in the background and then the pattering of paws over the hardwood floor. "Maybe it's time to let this go and get back to your life. Leave the weird sex parties to others."

I assume Tam is making a joke, but I say nothing.

"And, uh, Liza? Maybe you might…" She clears her throat. "Maybe you might want to talk all this out with your psychiatrist. Explore why you feel the need to…uh…look into these kinds of things."

I'm about to bite back. Argue that I don't feel the need to look into anything. That it's not her place to tell me what to discuss with my shrink, but I restrain myself. For all I know, Tam is right, and it's not fair to unleash my anger on her. Without her, I wouldn't know any of the details I've just learned.

"Thanks for calling Officer Cho for me," I say. "That was cool of you."

We end our call on a good note, but my mind is in turmoil. Am I on to something with Theo and Fiona, or have I simply created a flurry of drama? It seems I've made nothing but wrong assumptions so far, starting with Demetri killing Fiona (his solid alibi suggests otherwise) and ending with his son being the murderer. But now that son is dead. Is he dead because he *did* kill Fiona? Or is he dead because he knows who did?

Or maybe I'm just wasting my and everybody else's time.

Maybe I'll just always be a weirdo who spends too much time in her own head.

Maybe a part of my mom is inside me, and I can never be truly sure of what's real.

Maybe I—

A crash in the hallway outside my apartment makes me jump.

I leap off my bed and hurry to the door. Is it April? Jasmine? Did Chopper come to hurt them, not satisfied with my ten grand?

I yank the door open.

If it's him, I'll grab him by the throat and—

It's not Chopper down the hallway, but it's someone almost as despicable: Pete Parsons.

He grins at me, a box in his arms and another one toppled on the floor, its contents of cords and cables strewn all over. His dark hair sits thicker than a bear's pelt, and the shadows under his eyes are as pronounced as ever.

"Hey there, Liza," he chirps as if we're best buds. "Sorry for the noise. I'm such a klutz."

He's not sorry at all. My astute psychopath radar knows that. He no doubt dropped his box of crap on purpose to get my attention.

"What're you doing?" I dig my fingertips into my palms. My nails have grown too long, and they stab my flesh like tiny blades.

Pete steps over his scattered belongings and strolls closer. "I'm moving in. We're neighbors now. How cool is that?"

My brain screams every curse word in the book.

"Just dropping a few things off tonight," he says, "but I'll be driving the U-Haul over tomorrow." He makes a *vroom vroom* noise with his stupid lips.

"If you think you're getting to me by renting a place here, you're wrong," I tell him. "I couldn't care less where you park your ass. I only care that you stay away from my mom."

He mimics Goofy's voice. "Well, uh, that's kind of hard to do when I'm the orderly."

"You know what I mean. Don't harass her or any of the other residents for your own shits and giggles."

"Oh come on, I've been a very good boy since you tattled on me to Daddy."

He means Dr. Dhar, my mom's psychiatrist and the head of Home and Hearth Healing. He continues to watch Pete closely.

I head back inside my studio. "Just leave me alone, and we'll get along fine." I shut my door, not quite a slam, but definitely not quietly.

He won't leave me alone, of course he won't. His whole reason for moving here is to mess with me. That's at least one drama I'm not inventing.

Whatever.

Pete Parsons doesn't scare me. I can handle guys like him just fine.

It's the uncertainty of my assumptions about Fiona and her death—and now Theo's too—that has me worried.

33

Inside my cubicle at noon on Thursday, I put the finishing touches on a PowerPoint presentation on the histopathologic findings of fungal infections. I'm due to give it next week.

When I finish, I grab my phone and wallet from my bag. A slice of ham pizza from the cafeteria and a chocolate mousse cup are calling my name. If only the kitchen staff didn't skimp on the whipped cream. Depending on how wilted the broccoli is, I might throw some of that in too.

Before I make it out of the residents' room, Waseem barrels in. "That mean-ass dude is here to see you again," he says.

My appetite vanishes. "Where?"

"Outside Dr. Thomas's office. Mrs. Dejean's lips are tighter than an elephant's underwear."

I curse under my breath.

"Is he your boyfriend or something?" Waseem asks.

"Hardly."

I sidestep Waseem to leave the room—I need to get to Chopper before he does or says something that could hurt me—but Waseem puts a hand on my shoulder. "Are you okay? Do you need me to come with you?"

"I'm fine, thanks. The guy is just…an old acquaintance of my brother. He looks worse than he is." *Not true.*

Waseem narrows his eyes. "Hmm, if you say so, but I wouldn't take any wooden pennies from him."

I think Waseem messed up the idiom—he does that sometimes for laughs—but I'm too focused on Chopper to be sure.

Outside the residents' room, I spot my blackmailer down the hallway. As before, he's leaning against the wall near Dr. Thomas's office as if it's his right to be there. His fingers are hooked through his belt loops, and the hard mask of his face is anything but cheerful.

I give him a rough wave to follow me. "Come on."

As we pass my program director's office suite, I avoid looking inside, but I imagine Mrs. Dejean's mind is swimming with all sorts of thoughts about who my repeat visitor is, and none of them good.

"You can't keep coming here," I seethe as I lead him down the hospital corridor to a consultation room. "What part of that can't you get through your buzz-cut head?"

Chopper pushes my shoulder from behind. Hard. "You're lucky I don't shank *you*, you stupid b—"

"Get in here." I yank him into the private room. Save for a water dispenser in one corner and a fake ficus tree in the other, a table with six chairs is its only furnishing. I close the door and stab a finger at him. "I paid you ten grand. Ten grand more than you deserve. So you and me?" I wave the finger back and forth between us. "We're finished."

"Finished?" Chopper barks an ugly laugh. "I don't know what you did to me the other night in that bar, but oh, Butch, we're far from finished."

"You drank too much and passed out. I helped you to your car. You're welcome."

"Bullshit." He plops his jeans-covered butt on the table. "You slipped me something. Trying to kill me? Is that it?"

"Trust me, if I wanted you dead, you'd be dead."

He holds up his hands and raises his voice to a falsetto. "Ooh, such a tough girl. I'm so scared." His pitch returns to normal. "You think we're over? We're just getting started, especially after your little stunt the other night. You still owe me forty grand."

"I don't have forty grand, dumbass. I'm a resident, not a heart surgeon."

Chopper cracks his knuckles. "But you will in a few years, so we're going to set up a recurring payday. A little something every month and then more when you're rolling in the dough."

"Oh, are we?" I scoff. "You're overestimating the salary of a pathologist. And how long, exactly, do you think this 'recurring payday' is going to last?"

"No expiration date, Doc. No expiration date."

I work my jaw back and forth. This is what I knew would happen. Stupid of me to think Chopper might let it go at ten grand. There's no way I'm going to pay this thug for the rest of my life. Time to unleash the rest of plan B.

I step closer to the consultation table where his butt is still parked and lean forward until our faces are a foot apart.

"Here's how this is going to play out." I flick my hand. "Everything ends here. You take the ten grand, put it into your little woodworking business, and be grateful I gave you anything at all. Then you never contact me or April again. Got it?"

"Oh no, there's Miss Scary again. I think I just crapped my pants."

He hops off the table, whacking my body with his own. He's taller than me and a whole lot stronger, but I resist stepping back.

He digs a finger into my sternum. "It ends when I say it ends."

I move away, feigning annoyance, but really, I want to be out of his threatening orbit. Guys like him smell fear like cats smell tuna. Leaning against the room's lone window, which offers a view of one of Titus McCall's scattered parking lots, I pull out my phone.

"Excuse me," Chopper says with a sarcasm I can't miss. "Am I boring you?"

I tap my photos app and open the album I've labeled *Plan B.* Not very subtle, I know. I scroll through the many images I took of Nyx doing deviant things to Chopper, things he wouldn't want anyone to see. I find a tame one. In it, Chopper is lying on his back on the padded table, wearing only his boxer briefs. He is fully erect. Nyx, dressed in her leather mask and studded bra, rubs his thighs. Chopper was too groggy to keep his eyes open or notice me taking photos, but he clearly enjoyed where the night was headed. Or at least he thought he did.

I send the photo to his phone. Thanks to his texts full of ticking-clock and knife emojis, I have his number.

He grumbles and opens the picture I sent him. "What're you—" He squints at the image, and his snarl deepens. "What's this?"

"That's you. With a boner. Isn't it obvious?"

"That ain't me. Must be a deep fake or something."

An emotion flickers on his face. Doubt? Uncertainty? Fear? I imagine he's combing through his brain, trying to remember last Sunday night.

While he's thinking, I text him another one.

Ping.

In the new one, Chopper is draped over a stool, his body too drugged to support itself but his face turned my way. His identity is clear. Nyx stands behind him, her whip on his back. Her strained expression and wildly parted red lips give the illusion of force, but in reality, she merely rested the whip on his flesh. Anyone looking at the photo, however, would think Chopper relished being whipped by a masked woman in thigh-high boots and a tight miniskirt.

He growls at me, his face pinking and his eyes bulging. "What did you do? I'll kill you, you crazy—"

I hold out my hand to keep him from jumping me. "Before you do anything you'll regret, let me show you this one. It's my favorite."

This time around, Chopper is locked in a pillory, his butt in the air, his confined head and hands close to the floor. Although he still wears his underwear—I'm not depraved enough to fully undress him; even a schizoid psychopath has her limits—Nyx grips the upper band of his boxer briefs as if she's about to yank them down. In her other hand, she holds an anal hook, a device whose function I don't wish to know. As in the previous photo, Chopper's face is positioned toward my camera. Although he'd fallen asleep by then, his peaceful expression gives the appearance of a man enjoying what's about to come.

Nothing happened, of course. Sexual assault, whether of a man, a woman, or any blend of the two, is a line I'd never cross, and I'd certainly never put Nyx in that position. She's a nice woman who's saving for a nursing degree. Who cares if her hobbies are different from mine? We only gave the *illusion* that Chopper was enjoying a little BDSM. No nudity. No actual sexual contact.

Too far? Maybe. Probably. And I don't feel good about it. That's why plan B will never be discussed with my shrink or anyone else. Like that anal hook, they'd rip me a new one, and rightfully so, but I had to have a backup. Had to have some kind of insurance to keep Chopper away from my finances, and, more importantly, away from April and Jasmine. They've suffered enough of his abuse. So, no, I'm not proud of what I've done, but it was justified to protect my inner circle, at least in my playbook.

Chopper stands before me now, wordlessly sputtering. He looks like a man who's been flung onto an electric fence.

Just as *he* did earlier, I plop myself onto the consultation-room table. After the voices of passing hospital staff fade in the hallway, I say, "Imagine what the tourists visiting your future souvenir shop would say if they saw those pictures. All those rich tourists who come to Morganville, a home you don't want to leave." I examine my fingernails. "And what about your mom? What would she think? Her baby, a perverted degenerate."

Chopper's eyes widen at this, and I think I see real fear in them.

I continue. "I'm tech savvy, you know. Ridiculously so. One hack into your shop's website, which, of course, you'll have to create to drive business, will dump all these photos onto it."

This is a bluff. I *am* tech savvy, but mostly when it comes to graphics and photo alteration. I'm no hacker. But Chopper doesn't need to know that.

"And then the photos will find their way to your mother. Her sweet boy, who finally got out of that awful prison."

Chopper shakes his head at me, his knuckles a white death grip on his phone. "I'll kill you. Cut your heart out. Chop you up and feed you to the ocean."

"If you do, these pictures will surface—even if I don't. They're backed up on a hard drive, a thumb drive, you name it. If anything happens to me, they'll land in the hands of my cop friend, along with my statement that you killed Sam Donovan last year and tried to blackmail me for it. Did you think I'd be stupid enough not to record our conversation back in the hospital gardens?"

"No…wait…I implicated you in his murder. April too. Your recording is worthless."

Has he just confirmed he set this whole thing up? That April never asked him to kill Sam Donovan on my account? Maybe. But there's no way to be sure. I can't risk any finger-pointing at April. Can't risk her getting arrested and losing her daughter all over again.

I tap my head. "Tech savvy, remember? I've edited the recording." This part is true. "Yours is the only confession. So, even if you kill me and toss me into the Atlantic, your life—and any hopes of a woodworking business—are gone. You'll be in prison until death do you part. No more homemade dinners with Momma. No more powerlifting as a free man. Imagine how much the boys inside would enjoy these pictures. Trust me, there are plenty more shots of you."

Chopper grinds his teeth. Flares his nostrils. His face reddens even more, and I can practically see his mind churning with everything I've smacked him with. Compromising photos. Cop friend. Voice recording of him confessing to shanking someone. Truth be told, he seems like a smart guy, so hopefully he's got enough intelligence to know when he's been outplayed.

I hop off the table and replace my phone in the back pocket of my chinos. "So I repeat, this ends here. You don't contact me again. You don't contact April or Jasmine again. You don't contact anyone circling my world. You go start your new business and your new life, and we go our separate ways."

His tongue probes the inside of his cheek as if he's got a herpes sore, which, maybe he does. Or maybe he's simply trying to process this whiplash change of events.

After a few long minutes, minutes I worry he might actually call my bluff, he grabs the doorknob and says, "Fine. But I'm keeping the ten grand, you crazy psychopath."

His noun choice for me isn't wrong. Maybe not even his adjective. But at least my plan B has worked.

Chopper flips me double birds and stomps out of the consultation room.

That's one problem solved.

Chopper has left the building.

34

———

I spend the rest of the workday feeling pretty good, not so much about what I had to do to Chopper at the Wicked Wonderland to achieve plan B, but because it seems to have worked.

When I see Mrs. Dejean, I apologize. "Chopper was an old acquaintance of my brother's and didn't know how to reach him," I lie. Then I truthfully add, "I promise he won't be back again."

Unfortunately, my cherry of contentment gets popped a few hours later. When I leave Brian's Gym and return home with my Chinese takeout, an envelope taped to the outside of my window catches my eye.

That can't be good. Anyone I know would text or call.

I pull out my phone and make sure I haven't missed anything. Nothing.

After tossing a piece of garlic chicken into my mouth, I head outside to the back of the apartment complex and retrieve the letter. When I return to my studio, I lean against the counter and inspect the envelope. Nothing is written on either side of it.

My fingertips dance over the seal. I picture anthrax spores flying into my nose the minute I open it. Realizing I'm being dramatic, I tear off the end of the envelope.

No white powder, but the typed words on the single sheet of paper are just as threatening. I know where you live. I know where your family lives. Back off before someone else dies. Talk to the police and someone dies.

The chicken sits like a brick in my gut. Who left this? Someone involved with Fiona? I swallow the sting of garlic and work through other possibilities.

Chopper was raging when he left me. Was it him? But why? The moment he messes with me, I'll release those photographs. He knows that. Maybe just an intimidation tactic then? Something to make me continuously look over my shoulder?

It could be Pete Parsons, but as a new tenant, he has access to the building. Why wouldn't he simply slip the note under my door? To avoid incrimination? Maybe he wanted to throw me off his scent. He obviously knows where I live. Given he's an orderly at my mom's center, he also knows where she lives. Probably my brother too. Ned's address would be in my mom's contact information.

But the note also says, Back off before someone else dies. Who in my orbit with Pete died? No one. Plus, why would he mention the police? No, it doesn't make sense. Pete Parsons *will* try to mess with me, of that I've no doubt, but this isn't him.

Which can only mean one thing. Someone, likely the person who killed Fiona, knows I've talked to the police. They know I'm getting close. Close to what? The fact that Fiona's death wasn't accidental? The knowledge that Fiona led a double life—sexually, anyway? The trail of counterfeit drugs?

Two people related to Fiona have died, her being one of them. The other is Theo Pappas. Whoever left the note is likely referencing one or both of those deaths. That would imply he—or she—knows I outed Theo. As I suspected earlier, that means I might have played a role in his death.

I place the ominous note on the counter and smooth the crinkled edges my tight grip created. If I don't back off, this person is threatening to kill me, my family, or both. Could be a bluff. Probably is a bluff. But am I willing to risk that?

My mind flashes to all those dead bodies our autopsy tables have seen of late. People I've cut open. Young people. Teenagers. Sons. Daughters. Parents. Overdosed on tainted drugs. Some maybe never did any kind of drug before in their life. Just made the tragic mistake of popping a friend's pill into their mouth at a party. A pill that if tainted with a non-opioid couldn't be reversed with naloxone. If Fiona's and Theo's deaths are tied to the sale of these drugs and I let it go, then more people will die. Their deaths would be on me too. If I can do something to stop it, shouldn't I? Isn't that the epitome of being a helper?

But what can I do? If the threatening letter isn't a bluff, am I willing to put my family in danger by going to the police? And what would be the outcome? Someone who kills people to keep them quiet is someone who would cover their tracks: wear gloves to avoid fingerprints on a letter, dodge security cameras, wear a disguise. The cops would never find the person behind the note. Probably wouldn't even check. As Tam said, they aren't exactly playing board games and singing camp songs. They're busy, and I have nothing concrete to offer them. Pictures of a blurry Theo through a window with a bag of what looks like candy isn't enough.

If I go to the police and put my family at risk, then I better be guaranteed something will come of it. Like getting tainted drugs off the street. Like future lives saved. Like getting justice for Fiona's death. Theo's, too, if he was murdered. To do that, I need to find who's selling the pills. It might be the same person who silenced Fiona and Theo.

How to get that proof is the question.

By now my Chinese takeout is cold and my mind painfully conflicted. I need my father to help me. His absence weights me like a stone.

I'll have to rely on Dr. Lightfoot. My appointment with him is tomorrow. I won't mention specifics, won't get too detailed, but his normal cerebral circuitry will help guide my aberrant wiring toward the soundest decision.

I rise and put my cold food in the fridge.

I'm no longer hungry.

35

———

R ight before I pull out of the hospital parking lot for my psychiatry appointment in Boston, my phone pings in the cup holder. A text from Megan. Given Dr. Lightfoot said the people in my life might feel undervalued if I ignore their messages, I've been trying to do better with answering. My brain maturation at play.

Join us for drinks at O'Dell's when you're back from Boston? Megan asks.

Can't, I respond, not only because I don't want to but because I don't want to tell her what I might be doing after my appointment: returning to the condo under renovation to find proof Theo was involved in something that led to Fiona's death. The police might be restrained by rules and regulations for home searches, but I'm not.

First, though, I need to run it by Dr. Lightfoot. My head is too jumbled and my thoughts too confused to skip his insights. Been there, done that, and the consequences almost killed me. The new me is trying to learn better ways to navigate life. I won't share the exact details with him, just enough hypotheticals to get his advice.

Why not? Megan texts. It's Friday night.

Have something on my schedule. Sorry. About to drive now. I withdraw a learned response from my platitude bank and add, Have a nice weekend.

If Megan texts anything else, I'll have to ignore it. Dr. Lightfoot never told me *how* many messages I have to answer.

After more than an hour of painful rush-hour traffic, I'm seated in my shrink's comfortable office. His hair boasts a recent trim, and a blazer tops his tieless shirt. Two mugs of tea rest on wicker coasters on the coffee table between our deep chairs. As I sink into the faux-leather fabric, we begin our opening banter, which, with a person like me, is probably about as much fun as conversing with a turnip. After a few minutes, I dive into what I came to discuss before I can change my mind.

"Can I present a hypothetical to you?" I ask.

"Of course."

"Well, I guess it's more of a metaphor." I pull up the words I rehearsed in the car. "Let's say you're worried some dogs inside a house are being hurt, or that they might be in the future. You report it, but because there's no proof, nothing can be done."

My hypothetical scenario sounds weak and unimaginative, even to my ears (I could use Waseem's screenwriting skills), but there's no backing out now. Dr. Lightfoot frowns but, ever the professional, doesn't interrupt. He simply indicates with a slight nod that I continue.

After a sip of my tea, which is really good because Dr. Lightfoot buys the best stuff, I do. "So now, with you being the only person who thinks the dogs might be hurt, isn't it your moral obligation to check on them yourself? Even if technically you're not supposed to?"

Dr. Lightfoot's frown deepens. "Liza, what's going on here?" When I don't answer, he says, "Are you in trouble?"

"No, not at all." It's true. I haven't done anything yet.

He eases back in his chair but still holds a stiff posture. "How about we leave the metaphor for a bit, and you tell me what's really on your mind?"

"I don't want to do that."

"Then I don't know how to guide you." Dr. Lightfoot grabs his mug. "Look, I'm your psychiatrist, and there are professional boundaries inherent in that relationship, but we've known each other for a long time, right?"

I nod.

"And although I'd never try to replace your father or step into his shoes—how could I?—I can't help but feel some parental duty along with my professional duty." He swallows some tea. "I probably shouldn't admit that, but it's true. I can't deny worrying about you. So if you're in trouble or danger, I need to know."

"I'm in neither. Honest. I just have a feeling about something, but the people who could help me need more proof."

"Are we talking about the police?"

I don't answer.

Dr. Lightfoot sighs. "Okay, fine. We'll play the vague game. But before I can offer any opinion, I need you to answer a few questions."

"Shoot."

"Are you going to hurt yourself?"

"Purposely? Of course not."

"Are you planning to hurt someone else?"

I snort. "No, the opposite. I want to help—" I almost say *help prevent more overdoses* but revert back to my pathetic metaphor. "I want to help prevent any dogs from getting hurt."

"Because if you're planning to hurt yourself or someone else, I have to report it."

Dr. Lightfoot sounds sterner than I've ever heard him, which is probably inappropriate for a psychiatrist, but from my father, I've learned that tone comes from a place of concern.

"I promise you, neither of those things is on my agenda," I say.

"Okay, good, that's good." He lowers his mug to the coffee table. "Question number three: Could what you want to do get you arrested?"

I consider this. I don't want to lie to my shrink. I rarely do, because what would be the point? Without his help, especially since my father died, I wouldn't be where I am today. Omission is more my style with him, so I need a moment to formulate my response. I shake my head. "No, that's unlikely. Especially if no one catches me…checking on the dogs."

Dr. Lightfoot rubs his eyelids. "You're not making this easy for me."

"I'm sorry. I don't mean to be irritating."

"You're not irritating me. You're just scaring me."

"You don't need to be scared. Really. I haven't expressed myself well. Big surprise there, right?" I'm going for a laugh, but he doesn't bite, so I carry on. "What I'm looking for is your opinion on whether we have a moral obligation to protect others from harm if we can foresee it. From everything you and my dad have taught me, it seems we do."

"Why do I feel like you've just boxed me in? Yes, when you put it like that, I believe we do." He holds up a finger. "But not if our life is at stake."

"Really?" I say. "What if we could save a hundred children from dying by landing on the grenade ourselves?"

"I…uh…" Dr. Lightfoot smooths his dark jeans. "You're really…"

"Making you crave a Friday-night drink?"

This time my psychiatrist does laugh—a hearty one at that—and I'm happy I've lightened his mood. I don't enjoy being the source of his stress.

He stares out the window, the sun low on the horizon now. After a beat, his gaze returns to me. "Just promise me this. If you feel the need to save the world, could you bring someone with you? Just to be safe?"

Knowing he won't let me leave his office until I do, I give him what he wants.

"I will," I say. "I promise."

36

———

With my car idling outside a Panera Bread not far from Dr. Lightfoot's office, I tap my fingers against the steering wheel. Scents of a hastily eaten chicken noodle bread bowl linger in the air.

The last thing I want to do is break a promise to Dr. Lightfoot, but who, exactly, am I supposed to call to help me do something that borders on illegal?

"Borders" on illegal? I hear my father say.

Okay, breaking into someone's place is flat-out illegal, but I'm not going to steal anything. I just want to look around. Likely a fool's errand, but maybe I'll get lucky and find something Theo left behind. Something that might convince the police to reconsider Fiona's death as something other than a tragic accident. Maybe Theo's too. It'll take ten minutes. Fifteen at the most. In, out, bada bing, bada boom.

My mind flashes on the last time I broke into someone's house. Didn't go so well. But I survived, and everything turned out for the best. I caught a killer. If I can do that again, shouldn't I?

But how to keep my promise to Dr. Lightfoot? I can't ask any of my colleagues to go with me. Too risky for them and unfair of me to put them in that position. Same goes for Shawna and Tam, not to mention Tam is a cop and would try to stop me.

My brother? Wouldn't take him long to get here from Providence, but his band is on a New England tour until mid-October. He could be anywhere.

Nyx?

No way. Our business is concluded. She shouldn't have to cross another line for me just because she's eager for cash.

My neighbor April?

God no. She needs to stay far away from anything involving the police. She and her daughter are the whole reason I did what I did with Chopper.

But that's my full circle. No one else to ask other than my mom, and I'm not about to bring along a schizophrenic woman who lives in a mental-health facility.

Another option flits into my brain. It's not a pleasant one. In fact, it's a despicable one. But at least the man has no problem breaking the law.

Fuckity fuck fuck.

I pull out of the Panera Bread parking lot and drive to the nearest ATM.

"You must have a death wish to contact me again," Chopper says.

"You're here, aren't you?" I shoot back.

My partner in crime—literally—stands rigid against his Subaru on the narrow street near Fiona's condo building. My Civic is parked two cars away. Despite the dark night, its bold blue paint shines like a beacon under the streetlight.

Chopper's expression is that of a bull who's been poked one too many times. "Get rid of those pictures and maybe I'll consider helping you."

"I won't do that. If you don't want the cash I'm offering, then leave."

It's almost 10:00 p.m., much later than I'd like, but I had to wait for Chopper to drive to Boston from Morganville. I doubt he'll hurt me, not with those BDSM pictures of him saved on a thumb drive, along with an audio recording of him confessing to the murder of Sam Donovan, but I distance myself from him nonetheless. My work loafers aren't the best for running, but I'd manage.

Chopper remains silent, fisting and unfisting his hands.

"Do you want the thousand bucks or not?" I ask him.

My paycheck was deposited today. Good thing, too, because after paying Chopper the ten grand from my savings account and the other three for Nyx, I'm tapped out. Dipping into my investment accounts is not going to happen.

Chopper the bull stares off across the street. "I should kill you right now."

"You could, but we've already had that conversation. Compromising pictures, audio, cop friend—remember? Even if you kill me, the photos and recording will surface. It's time to move on. You going to help me or not?"

His gaze burns back to me. "And all I gotta do is stand in the alley and whistle up to you if somebody comes?"

"That's all. The easiest grand you've ever made. Five hundred before I go up. Five hundred when I come down."

"Seven up front. Three after."

Whatever. Let him feel like he's in charge. "Deal," I say.

We wait for a car to pass and then cross over toward the alleyway that houses our destination: the fire escape outside the windows on Fiona's side of the building. A backpack hangs over my shoulder. It contains two flashlights, a small crowbar, and a Swiss Army knife. A bag of cashews too. I make Chopper walk ahead of me. There's no trust here.

The alley dumpsters are especially pungent tonight. Scrunching my nose, I check to make sure we're alone. Once my foot is on the first rung of the fire escape, I pull ten one-hundred-dollar bills from my pocket, peel off seven, and hand them to Chopper. Hopefully he won't jump me for the last three and take off.

He doesn't. Out of honor? Doubtful. More likely out of fear of the thumb drive that's in an envelope labeled with Tam's name inside my lockbox. Just as Shawna has a spare key to my apartment, she has one to the lockbox in my closet. Social Security card, passport, birth certificate. Those types of things. Save for Dr. Lightfoot, there's no one I trust more, not even my own brother. Ned would lose the key within days.

Chopper stuffs the seven Benjamins into his pocket. "Just hurry up."

Having every intention of doing that, I scramble up the fire escape while gripping the handrails firmly. A tumble onto the concrete or into the reeking dumpster is not part of the plan.

Once I get to the top unit that Theo was holed up in, I peer through the window. With the lights off, it's difficult to see anything. Mostly just shapes and shadows of the debris inside.

Below me, a streetlight from the main road illuminates Chopper at the base of the fire escape. Talk about a poor choice to have watching my six.

It'll be quick, I tell myself.

Hoping to climb through the window as easily as Theo did, assuming he's the one who tampered with the lock, I'm soon disappointed. Someone, probably the condo owner, has wedged a wooden bar across the interior frame, similar to how Theo did the day I spied on him. The window can't be raised.

Perched on the metal platform of the fire escape, I remove my backpack and withdraw the small crowbar. Maybe I can break the seal along the side of the window and push the entire lower pane in. Earlier, I decided against wearing gloves. It would only make the job more difficult, and there's really no point. The place is under renovation and is full of dust and debris. Plus, if I find something important, I may need to use it. Denying I broke in would be pointless.

After another glance down to confirm Chopper still mans his lookout post, I wedge the crowbar into the side of the lower frame. It takes some muscle at first but then gives way easily. Gingerly, I push the window in, but despite my gentle maneuvering, the glass shatters against something hard. The noise rips through the quiet night.

I freeze, my heart pounding. Below me, Chopper swears.

"This isn't what I signed up for," he says in a harsh growl, his voice carrying up from the empty alleyway.

"This is exactly what you signed up for," I hiss back, praying no one is listening.

I hoist my backpack inside and climb in behind it. Then I lean out the window and call down as quietly as I can to Chopper while still being heard. "I'll be quick."

"I'm not going back to jail for you."

"I'll give you an extra two hundred."

He growls again but stays put at his watch near the dumpster. A second later, he flicks a lighter, and a cigarette flares up in his hand.

Leaving the window, I crouch inside the dark room. I replace the crowbar in the backpack and remove one of the flashlights. With its beam, I search for a camera near the ceiling. Seeing none, I sweep the light over the chaotic bedroom. As before, wood planks lie in a haphazard fashion. The same worktable is off to the side, but just as Tam told me, the foam mattress Theo was using is gone. His duffel bag and clothes too. He probably gathered everything in a flurry and ran off.

I'm about to move deeper into the condo toward the hallway when a male voice in the alley down below bellows, "Hey, what're you doing there?"

Crap.

I hurry back to the window and look down. A man toting a garbage bag approaches Chopper. In the streetlight, I recognize his beefy build. He's the guy I saw leaving the building the day we found Fiona dead. Unlike the other vultures gathered on the sidewalk, waiting for the body to be wheeled away, he'd shown little interest in the commotion. I also rode the elevator with him when I went back later to pack up Fiona's things but got clobbered by a jewelry box instead.

"Just having a smoke," Chopper says.

"You live here?" the guy asks.

"No. I'm waiting on a friend who does."

"Oh yeah, who?" No warmth in the guy's voice. Just a challenge. "Because I live here, and I've never seen you around."

My mind races for what I should do. Stay put? Go out the front door?

Chopper drops his cigarette and stomps on it. He pulls out his phone. "Never mind. Looks like he's not coming. See you around, buddy." He leaves his post and heads toward the street.

"I'm not your buddy," the beefy guy calls out.

After the man dumps his trash bag into the dumpster, he looks up.

I jerk my body back inside the window and pray he didn't spot me. When I hear nothing but footsteps walking toward the front of the building, I exhale in relief. Why did he hand deliver his trash to the dumpster, anyway? Doesn't the building have a chute? Whatever the reason, it sucks for me.

Once his footsteps disappear, I peek out again. Chopper doesn't return. Guess the promise of more cash wasn't worth the risk of a call to the police. Can't say I blame him.

But so much for my helper.

Sorry, Dr. Lightfoot. I tried.

37

Once I confirm Chopper isn't going to return and serve as my alley lookout, I pull away from the window and sling my backpack over my shoulders. In case I need to make a quick exit, either down the fire escape or through the front door, it's best to keep it with me.

Returning my attention to the disaster zone that is the bedroom in front of me, I sweep my flashlight around. From what I can tell, part of the far wall has been knocked out, maybe to enlarge the space or connect it to the bathroom across the hallway. The flooring has been ripped out as well, and wires poke from a hole in the stippled ceiling where a light fixture once hung. An old dresser abuts one of the corners.

The fact Theo was able to squat here makes me wonder if the renovation had been put on hold, either by the contractor or the homeowner. Otherwise, wouldn't someone have spotted him? At any rate, searching the disarray seems impossible. Makes me question what exactly I expect to find. Could be dangerous, too, not only because someone might catch me, but because I risk tripping over loose boards or stepping on a hidden nail.

Moving cautiously, I cross over to the hallway and then into the living room, which is every bit as chaotic as the bedroom. Another wall has been torn down, this one separating the living room from the kitchen, giving the unit an open floor plan. My flashlight makes out a fridge on the right and a central island minus its countertop. Somewhere in Boston a big slab of granite or quartz is on order.

To the left is the living room. As with the bedroom, furniture has been cleared away, floorboards ripped out, and light fixtures removed. Some wooden planks lie in orderly piles. Others sprawl at odd angles. Whether they've been removed from something or are yet to be used, I don't know. A flashlight doesn't make for the best visual inspection, but I don't dare turn on any of the work lamps. At least my flashlight doesn't find any cameras.

There seems to be no systematic, room-by-room approach to this renovation. It's as if a team came in and razed everything all at once. At least they protected the windows with cardboard slabs. Or maybe they're there to prevent Peeping Toms in the nearby buildings from noticing the place is deserted. Theo must have removed the window covering by the fire escape in order to easily climb in and out. The living room's only intact original structure seems to be the fireplace on the side wall, its surrounding tile a slate gray.

Wondering where to start, I make a slow turn. Without Chopper to watch out for me, my stomach clenches into a tight ball. At least the windows are covered, and nobody knows I'm here.

Carefully, I step over the rubble and return to the bedroom where I first spotted Theo. My foot strikes a metal object. It clatters over the floor, but by the time my flashlight beam hits the area, the object has disappeared under a pile of boards.

I hold my breath, worried someone in the unit below might have heard me. If the renovation *has* been put on hold, any noise from this condo could rouse suspicion.

When nothing follows—no running footsteps, no knock on the apartment's front door—I resume my search. The only piece of furniture left behind in the bedroom is the dresser in the corner. When I look inside it, I find nothing. Same goes for the big hole in the wall. Nothing beyond metal studs and insulation.

Damn. I was hoping Theo hid something here that proves he was squatting illegally. Something to show the police I didn't misinter-pret things. Officer Cho told Tam that neither the police nor the unit's owner found evidence of a squatter, but I know what I saw. A mattress, blankets, clothes, belongings. All signs that Theo was living here. Is it possible the homeowner never checked in while Theo was squatting? If it were my place, even with the renovation on hold, I'd pay my condo a visit now and then. Make sure no one was messing with things.

I make some mental calculations. I first spotted Theo on the fire escape on the first Saturday of the month, the day Megan and I found Fiona dead in her piano bed. When I spied on him through the window and caught him with the bag of drugs, it was just over three weeks later. That's at least how long he was living here. Seems a good chunk of time for the homeowner not to check in.

A weird thought occurs to me. What if the condo owner knew Theo was squatting in his or her place? What if they let him do so willingly but didn't tell the police because they were worried about liability?

I close my eyes and try to remember if Tam mentioned the name of the homeowner. I don't believe she did, and I didn't ask, because I didn't think it was an issue. Probably still isn't an issue, but any possibility could be important.

In the darkness, with nothing but my flashlight, I shuffle into the bathroom, my backpack hitting the doorframe. The tub has been hauled away, the vanity removed. Nothing but an empty linen closet and a toilet remain. I squat and feel around the commode for anything that might be hidden back there, trying not to gag at the notion of someone's ass sitting inches away from my face or at the texture of grossness beneath my fingers. Then I lift the tank and shine my light inside. Nothing but a rusty basin partially filled with water.

For the hundredth time, I ask myself what I'm doing.

Mindful of the debris, I trudge back down the hallway and weave my way into the kitchen. The cabinet doors have been torn out, and the empty shelves await their updated counterparts. Definitely no place to hide things on them. A peek inside the oven reveals the same.

On my way back to the living room, my phone buzzes. Megan.

Where are you? she asks.

Why?

Because I'm worried about you.

Don't be. I'm annoyed at the interruption. I need to haul my butt out of this residential mosh pit.

A quick succession of texts from Megan follows. **Drove past your apartment. Your car isn't there. Isn't at Brian's Gym either or at your mom's place.**

My irritation grows. **You stalking me now?** I stab out.

Not stalking. Concerned. Worried you're in Boston taking matters into your own hands again. A trio of dots undulates, indicating she's still typing. **Because you refuse to ask for help.**

I roll my neck, massage out the tightness. Why is she so creepily perceptive? And who says I didn't ask for help? I had Chopper here, didn't I?

Everything's good. I pause and think of what to add. **Just running errands. See you Monday.**

Then I put my phone on *Do Not Disturb* and pocket it.

Using my flashlight beam, I scan the rubble of the living room. No place to search because there's no place to hide anything. No holes in the wall like in the bedroom, and nothing but ripped-out boards on the floor.

A thump somewhere beyond the condo startles me. I freeze and hold my breath. It's probably just somebody across the hallway or below. Regardless, a voice inside me tells me to get the heck out.

Doing just that, I backstep to return to the bedroom's escape window, but when my flashlight catches the fireplace, which is untouched by the ravages of renovation, I stop.

After listening for more noise that might indicate someone is coming, I shuffle as silently as I can to the fireplace. With my flashlight, I inspect the surrounding slate tiles and then the gas firepit itself. Nothing inside it. To be thorough, I squat and push around on the floor tiles that extend two feet beyond the pit. In the middle of the grouping, one shifts.

Pulse quickening, I place my flashlight on the floor and aim the beam at the shifting tile. With both hands, I wedge my fingers into the grout on either side of the slate square. I still haven't clipped my nails, and I almost rip one off trying to pry up the tile. Pain shoots through my fingertip, and I yank my hand back. The motion dislodges the tile.

Ignoring the pain beneath my fingernail, I lift the tile and slide it over. I shine my flashlight on the floor below it, and my heart rate climbs even higher.

There, in a shallow groove, lies a gallon-size bag of pills.

Colorful round pills. Maybe even counterfeit fentanyl.

I lift the bag and examine its contents through the plastic. A score line marks the middle of the pills, and above that, a numbered milligram marking.

Last I checked, candy didn't have score lines or milligram markings.

These aren't sweets, Officer Cho.

I sink back on my haunches, processing my stroke of luck. It's the proof I need. Proof Theo was squatting here and proof he was selling drugs. No one who isn't dealing leaves this many pills lying around.

But why did he leave them *here*?

If he got spooked after I spotted him through the window, wouldn't he take the pills with him? That's a lot of money to leave behind. Maybe he worried he'd get caught with them. Figured he'd sneak back later and retrieve them when the heat died down. In the meantime, he hid them in a great spot. The one area the contractors haven't ripped up.

I stare at the pills, trying to imagine Theo acquiring such a heavy score. Fifty pills alone would net him a big payoff, but this bag promises an enormous sum. I didn't know him, but the little I saw of him, the little I learned about him from Demetri, didn't exactly scream mastermind.

So what now? I can't take the pills. That won't show proof to the police of where I found them. They could say I planted them, though why they'd think I would I don't know.

My brain scrambles for the best solution. A photo didn't convince the police before, but it was a crummy one taken through a window in front of a heavy reflection of sunshine. This time I'll snap a good one, one that doesn't mistake the pills for candy.

I return the bag to its hiding place and take several pictures from multiple angles to illustrate the tablets' round shape and rainbow colors. With the phone camera's flash, they come out perfectly. After I finish, I replace the tile and smooth it back down.

I have to go straight to the police. I'll be in trouble for breaking in, and an arrest on my record almost makes me want to forget the idea, but I can't risk the pills being moved and then sold. I can't risk one more teenager's death.

I start to weave my way out of the shambled living room. What if I make an anonymous call? Leave my name out of it? The police would still have to investigate it, wouldn't they?

Yes. That's what I'll—

The click of a key stops me dead.

A doorknob turns.

With my heart in my throat, I will my frozen feet to life and hurry as best as I can down the hallway toward the bedroom. A loose plank catches my shoe, and I fall onto my knees. I stifle a cry of pain.

The condo's front door opens.

A light flicks on.

From my fallen position, I look over my shoulder toward the door. A man in a suit and tie stands in the frame. He's got a hand in one of his pockets, as if he's ready to pull something out. The other pocket holds something long and white.

I scramble to an upright position.

"You just couldn't back off, could you?" he says.

He moves toward me.

38

Limping from the pain in my knee, I scramble through the rubble toward the bedroom's escape window. The straps of my backpack slip down my shoulders, and the weight of the small crowbar and second flashlight inside it thump against my butt. I dropped the other flashlight when I fell and am now running blind.

Just when I reach the bedroom door, the man nabs me. Pulls me back against his body and restrains my chest with his arm. Facing away from him, I'm able to free one of my own arms. I reach up and dig my fingernails viciously into his face.

He yelps and jerks his head away but doesn't release his hold. I go for his kneecap, kicking it with the heel of my shoe. My backpack squishes between his stomach and my back, and when his knee buckles, I have enough leverage to squirm away from his grip.

Once again I hurry toward the window, and once again he makes contact. This time he shoves me hard, and I fly face-first onto the floor. My cheek smacks a ripped piece of drywall, and my elbow bangs into a wooden plank.

Despite the stinging pain, I whip my body over, the backpack now pressing into my lower spine. As I scoot backward, I wriggle out of the straps. I don't need the bag or its contents. I just need to get to that window and bolt.

My attacker switches on a work lamp in the corner of the room. The glow lights up his face. I've seen him somewhere before, but in my flustered state, I can't place where. I just know his wavy blond hair looks familiar.

I rise to a stand, my knee buckling from my earlier fall. Judging by the man's limp beneath his suit pants, I did a number on his kneecap as well.

"You just couldn't back off, could you, Liza?" he repeats.

How he knows my name I have no idea.

I sidestep another pile of drywall and shuffle back to the window. He, too, keeps advancing. When I reach my escape hatch, I start to crawl out, having broken the window earlier, but a click behind me and a pressure in my back stops me cold.

"Make one more move and this knife goes into your spine."

At the word *knife*, I remember I have my own.

Yes!

My relief quickly fades. The knife is in my backpack, which I wiggled out of so I could move faster. Had I known I'd need the Swiss Army knife as a weapon instead of as an all-purpose tool, I would have kept the bag on me.

His blade pokes my lower back through my hoodie and sweater. I imagine it's what he was reaching for when he first came in.

Slowly I turn around. He pulls the knife back, but it's still dangerously close to my gut.

"How do you know my name?" I croak.

"Why are you in my condo?" His free hand waves around the room's disarray. "Can't you see it's dangerous in here?" He raises the blade higher, his double meaning loud and clear.

I study his face. How do I know him? Feverishly, I run through the places I routinely go, everything from the hospital to Brian's Gym. But this is Boston. Aside from Dr. Lightfoot, I interact with few people here.

Then it hits me. I don't know him. I saw him.

Like the beefy guy who chased Chopper away, this man was

near the building when the body-removal technicians transported Fiona's body out on the mortuary cot. I remember thinking his attractiveness put him more in Fiona's physical league than her meal-sharing neighbor, Chuck. I also remember I had to pull Megan aside so he could get through. Did she say my name? Is that how he knows it?

If that's the case, he has a good memory. Too good. The kind of memory a person who'd just committed murder and doesn't want to be found out would have.

"Did you kill Fiona?" My tone is accusatory, but my voice is shaky.

He responds by roughly grabbing my arm and dragging me to the wall with the gaping hole. At five eight, I'm tall. Strong too. But he's bigger, and he has a knife, and that makes escape tricky. When he plucks plastic zip ties from his pocket—the white objects I noticed when he first came in—I have no choice but to try.

With a hard fist, I punch him in the neck. His grip on my arm releases. I bolt toward the window, but he sticks out his leg. I trip and smack down on my face again. Something slices my cheek. Warm fluid drips toward my chin.

I scramble upright, but he slams his fist into my stomach before I can get away. I crumple in pain and wheeze to catch my breath.

He drags me back to the wall. Still struggling to breathe, I flail my arms, but my attempts at self-defense are laughable.

He shoves me down and presses his knife against my neck. My heartbeat hammers against the steel blade. Rather than slit my throat, he bashes me in the temple with his fist. The work lamp across the room bursts into a thousand stars.

Weakened and stunned, I feel rather than see him yank my arm toward one of the metal studs in the damaged wall.

Zippppp.

He's tied my left wrist to the stud.

While I fight the urge to vomit from his head blow, he shoves my body sideways on the floor.

Zipppppp.

There goes my right wrist, restrained directly below the left one on the stud. My legs bend uncomfortably on the rubble, and the binds dig into my flesh.

"How did…you…?" My voice refuses to work, silenced by the hits to my head and stomach.

"How did I know you were here?" he asks. "Ever heard of cameras?"

I shake my head, indicating I didn't see any, but the motion makes me dizzy.

"After I learned I had a squatter, I hid a couple." My attacker leans back on his haunches, the switchblade still open in his hand. "I don't like rats in my home, especially ones who snoop."

"No." I force the words out. "Wasn't me. I wasn't the one squatting here."

"You think I don't know that? For the record, things didn't end too well for the last guy who crashed here."

"You killed Theo?"

A blond wave flops over my captor's forehead. He puffs it out of his eyes but doesn't answer.

"Why? Why would you do that?"

He stabs a finger into my shoulder. "You're the one who got him killed. Got him all spooked with your poking around. He was a loose end, and loose ends are…risky."

The man tugs at his tie as if it's choking him. When he does, his suit jacket shifts, and a name badge attached to his shirt pocket pops into view. Thanks to the work light he turned on, I can make out the name: Brad Marshall.

Where do I know that name from?

And if Theo was simply a squatter, why did he kill him?

Nothing makes sense, my head too foggy. I must stare at his name badge for too long because he yanks it off and stuffs it in his pocket.

He stands and flexes his knee a few times, as if assessing the damage my backward kick caused. While I study him, it hits me.

I know who he is.

39

Brad Marshall is Demetri's partner at the pain clinic. He's also the doctor who volunteers at the Hands of Hope addiction center, just like Fiona did. I recall my conversation with the stringy guy outside the facility, the one who accepted my cash for information. He mentioned that "Dr. Brad" volunteered on Friday nights. At the time, I was more interested in Demetri, so I paid little attention to that piece of info.

It's possible the doctor came directly here from the center. It's Friday night, and he's still dressed for the job. When his phone alerted him that his hidden camera picked up activity, he zipped on over with his pocket full of zip ties.

"You work with Demetri Pappas," I say.

He halts his knee flexing. The shock on his face is obvious (text-book emotion card), and that surprise tells me I've guessed correctly. Everything starts coming together in my mind, especially the fact that as a pain doctor, Brad would know all about fentanyl.

I shift on the floor, moving closer to the wall stud so I can bend my arms. My face is still bleeding from my fall.

"You knew Fiona Carlson," I say. "She lived in your building. Was it you who got her interested in helping out at the center?"

He doesn't answer, just stares at me, the knife in his hands.

I continue piecing it together. "That's why she was researching counterfeit pills. While she was volunteering at Hands of Hope, she heard about all the young people overdosing on fentanyl, or what they thought was pure fentanyl. She started looking into it." I pause, my understanding deepening. "Somehow, I don't know how, she realized *you* were the one selling it."

"Shut up," Brad orders.

"Who better to sell fentanyl than a pain doctor who volunteers at an addiction center? Nice protective cover. No one would suspect it. Did you know the pills are tainted with other drugs, some with a veterinary tranquilizer that doesn't respond to naloxone? That's why so many people are dying."

"Shut up." Louder this time.

I know I'm right. I can read it on his psychopathic face, just like I can read Pete Parsons and just like I can read Chopper, most of the time anyway. We're able to sniff each other out like dogs. Maybe Brad doesn't know the pills are tainted, but I'd bet my next five paychecks that he's the guy selling them. Or getting his minions to do it. Minions like Theo.

It seems obvious now. How did I get it so wrong? First suspecting Demetri and then Theo. If what Brad says is true, that he killed Theo because Theo got spooked and was a liability who might sing, then I *am* responsible for Theo's murder. If I hadn't been tailing him, Brad might never have found out I was looking into Fiona's death.

My wrong assumptions got Theo killed. Not even out of his twenties yet, and now he's dead. Brad made it look like an accidental overdose, but I was the trigger all the same.

"Did Theo come to you or did you recruit him?" I ask, my wrists raw from the zip ties but my guilt rawer. "You knew Demetri's kid was a drug seeker. Instead of helping him through his addiction like a doctor should, you involved him in your drug dealing. As a pain specialist, you must have all sorts of clients willing to pay for an extra prescription on the side."

Brad says nothing, just keeps squatting in front of me while I talk, his jaw hard.

"Your side gig made you rich. This condo is probably only one of many. Theo learned you were renovating it and jumped at the chance to squat. Bonus? He could rob other people's places from that fire escape."

A new thought comes to me. What if Theo *stole* that bag of drugs from Brad? Decided to make a little extra cash on his own. If that's the case, maybe I'm not the sole reason for his death. It's a thought that brings little comfort. The skateboarder is dead either way.

When I fall silent, Brad stands from his crouched stance, leaving me tied up and sitting on the floor. He neither confirms nor denies anything I've said, which makes me think I'm close to the truth. He rubs his neck and paces a patch of uncluttered floor in the room's rubble. It seems I've thrown him off his game.

It dawns on me that Brad is probably the one who stuck the warning note on my window yesterday. I used my real name at the addiction center, and he could have found out I was asking around. Wouldn't be hard to track down my address. Stupid of me to have given my name, but at the time I wasn't expecting a killer to be one of their volunteers. I'd just wanted to learn more about Fiona's work there.

Brad stops pacing and stares at me for a long moment. The claw marks I left on his face during our struggle are now fat crimson streaks.

Maybe he'll let me go. Maybe I've got him and everything I've accused him of wrong. Simply more malignant assumptions on my part.

Just as I start to convince myself of this, he startles me by unleashing a torrent of expletives. He fishes what looks like a cheap burner phone out of his suit jacket and calls someone.

"I've got a problem," he says into the phone while eyeing me. "Need you to come solve it. The condo. No overdose this time. Too suspicious." A pause. "Keep it clean and quiet and dump her back in Morganville. Find her car too." Another pause, then, "Fine, double the fee. Whatever. Just get over here."

He hangs up. We study each other, me still turned sideways and secured to the wall stud, him still with a knife in his hand. I pull at my wrists, but there's not a morsel of laxity.

My breathing shallows, and I realize two things. One, I'm going to die. Two, it won't be at his hands. He's the kind of guy who hires other people to take out the trash.

Which means I only have one option available to me while we wait. It's a residential building, after all.

I scream for help.

40

I don't remember the last time I screamed. The act isn't natural for me, and even as I holler for help and kick at the ripped-up floor, it doesn't sound like me at all. But this man plans to have me killed, and given I'm zip-tied to a metal stud, my only hope is that someone inside the building will hear me and call the police.

So I scream, no matter how foreign it sounds to my own ears.

It doesn't last long. Brad Marshall, the drug-dealing pain doctor, hisses at me to shut up. When I don't comply, he grabs a roll of duct tape off a corner workbench, rips off a piece, and smashes it over my mouth. I bite at it with my teeth, hoping to catch his fingers. Blood from my cheek wound catches on the tape, and the taste of copper fills my mouth. Soon my screams are nothing but a muffled gag.

He stands up, cursing again. Whatever hold his hair gel had on those blond waves is long gone. They flop over his forehead like strings of a mop.

"These floors are concrete. You think anyone's going to hear you?" His tone is venomous. "Trust me, if someone does, I'll—"

A knock on the door cuts him off. Hope ignites in me. I scream from behind the duct tape, but it comes out a harsh and muffled moan that burns my throat.

Brad silences me by sticking his switchblade against my neck. "Scream again and I'll sever your carotid."

When the knocking continues, Brad rubs at his temple with his free hand like a rabid dog. A male voice outside the door bellows, "I know someone's in there. If you don't answer, I'm calling the police."

"I'm going to answer that door," Brad whispers forcefully into my face, spraying me with spittle, "but if you make a sound, you'll force me to kill whoever it is. You want that on your conscience too? Another death caused by your prying?"

I stare into his wild eyes, my breaths choppy, my dizziness from his earlier head blow still pronounced. He might be bluffing—it's hard to tell—but I can't risk someone's life to find out.

He presses the knife once more against my throbbing carotid in warning and then leaves the bedroom. Moments later, I hear but can't see the front door open.

"What's going on in here?" the knocker asks.

The voice is gruff and familiar, because I heard it less than an hour ago. It's the beefy guy who threw his trash in the dumpster and scared Chopper away. His unit must be next to or below this one.

"Hey, man, sorry for the noise," Brad says. I imagine him swiping his loose locks off his forehead. "Working on some renovations, as you can see."

"At night?" the visitor asks. "In a suit?"

I consider thrashing about again, creating any noise I can, but do I dare risk it? Brad has a knife, one with a good-size blade that can do good-size damage. He's also a man with a lot at stake, a man who would probably do anything to protect himself. I'm the one who was stupid, not this unsuspecting good Samaritan. He shouldn't have to pay for my ignorance with his life. Brad's minion is coming to take care of me. One more body simply means one more bundle of cash for the guy.

"Just moving stuff around." Brad sounds jovial enough. "Gotta clear things away. Again, sorry if I disturbed you. I haven't owned the place long. Don't know all the rules yet."

The guy I saw outside in the alleyway was big. Could he take Brad, even if Brad pulls his knife? Maybe, but what if it isn't the beefy guy? What if I'm wrong about the voice? What if it belongs to some skinny old guy who doesn't stand a chance? My drawing attention could get him killed.

My mouth dries to desert levels. *Dad, what should I do?*

"Yeah, well," the knocker says, "I haven't heard anyone working here for a while."

Brad laughs. "Tell me about it. Trying to get contractors to finish anything is the bane of human existence."

I decide to risk it. Otherwise I'm dead for sure. But just as I start kicking at a piece of wood to make noise, I hear another laugh, this time from the good Samaritan.

"Don't I know it," he says. Suspicion seems to have left his voice. "Have a good one."

Brad closes the door. I've lost my window.

My captor storms back into the bedroom, pieces of wood clunking together as he steps through the disarray. He grabs the duct tape and approaches me, his face a furious red. Without saying a word, he forces my legs out in front of me and pushes them flat. I'm positioned sideways against the wall—it's more comfortable that way—and he uses this to his advantage. After binding my ankles together with duct tape, he raises my feet and tethers my taped ankles to the same metal wall stud that restrains my wrists. Seated only on my butt now, I'm left in a deranged yoga boat pose, my hands and feet useless. My unreachable phone in my back pocket pushes into my glute.

Standing back to study his work, Brad wipes sweat from his forehead. "Let's see you try to stomp around now."

Though he speaks with bravado, I don't miss his shaking hands or the way he keeps pushing his hair back. He might be a high-class drug dealer, but it seems tying women up and threatening them isn't in his comfort zone. He's a doctor who pays other people to do his dirty work.

His phone chirps. "You here?" he asks the caller. "Good. Let me leave first. I don't need to see this."

Brad returns his phone to his suit pocket and shakes his head at me. From my hog-tied position, I have to look over my right shoulder to see him.

"It didn't have to come to this," he says. "Good God."

A few seconds later, he's gone.

I swallow. Even though the duct tape covers only my mouth, I struggle to breathe. My heart pummels my ribs, and in my forced V-sit, movement is awkward and futile. My core already feels the strain.

What have I done? Why am I such a messed-up, clueless excuse for a human being?

My brother used to tell me I was self-absorbed, blind to everyone else's needs. "Other people have lives too, you know," he'd say. "Lives full of problems and emotions and chaos. That's normal, Liza. But you? You're not normal."

More recently he's seen me in a new light. Says he now understands that my brain works differently, that my means of helping people are different from his. But a lifetime of his earlier, harsher words remains, buried deep within my cerebral pathways, and two things can be true at once: I can be blind to others' needs, and I can also be a helper.

Right now I'm the one in need of a helper. I assumed I could do this on my own. Get in, get out, no problem. I didn't even believe I needed Chopper. He was only there to keep my promise to Dr. Lightfoot. I've always been an island, and islands don't need help to stay afloat.

But now? Tied to a wall stud and about to be murdered? I should have listened to Megan. I should have involved her—or someone—in what I was doing.

I should have asked for help.

41

Despite my hopeless thoughts, I try to free myself. My killer will be here any moment.

I strain to pull my wrists from the zip ties, but the plastic tears into my flesh. I shift my butt back and forth, desperate to loosen the tape around my ankles, but it's impossible. Brad taped my feet so tightly to the stud and cinched my wrists so firmly against it that I remain in my V-shaped boat pose, muscles cramping and mouth muzzled.

Finally, I let my exhausted body fall lax. I am not going to survive this. Brad is gone. His problem-solver is coming, and when he gets here, I'll be an easy obstacle to clear. Defending myself isn't an option, not when I'm tethered like a pig for roasting.

My backpack is a few feet away, abandoned after I wriggled out of it in order to bolt. Even if I could get to my Swiss Army knife—which I can't—it would be no match for whatever Brad's problem-solver has in mind. *Keep it clean and quiet,* Brad told him on the phone.

I lean my head against the shredded drywall. *I'm sorry, Dad.*

My father did his best with me. Dr. Lightfoot too. But some things aren't fixable.

I am one of those things.

The world won't miss me, but I'll miss parts of it. My work. My computer. Shawna and Tam. Dr. Lightfoot. Brian's Gym. My brother. April and Jasmine and their cookies. Maybe even my colleagues. But mostly I'll miss my mom. Who will look after her now? Who will visit her three times a week? Take her out for a Sunday pass when she's having a good day? Listen to her when she's Meryl Streep? Fear for her when she's Anna, the Holocaust victim? Ned will try, but he doesn't live in Morganville, and he doesn't have the stomach for it. He's told me as much.

The thought of my mother wondering whatever happened to that young woman with the short hair who always came by to see her pinches my heart more painfully than the plastic zip ties pinch my wrists. The idea of her mourning her daughter during lucid moments is even worse, and any breath I managed to find now chokes off like a flame. Maybe I'll die from asphyxia before he even—

A key unlocks the condo door.

My body freezes in its bound hold.

Brad's problem-solver is here.

"Yes, yes, I just got inside," he says, presumably into his phone. "I'll take care of her, don't worry."

I don't hear the door close all the way behind him, but even if he is just standing there, finishing his conversation, he'll be in the bedroom soon.

The duct tape over my mouth is suffocating. I force myself to remain calm and deliver a pep talk in my mind: *Your nose is open. There's plenty of air. Relax. You need to be sharp.*

"Clean and quiet, just like you—"

I hear a strangled choke. The problem-solver's voice cuts off. Several seconds of zapping follow, and from inside the bedroom I have no freaking clue what's going on.

Then a thud, like someone falling.

Footsteps tap over the flooring. Wooden planks bonk against each other. I crane my neck to look over my shoulder at the open bedroom door. With my body facing the window, this isn't an easy task, and my neck muscles scream in protest.

But someone is here. Someone who isn't Brad or the problem-solver.

The footsteps are soft, cautious even, and I imagine the person tentatively walking through the debris, heading toward the source of the light, which is the work lamp in the bedroom that imprisons me.

Is it the beefy guy again? Maybe he called the police. Wouldn't they announce themselves?

The footsteps keep advancing, and my forced calm shatters. My neck nearly breaks as I continue to eye the door.

A woman's voice says my name. I must be hallucinating, like my mom when the king speaks to her.

"Liza?" the voice repeats softly. "Are you here?"

Megan?

Snapping into action, I holler as loudly as I can against my duct-tape muzzle. I scrape my butt back and forth over the flooring, anything to create as much noise as possible.

Megan's footsteps quicken, and within seconds she hurries into the bedroom.

"Oh my God, Liza!"

She rushes toward me, stumbling over a wooden plank. Never have I been so grateful to see the annoyingly social woman. I owe her five nights out and three trips to Nordstrom. At least.

She drops down beside me. "It's okay. You're safe now." She peels the duct tape off my mouth.

I nod. I want to ask how she knew I was here, but speech doesn't come. Death was too close. My mind needs a minute to catch up.

She studies my bindings, her eyes wide and darting back and forth. "I need something to cut these with."

She looks over her shoulder, her breaths rapid. I notice something in her hand. Fiona's stun gun. The one Megan removed from Fiona's purse because it wasn't registered. Megan must have kept it in her tote bag.

Still staring back at the bedroom door, she says, "I zapped him good, right on his neck, but he'll be moving soon."

"My backpack," I croak. "Swiss Army knife. Front compartment."

In her cream-colored pants, she scoots across the dirty floor and grabs the bag, all the while watching the door. I do, too, despite the painful torque in my neck. My hired killer could enter any second.

Megan pulls out the small knife, sets the stun gun on the floor, and starts cutting the plastic ties around my wrists. It takes forever, and barely has she cut me free from the restraints when a rustling and scraping noise comes from the condo's entryway.

"Oh God, he's moving." Megan's tone is high pitched.

She slices away at the duct tape around my ankles. Her alarmed eyes and frantic cutting show her panic.

Footsteps thump down the short hallway. An unsteady voice calls out, "You're dead. Both of you."

Megan's eyes grow wider, and her hands cut faster. Just as a figure reaches the doorway, the duct tape gives way. My feet thud to the concrete floor, my core spasming with the sudden movement. I'm free.

Brad's problem-solver barrels into the room. A ponytail swishes behind his squarish head.

Megan gives a loud cry and shoots forward for the stun gun, but he's too quick. He kicks her crouched figure, and she stumbles back, inhaling sharply. The Swiss Army knife flies out of her hand and disappears into the rubble.

I snatch the stun gun off the floor but don't make it all the way to my feet before the killer lunges for me. I zap his abdomen, but the electric jolt barely penetrates his flannel shirt. He wrestles the gun from my hand and flings it across the room, where it cracks into the metal work lamp and smashes onto the floor. He grabs me by the neck and forces me back against the same wall I was just tethered to.

He's big. He's pissed. He's pounds of muscles stronger than me. This time my airway chokes off for real in his grip. I can't breathe. I can't think. I can only feel my face fill with blood. The guy's hair is dark red and his eyes a pale gray. He's the most sinister-looking man I've ever seen.

Megan pounds on his back, but it does nothing. She should have called the police when she first spotted me. Then again, if she had, I'd still be tied up, and we'd both be dead.

I sputter, and my glottis makes an inhuman, strangled cry. My legs are like noodles, and my fingers scrape at his thick hand to loosen it from my neck. It doesn't budge.

"This clean and quiet enough?" he says through gritted teeth, his expression that of a lion devouring a gazelle.

Megan stops pounding on his back and disappears. In my low-oxygenated state, I can't process what's happening. When I see her reappear with her giant purse, it makes no sense. Is she leaving me?

She pulls something out. Something long and thin.

It's her goddamn knitting needle.

She rushes forward, and with a keening screech and wild eyes, she lifts the man's flannel shirt from behind and stabs the aluminum needle into his back. His body jerks and stiffens. His hold on me releases, and I slump against the wall, my fingers raking at my neck, trying to force in the air.

Brad's murderous problem-solver swivels around, the knitting needle plunged deeply into his flank, so deeply it's probably stabbed right through his kidney. Before I can catch my breath, Megan yanks my arm and drags me across the room. My shoes trip over the rubble.

"Hurry," she cries. "Hurry!"

She doesn't have to tell me twice.

My feet start flying.

42

———

Megan and I race down seven flights of stairs and out of the condo building. We don't dare hole up on the fourth floor at Fiona's place, not with a killer on our heels.

When we spill into the cool night air, I suck it in like an asthmatic. If the giant with the impaled kidney is following us, I don't take time to find out. I only want escape.

"Your car is closer," Megan huffs out.

I have no idea how she knows this, but it doesn't matter. I follow her lead toward the side street that holds my Civic. Her big purse flaps against her back as she runs. My bag remains in Brad's condo.

Once we reach my car, breathless, I fumble with the key fob, and we both dive in.

"Drive," Megan orders.

"Where?" My brain struggles to focus. Two times in as many years I've come close to dying, and I can't seem to clear the shock.

"To the police."

"But we don't have—"

"Drive, Liza!"

Never has Megan barked orders like this. Not unless it involves party planning or team projects.

When I near the same police precinct I visited before, I pull into a gas station and put the car in park.

"What are you doing?" Urgency floods Megan's voice.

"Just…let me catch my breath." I mean this figuratively. My breathing is almost back to normal.

"We need to report him. Before he leaves." Megan's honey locks are wind-whipped and tangled, and her eyes carry the feverishness of a flu.

"He's already left. He's not going to stick around with a knitting needle buried in his kidney." I rub my eyes. "I need a minute to process things. I work best that way."

"What, exactly, do you need to process?" Megan asks sharply. "That you were duct-taped together like a broken doll? That you almost died?"

"Well, yes, but also, how did you know I was there? I thought I was hallucinating when I saw you."

"Not rocket science, Liza. For someone so smart you can be pretty dense."

Not the first time I've heard that, but I let Megan continue.

"I knew you were up to something. Your stupid vague texts tonight, saying you had things to do, running errands. Yeah, right. The only thing you do on a Friday night is hit the gym and mess around on your computer."

Again, not wrong.

"So I drove around Morganville—your place, the hospital, Brian's Gym, your mom's center—didn't see your car anywhere. That vibrant-blue Honda sticks out like a neon pimple."

For once I'm grateful for its distinct coloring. *Your car saved my life, Dad.* Not to mention the quick-thinking Megan.

"I knew you had your appointment tonight with Dr. Lot…Dr. Lit…"

"Dr. Lightfoot," I finish for her.

"Right. Lightfoot. I knew you had your appointment tonight, and I know you're convinced my aunt's death wasn't an accident. So I put two and two Lizas together and figured you'd go back to Aunt Fiona's place and snoop around again. Sure enough, there was your car." Megan's rapid speech still shakes with adrenaline. "Of course, I thought you'd be in my aunt's place. When you weren't, I was scared to death you went back to the top floor to spy on that guy." She slaps the dashboard. "What were you thinking going in there alone? That was ludicrous."

"I know that now."

"What did I say about asking people for help?"

"I didn't want to get you involved. Not until I knew for sure. I needed more evidence that Theo was caught up in this."

"And did you find it?" Megan's manic gaze drills into me.

"Well, maybe, but not Theo. It's—"

"I'm freaking out here, Liza." Megan squeezes her thighs with both hands and rocks back and forth in the passenger seat. "I just stabbed a guy with my knitting needle. We need to go to the police. Now!"

I hold up my hands. "Just give me a sec. I haven't told you everything yet."

"What else is there?"

"Theo. At first I thought it was him, but it wasn't. He's…he's dead."

"Oh my God, what have you gotten yourself mixed up in?"

"It's a guy named Brad Marshall. He lives in your aunt's building."

Megan wipes at her forehead, and from the lights of the gas station parking lot, I see she's perspiring. She unzips her fleece sweater. "I don't understand anything you're saying."

Forcing myself to think chronologically, I start over and tell Megan everything that's happened since I learned Theo died from an overdose.

"Remember those drugs I saw Theo holding?"

"Of course."

"I assumed he was selling them for himself, and when your aunt found out, he killed her. But it wasn't Theo. It was Dr. Brad Marshall, the man who lives in that condo. Your aunt discovered he was selling drugs to the very people he should have been helping."

"A doctor? Really? Haven't you played this card before?"

Touché.

"He's a pain specialist in Boston," I say. "A partner of Demetri's."

"The same Demetri you first thought murdered my aunt? Then, when he had an alibi, you thought his *son* murdered my aunt. Now, apparently, it's his clinic partner."

Her sarcasm is obvious, even to me.

I shift in the driver's seat. "You're right to be skeptical. I deserve it. My assumptions were wrong until now because the three men tie together. I got confused. But it's clear now. Brad Marshall knew about Demetri's deadbeat son and recruited him to sell drugs. Whether or not he knew Theo had been crashing at his condo, I don't know."

"And you have proof this Brad guy killed my aunt?"

"Absolute proof? No. But he volunteers at the same addiction center Fiona did."

At this news Megan stills her agitated fidgeting and stares at me in what I assume is surprise.

"They live in the same building," I continue. "They knew each other. He's the one who encouraged Fiona to volunteer at the center. Or, at least, he didn't deny it when I asked. Nor did he deny killing her when she found out he was selling counterfeit drugs. He—"

"So the guy wearing my knitting needle is Brad Marshall?" Megan points to my cheek. "He did that to your face?"

I rub the now-clotted cut on my cheek. "No. That was from a board or drywall or something. I fell. The guy you stabbed is Brad's hired help. Brad tied me up and then called his man. Too chicken to do it himself. Either way, I sucked at defending myself." The words taste bitter on my tongue. I'm furious with myself for not being better prepared. I rub my still-sore knee and examine my too-long fingernails. "At least I managed to carve Brad's face up."

"You think his hired help killed my aunt?"

"Yes. He does things 'clean and quiet' for Brad. Like suffocating a woman and letting her Murphy bed take the blame."

Megan winces.

"And if you hadn't shown up, I would've been the next 'clean and quiet.'"

Megan gazes out the car window and shakes her head. In a low voice, she says, "My aunt really *was* murdered. I can't believe it."

"But I have to prove it. Those rainbow pills are still hidden in Brad's condo under a fireplace tile—unless he knew Theo stashed them there. If that's the case, they're long gone, and the only proof I have they existed are the photos I took." I shrug. "Hopefully the police will believe me."

"They'll know you broke in if you show them."

"It is what it is. I'm going to have to accept the punishment. Better than more people dying from bad pills."

Megan rests her hand on my forearm. I don't much like it, but I know better than to shake it off.

"You're a good egg, Liza." After a pause, she reverts back to business. "What about the guy I stabbed? That's proof. We tell the police he was going to kill you, so we stabbed him in self-defense. With an injury like that, he'll show up in an ER. They'll find him and connect him to Brad Marshall. Then they'll take another look at my aunt's death. Brad and his man will go down for murder. How much legal trouble will you really be in? Your actions will have stopped a murderer or two."

"What if it's not enough?" I say. "I've been down this path before. Confident I had enough proof only to find out I didn't. Then Brad gets away with murder. I can't prove he's the one who tied me up and left me to be killed. It'll be my word against his. Even if his problem-solver talks, Brad will hire a great lawyer and deny all charges."

I lean back against the headrest, exhaustion and failure wilting me. What a jumbled mess. I was so sure I could pull this off.

We sit in the front seat of my car, watching people exit the gas station, their arms loaded with soda and chips. A guy getting out of the vehicle next to us blows Megan a kiss, but she ignores him. Maybe she, too, has accepted defeat.

Without warning, she shoots up in her seat. I startle so hard I bang my sore knee against the steering wheel.

She pivots her body toward me. "Your hands, Liza." She seizes them. "Your hands."

I frown. What is she talking about?

She pulls my hands toward her and inspects them over the center console.

"Um…Megan? What—"

"You told me you clawed up Brad Marshall's face, right?"

"Yeah. So what? He'll just deny it. He'll say—"

I cut myself off. Megan is grinning like a chimp who's just eaten its owner. I now understand where she's headed. Leave it to the budding forensic pathologist to figure it out before me.

"Your fingernails," she says. "They're teeming with Brad's DNA."

43

———

With a pint in my hand and a basket of pretzel bites in front of me, I sit at a high-top table at O'Dell's and listen to Megan tell my transfixed colleagues about our recent nightmare. Considering she saved my life, I owe her a Saturday night out. John, Waseem, and Jen are seated across from us.

Thanks to a lawyer at my late father's firm, my breaking and entering at Brad Marshall's condo was reduced to a trespassing charge. In Massachusetts, that means a hundred-dollar fine or up to thirty days in jail. I got the fine. Being bound, gagged, and nearly killed made for a few nights of poor sleep, but eight days separate me from the incident, and things are smoothing out. The perks of being a robot.

John shakes his head. "You were ballsy going in that place alone."

"Most would say brainless," I reply.

"This pain specialist killed your aunt?" Waseem asks Megan.

She sips a pink lady cocktail. "No. His hired help did. Or, as Liza and I call him, Knitting Needle Man."

I never once called him that, but if Megan wants it to be a bonding experience between us, so be it.

"The police went back to my aunt's place and swept for finger-prints and DNA. Glad I didn't have time yet to clear out the furniture or do a deep clean. They didn't find any prints on the piano bed. The guy probably wore gloves. But they found a dark red hair in it. Forensics matched it microscopically to Knitting Needle Man. The DNA isn't back yet."

"The root was still attached?" Jen's fingers drum against her wineglass.

Megan nods. "They think my aunt probably struggled with him. Pulled one of his hairs out in the process."

"So the bed was open when he came in?" Waseem asks.

"Yes. She was in her pajamas when she died. Probably getting ready for bed. That's maybe why her phone was still in her purse. She hadn't grabbed it yet. But then he came and..." Megan's words trail off, maybe too painful to say.

Jen reaches across the table and squeezes Megan's hand. "If this is too hard, we can talk about something else." She throws a glance my way.

Jen's look probably means I'm supposed to take over, but Megan resumes talking. Good. I want to sip my beer, chew my doughy pretzels, and remain on my island. Periodically I glance up at a ball game on the TV, but my attention remains on my colleagues.

"There was no sign of a break-in at my aunt's condo, so the police think Brad was the one who knocked on her door. She was probably surprised to see him at that hour, but since she knew him, she let him in. Reluctantly, I'm guessing. Especially if she'd learned he was the source of the lethal drugs." Megan jerks a thumb my way. "That was Liza's theory. Looks like she was right."

I shrug and eat another pretzel.

"Once Aunt Fiona opened the door for Brad, Knitting Needle Man slipped in and...killed her so she wouldn't report Brad to the police. Suffocated her and sealed her up in her old Murphy bed. Probably thought he was pretty clever to come up with it." Megan tugs at her silver earring. "Guess he was. Everyone assumed it was an accident."

"Everyone except Liza," John says.

I glance up from my beer at John. He's smiling at me in a strange way that catches me off guard. My gaze flits to the TV.

"If the DNA on that auburn hair matches the guy I stabbed, they can prove he was in my aunt's place and investigate him for murder. Liza's cop friend said he's been arrested for assault before. Been suspected of murder, too, but nothing's stuck." Megan's hands press together tightly, her knuckles white. "This time it will, thanks to my knitting needle. He'd pulled it out but then went to the ER the next day with severe flank pain. Probably had urine the color of his hair."

Waseem swirls the ice in his diet cola with a straw. "This would make a great film for my channel. No names, of course, and I'll change things up."

My colleagues laugh, but I don't think Waseem is joking. Let him make his film. I don't care. I'll leave it a great review. Or two.

"But they can't prove Brad Marshall instigated it, can they?" Jen asks.

A waitress buzzes by, and we all order another round. The thought of Brad getting away with everything leaves an all-too-familiar rotten taste in my mouth.

Once the server is gone, Megan says, "That's going to be trickier. Even if he entered Aunt Fiona's condo with Knitting Needle Man and left traces of himself behind, he'll claim he and Fiona knew each other, and he'd visited her place before."

"But you said his skin was under Liza's fingernails," Waseem counters.

"It was—or at least, when the DNA testing is back, they'll prove it's his tissue—but he'll claim he was defending himself against Liza. That she broke in and attacked *him*."

This is mostly speculation on Megan's part. Tam couldn't divulge her full conversation with Doris Cho of the Boston PD. "Detective interviews are confidential," she said. "I can't give you all the details."

But Tam gave me enough to piece things together, and I passed them on to Megan. It was her aunt who was killed. Her aunt whose life was ended prematurely by an entitled man who expects the world to spin his way. Injustices like that burn me hotter than any scorching fire could do.

"But how," Jen says, "will Brad Marshall explain the man you stabbed with the needle? That the guy just happened to break in, found Liza there, and decided to kill her? That's too far-fetched for any jury."

Megan pushes her salad plate away, everything eaten but the croutons. "Maybe, but here's the thing. Brad wasn't aware Theo hid the bag of pills in the condo. Liza found them, took pictures, got the cops involved. What's happened since then we're not sure, but Liza's friend, Tam, hinted there'll be an investigation into Dr. Brad Marshall's involvement. Looks like he found a lucrative way to make extra money. A penthouse condo in Boston isn't cheap, even for a doctor. Who knows what other luxuries he owns?"

Waseem grabs one of Megan's croutons. "Do you think they'll be able to prove he had Theo killed?"

"Maybe, maybe not," Megan says.

Jen returns to drumming her glass, as if she's unable to hold still. "Even if they don't find him guilty of murder, they can get him for selling drugs. Should be a stiff prison term."

John, who's barely more talkative than me, says, "You okay with that, Liza? Brad Marshall not being brought to justice for murder?"

I brush pretzel salt off my fingertips and think about the mess with Chopper, a mess that came about because a year ago, I couldn't stand the thought of an evil man going free. I can't risk something like that again. Can't risk more blackmail. Can't risk facing another Chopper.

I finally answer John, my gaze back on the television.

"Guess I'll have to be."

44

Despite my ill-fitting relationship with social gatherings, I'm oddly satisfied as I drive away from O'Dell's. Knowing Fiona Carlson's mysterious death is no longer so mysterious quiets my roving brain and gives it some much-needed rest.

Traffic in Morganville is its usual Saturday-night buzz—people headed to dinners, movies, dance clubs. As I begin to make a left turn toward home, a driver sails through the intersection. I brake in time but narrowly miss a collision that could've totaled my dad's car.

I curse loudly and complete my turn.

It's not my car anymore, tiger, my dad whispers in my head. *I've been gone for five years.*

I rub my hands over the steering wheel and imagine him doing the same. Or him flipping on the radio to his favorite jazz station. Or turning up the heat for my mother, who was always cold.

It's ridiculous, I know. I'm a doctor, a scientist, a concrete realist. I don't believe in God or an afterlife or anything more spiritual than the rush of endorphins after a heavy workout. Yet I still feel my dad's presence in this car. Still feel his wisdom guiding me every day, his patient advice as I stumble through life. I hope I didn't tax him too greatly.

What a pair he got stuck with. My mom and me, two messed-up brains, hers starting to quiet of late, mine starting to mature. Two cerebral cortices coming into their own.

I scoff. That's horseshit. The two beers in my belly are muddling my thoughts, because people like me don't change.

Sorry, Dr. Lightfoot.

At least I helped Megan. Her aunt is still gone, but she has answers, and that counts for something. Doesn't it always come down to evil men doing evil things? Brad Marshall for money, his redheaded accomplice for…what? Enjoyment?

Whatever his motive, hopefully justice will follow.

As I pass the run of strip malls leading to my building, I think about what Tam asked me two weeks ago. Why I feel the need to "look into these kinds of things." If she's expecting deep soul-searching from me, she'll be disappointed. It's simple. Being a helper eases the burdens of those in my inner circle. That's what I've been taught to do. Helping others helps my dad by showing him, or at least my memory of him, that I'm the person he wanted me to become. A kinder, brighter version of the daughter he loved rather than the darker version lurking underneath, the version where revenge and violence taste so good. The cruelest thing I could do to my dad's legacy would be to let his work with me go to waste. I might as well spit on his grave.

Besides, I can't stand seeing bullies win. Ever.

John's question at O'Dell's floats back to me. Am I okay with Brad Marshall not being charged with murder if the police can't prove he instigated Fiona's death?

I think so. I colored within the lines this time. Well, mostly, if you don't count the B&E or what I did to Chopper. But if I stray too far outside those borders, like I did last year, then Dark Liza threatens to rise. Without my father here to help me, she might enjoy sticking around.

So, yes, knowing I helped Megan will have to be enough for now. Dark Liza is best kept dormant.

I helped April and Jasmine too. They don't know it, and hope-fully never will, but thanks to my compromising photos of Chopper, he'll stay out of their orbit. He got ten grand out of me, plus an extra seven hundred for running away like a scared poodle in the alleyway. That's far more than he deserves, and he knows it.

Problem number two ticked off my list.

With the feeling of satisfaction still coursing through my blood, I pull into my apartment building's well-lit lot (*score one for Mr. Sinclair*) and swing around to my usual spot.

Just as I reach it, I slam on the brakes, my tires squealing.

Parked in my spot—an *assigned* spot marked with a painted number 103—is a black Jeep. A Home and Hearth Healing sticker mocks me from its back window, telling me exactly whose car it is.

Pete fucking Parsons.

I glance over at his own spot, which is marked 102. A red MINI Cooper with a license plate that reads *Candy* barely fills the space.

Like a crystal ball packed with grenades, my calm of satisfaction shatters. My jaw clamps shut, and an animal sound squawks from my throat.

I swerve my car back out in a wide arc and consider ramming into Pete's Jeep. At the last second I slam on the brakes again. My dad's car doesn't deserve that, and a smashed vehicle is the last thing I need. While I'm not proud my anger still erupts so easily, I do credit myself for not following through on it.

Instead, I breathe deeply in and out, putting Dr. Lightfoot's defusing technique to work. It barely reduces the boil. I yank the steering wheel and drive to the back of the lot, where four visitor parking spots exist. One of them better be empty.

None of them are empty.

Cursing furiously, I peel out of the building's lot and drive three blocks down to the nearest strip mall, which is the closest I can get, because there's no parking on the high-traffic road. After choosing a spot near a streetlight, I grab my windbreaker from the passenger seat and spill out of my car.

With the stomps of a giant, I march the three blocks back to my building and enter the secured access. Pete's unit is the first to the left. Eighties music pours from the gap beneath the door. I knock with more fervor than a firefighter clearing a burning building.

"Open up, Parsons," I holler.

At the same time, I force myself to calm down. I can't have Jasmine peeking out of her unit one door down and seeing the monster her neighbor can become. God knows why, but April's eleven-year-old daughter thinks I'm cool. Maybe because I can solve a Rubik's Cube in under a minute, and I have a "creepy brain poster" on my wall.

With more control, I knock again.

The door opens.

A grinning, dark-haired, shadowy-eyed Pete Parsons greets me.

"Hey, Liza, how's it going?" He puts a hand over his mouth in an *oops* fashion. "I'm sorry. Is the music too loud?"

"It's not the music, and you know it. You parked in my—"

From the living room, a woman's voice cuts me off. "Hurry, Petey, this is the best song."

Seconds later a blonde in a pink dress scurries up to the door with a microphone in her hand. A Madonna song croons in the background. It appears Pete Parsons and his visitor—a carbon copy of his dead ex-wife—are doing karaoke. The notion seems absurd. Pete Parsons singing karaoke would be like *me* singing karaoke.

He scoops the blonde toward him and plants a kiss on her rouged cheek. "I'll be there soon, Candy."

Candy. Oh she of the MINI Cooper.

Parsons has obviously planned this down to the last karaoke note. A nice little show for me. A preview of what's to come.

I cross my arms and widen my stance. "Either you or your candy needs to move their car."

"Oh man, I'm really sorry about that. The guest spots were taken, and since you weren't home, I figured you wouldn't mind."

I dig my fingers into the nylon fabric of my windbreaker. In the background, Candy starts warbling "Dress You Up." I want to warn her away from this guy. I have no beef with her, and she deserves better than Pete Parsons. I'll leave a note on her car telling her as much. My phone number, too, just in case she ever needs help if the two of them become a thing.

As for Pete stealing my parking space tonight? The urge to slug him is stronger than his cologne, but I hold back. My posture relaxes. One of my father's life lessons was learning to pick my battles.

This battle isn't worth fighting. Fury from me will only show Pete he's won this round, no doubt the first of many to come. He wants to see me lose my cool. Wants to know he's beaten me. Wants to make it clear I'm his next target, a target far more challenging and exciting for him than the medicated patients at Home and Hearth Healing.

But Pete doesn't know who he's entered the war with. Not really, anyway.

I plant a smile on my face that's faker than Candy's plumped-up lips. I wave the issue of the stolen parking spot away. "No problem. Enjoy your night. You've certainly earned it."

Pete studies me. His eyes narrow, and his head tilts.

"Welcome to the building," I say, heading down the hallway toward my unit on the opposite side. For good measure, I whistle while I unlock my door.

Nope. Pete Parsons has no idea the combat he's just unleashed.

But he will.

He most certainly will.

THE END

AUTHOR'S NOTE

The characters and story lines in *Malignant Assumptions* are fictional, as are Titus McCall Medical Center, the city of Morganville, and many of the businesses named within. They are figments of my imagination, created my me, without the use of AI. In keeping with this make-believe, I've chosen not to mention the Covid pandemic, even though *Malignant Assumptions* technically takes place in 2020. (The first book in the Liza Larkin series, *Fatal Rounds*, was set in 2019.) I think we're all tired of reading about the virus so I made it disappear. Fortunately, in fiction we can do that. If only we could in real life too.

ACKNOWLEDGMENTS

A big thank you to my editor, James Gallagher of Castle Walls Editing, for his thoroughness and keen eye. After my former editor retired, I experienced a bit of a panic knowing I would need to find someone new. I'm so pleased James was available for the job. Another heartfelt thank you goes to my beta reader, Alex Whitmarsh of Whitty Editing. Her feedback helped strengthen the book, and she was a pleasure to work with. Thank you as well to Susan Marlowe for her wonderful audiobook narration and to Lance Buckley of Lance Buckley Design for his eye-catching cover art. And as always, I want to thank my online friends, both writers and readers alike, for your ongoing support and engaging interactions. Many of you have been with me from the start, and I consider you my "real-life" friends.

Finally, thank you, reader, for your interest in reading *Malignant Assumptions*. I truly appreciate your support and am grateful for each and every reader and review.

ABOUT THE AUTHOR

Carrie Rubin is a physician turned novelist who writes medical-themed thrillers. She enjoys exploring other genres as well, so she has a novel of magical realism published under the pen name Dannie Boyd and a cozy mystery under the pen name Morgan Mayer. She is a member of the International Thriller Writers association and lives in Northeast Ohio.

For more information, visit:

www.carrierubin.com

BOOKS BY CARRIE RUBIN

The Liza Larkin Series:

Fatal Rounds

Malignant Assumptions

The Benjamin Oris Series:

The Bone Curse

The Bone Hunger

The Bone Elixir

Other Medical Thrillers:

Broken Hope

Eating Bull

The Seneca Scourge

Pen Name Dannie Boyd:

Fractured Oak

Pen Name Morgan Mayer:

The Cruise Ship Lost My Daughter